PRAISE FOR
The Voice of Reason

"The Voice of Reason is a brilliant, beautiful,
important love story you do not want to miss. Pick
up this book, and savor it slowly—it will feed your soul."

—HOLLY KAMMIER
Best-Selling Author

D1297438

the voice *of* reason

KAT CLARK

FROM THE TINY ACORN ...
GROWS THE MIGHTY OAK

The Voice of Reason

First Edition
Copyright © 2020 Kat Clark

This story is a work of fiction. References to real people, events, establishments, organizations, or locales are intended only to provide a sense of authenticity and are used fictitiously. All other characters, and all incidents and dialogue are drawn from the author's imagination and are not to be construed as real.

This book contains depiction of a suicide attempt. Content may be triggering to some readers. If you or someone you know is having thoughts of suicide, please contact the National Suicide Prevention Lifeline: 1-800-273-8255, text HOME to 741741 in the US, or go to your local emergency room.

Book interior design and digital formatting by Debra Cranfield Kennedy.

www.acornpublishingllc.com

ISBN—Hardcover 978-1-947392-84-7
ISBN—Paperback 978-1-947392-83-0
Library of Congress Control Number: 2020906937

This book is dedicated to all those impacted by mental illness. You are not alone.

THE
VOICE
OF
REASON

PART ONE

Chapter 1

J osh Everett was twenty-one years old the first time the voices
spoke to him.

That ordinary summer morning, he ran a comb through
his shaggy, almost shoulder-length black hair as he checked his
reflection in the small bathroom mirror. Later, he'd wish he'd
looked harder; stared into the pool of his own eyes, attempting
to see straight into his brain. Maybe if he'd watched closely
enough he would've seen it happen; something misfiring deep
within the recesses of his brain, an almost imperceptible ripple
in the calm waters, a subtle precursor to the storm.

He hurried downstairs toward the aroma of coffee floating
up to greet him. At the threshold of the tiny kitchen, he paused
to take in the scene. Amy stood at the stove with her back to
him. His wife's long brown hair was secured behind her in a
messy ponytail and one of his T-shirts, which almost swallowed
her small frame. He watched her frying eggs, humming along
with the sizzling of the oil in the pan. She scooped an egg onto
a plate with a pancake and turned to slide it onto Caleb's
highchair tray. The baby pounded the tray with squeals of
excitement, his thick dark curls bouncing on his head. At one
and a half he still hadn't uttered a discernable word, but he was
always making noise and smiling.

Amy caught sight of Josh and broke into a grin. She made him feel ten feet tall just by the way she lit up when he entered a room. "Good morning, handsome," she said. "Have a seat. I hope Mrs. Crofsky's hens next door keep the eggs coming."

Instead, he walked up to her and snaked his arms around her from behind, kissing her slender neck.

She gasped. "Stop that! You'll make me burn the eggs. I'm trying to actually cook them right this time."

"It'd be worth it." He inhaled her strawberry scent before turning to greet his son, bending down to his level and ruffling his hair. "Morning, Caleb. High five." Josh held up his large hand. Caleb giggled and instead reached up with a sticky hand to tug Josh's hair.

"Oww." Josh pulled back making Caleb giggle harder. The baby lifted a piece of pancake as a peace offering and Josh bent his head and let him feed it to him. "Mmm," he said wiggling his eyebrows in exaggeration. "Mama's such a good cook it tastes delicious even with slobber on it."

Amy laughed and swatted him with a dish towel. "Sit down and you'll get your own. Slobber free."

Taking a seat at the narrow breakfast bar next to Caleb's highchair, he ran his hand over the distressed wood that he'd constructed with his own hands.

"Smells great," he told Amy as he picked up the knife and fork and began meticulously cutting his meal. Amy always laughed at his quirk of cutting up all his food before he ate it.

"It's like you've been practicing for fatherhood your whole life," she'd tell him, and as silly as it was, he liked the thought that somewhere in his subconscious he'd spent his life getting ready for Caleb. He poked one of the egg yolks, letting the yellow bleed across the red plate. Then it happened. A low, unfamiliar voice spoke.

"Watch your back."

Josh let go of the knife so fast he had to jerk back to avoid being hit by it as it bounced off the plate with a clatter and landed on the linoleum.

"Who was that?"

Amy turned from the sink to look at him, wiping her hands on the dish towel. "What?"

He glanced over at Caleb who was happily driving a piece of pancake through a puddle of yolk. He looked behind him as though the stranger with the low voice would be standing there. The accordion door leading to the family room was pulled back, offering a glimpse of scattered blocks and green shag, but no person. His eyes darted around the kitchen again. Who was here?

Josh vacated his chair abruptly and dashed into the family room. His eyes swept over the gold paint, worn plaid couch and green shag rug. The room was empty. The T.V.? He moved toward it, but the small tube was black and silent. The needle of the record player hovered in wait.

He circled the rest of the first floor before charging upstairs.

"Josh?" Amy called.

"Shh!" he answered, even though he was already halfway up the creaky wooden steps. The voice had been so sudden; which room had it come from? He stood still at the top, listening. The only sounds were of Caleb squealing and Amy's soft voice interrupted by the occasional clang of a dish. He shook his head. He was imagining things. Trying to even his breathing, he returned to his spot at the kitchen counter.

Amy stared at him, her head cocked toward her left shoulder.

"What's wrong? What are you running around for? It would usually take a crane to pull you away from breakfast."

Josh speared a bite of pancake and chewed before answering. "It's great, sweetie. I just ... didn't you hear that?"

She shook her head. "It's this old house. It's always making noises." The corners of her mouth turned down as her green eyes studied him. "Are you still having trouble sleeping?"

He shrugged, focusing on regulating his heart rate. "Everetts don't sleep, right, Caleb?" The baby looked up at the sound of his name and smiled at his father.

"Suit yourself. I enjoy going to bed."

Josh shifted his weight on the wicker stool. The reminder of the previous night helped him push aside the strange voice. Hell, it was more than lust. Amy's trust in him meant everything. He winked at her. "Thanks for putting that thought in my head."

Her cheeks flushed bright pink. "Behave yourself."

He shrugged. "Sorry, you're just so gorgeous I can't help it."

She set the dish towel on the edge of the sink and moved to the breakfast bar, leaning across the wood to kiss him. To his surprise she slipped her tongue in his mouth. He groaned. "You're going to make me late for work," he said as she pulled away, her forehead still against his.

"We have an audience," she whispered, jerking her head toward Caleb, who offered them an impish grin.

"We used to have to hide from our parents, now we have to hide from our son. Just wait little man. It'll be pay back one day," Josh grinned.

Laughing, Amy wiped her glasses on her sleeve before lifting Caleb out of the highchair and bringing him to the sink to wash his sticky hands and face. "I'm going to have to give you a full bath after this breakfast." The baby reached for her glasses, but she bent her head, covering his chubby belly with kisses. He squealed with delight.

Watching Amy with Caleb was one of his greatest pleasures. Whatever he'd heard, he wasn't going to let it shatter his idyllic morning. Maybe it was his imagination, or maybe a lifetime of exposure to the deafening grind of construction machinery was finally messing with his hearing. Whatever the case, it was only the three of them in the house.

He rubbed his forehead. Amy was right, he hadn't been

sleeping well. Work had been slow through the winter and he'd only just been able to pay the bills on time. But he'd pay them himself, without "help" from Amy's wealthy parents. He could take care of his own family. He worried about Amy sometimes, though. She smiled a lot and laughed easily but sometimes after Caleb went to sleep he heard her arguing on the phone with her parents. That's all this was; worry.

Shooing the thoughts from his head, he brought his empty plate to the sink and took his son from his wife's arms. "Daddy loves you," he said, throwing him up and catching him in a hug.

"Dada," Caleb said.

Josh's eyes widened in disbelief. One look at Amy confirmed that he'd heard correctly. Her eyes were misty. "Did you hear what he said?"

She nodded. "His first word. I have to get the baby book."

"Dada," Caleb said, poking a finger in Josh's chest.

Josh thought he might burst with joy. They worried about Caleb's lack of speech, and despite reassurance from the family doctor, he wondered if he'd ever hear that word.

Amy hurried back with the baby book. "What's the date?" She glanced at the calendar tacked above the counter. "June 25, 1979. Caleb's first word. I'm so happy I don't even care that he didn't say mama first."

Josh carried Caleb into the cozy family room and set him on the shag rug with a stack of rubber blocks. "He will. Dada is just easier. Now we know he *can* talk."

A single tear streaked down Amy's pale face. "I was starting to think maybe I'd failed him. I thought maybe I wasn't reading him enough books or—"

"Hey." Josh went to her and took her in his arms, brushing another tear away with his thumb. "You're the best mother there is. If I looked to the ends of the earth I couldn't find a more perfect mother for my child."

She looked up at him and smiled. "I'm sorry. This is a happy thing. I shouldn't cry."

He kissed her forehead. "I don't mind." He pulled himself away and headed for the door.

"Wait," she called, rushing to retrieve a brown bag from the refrigerator and bringing it to him along with a thermos of coffee. I packed you a sandwich."

"You're so good to me," he said taking it from her. "What would I do without you?"

She shrugged. "Starve."

"In more ways than one." He leaned down to give her one more kiss.

She touched his face. "Keep the boys in line and don't forget to eat."

He held up the bag and saluted. "Yes, Ma'am. Caleb, take care of Mama."

Josh drove to the job site with the windows of his 1968 white ford pickup down and Van Halen's *Dance the Night Away* playing on the radio. His son had said "Dada", his father had just landed a huge commercial project, and he had the most wonderful wife in the world. Life was good. Despite his weird experience, he had to admit things were looking up. Josh sang along with the radio, Van Halen's *Dance the Night Away* playing so loudly it was the only thing he could hear.

Chapter 2

Josh let himself into the double wide trailer that served as an office on the construction site. The welcome sound of a box fan whirring in the corner greeted him. He was already sweating.

"Hello, you must be Josh Everett."

Josh jumped, nearly toppling the carefully constructed toothpick model encased in a plexiglass stand.

"Sorry," a woman about his age said. Dressed in a lime green shirt under a denim jacket, red curls surrounded her head. Thick eyeliner and blue shadow encircled her eyes. *Too much.* Amy never did that. "I didn't mean to scare you. You were lost in thought there."

Josh steadied the case. What was this stranger doing at his work? He knew everyone that worked for his dad, and Bob Everett didn't hire anyone without consulting his sons. Although Bob was the boss, he'd treated them like business partners since they were old enough to work.

"This company will be yours when I'm gone. I might as well let you start making some decisions," he'd say.

"I brought you a coffee." The woman handed Josh a Styrofoam cup. It almost scalded his hand when he took it, though she didn't seem to be bothered. She took a generous sip of her own coffee and winced. "Strong. Like you." She nodded at him.

"Um, I'm sorry, who are you exactly?"

The woman smacked her forehead with more flair than necessary. "Oh, my gosh, I'm such a ditz! I'm Melissa. Your dad just hired me as the new secretary."

Josh stared at her outstretched hand for a beat before he remembered his manners. "Hi. Josh. Josh Everett."

"Oh, I know who you are." She giggled, poking him in the chest. "You're Bob Everett's oldest son." She blinked her cat-like eyes at him. "Anything you need, coffee, notes taken, phone calls made, you come to me. I'm your go to gal from now on. You boys work hard enough as it is. I like your tattoo. I don't know any guys who have tattoos." She reached out to trace the snake wrapped around his bicep.

Josh pulled away. "Um, thanks. Listen, Melissa, I don't mean to be rude, but, uh, my dad didn't mention he was hiring anyone." Even with the promise of an office building project, it was doubtful a secretarial position would make the budget.

Melissa waved him off. "Oh, it's my first day. I'm sure he was going to." She studied him so intently that it made him squirm. Women either made eyes at Josh or gave him a wide berth. At six foot two and two hundred pounds, he could be intimidating without intending it. It didn't matter to him either way. "Well," she said when he didn't respond, "I'm off to see if any of the other boys need anything. I'll see *you* later." She not so subtly brushed his arm on the way out.

Melissa didn't seem like a good fit. Josh made a mental note to talk to his dad about hiring her. He wandered over to the filing cabinet at the back of the trailer and set his coffee of top of it. He opened the top drawer in search of the office building's blueprint.

"You should sleep with her," a deep voice said. "Amy would never know."

Josh spun around as Jason came striding through the door.

His brother's jeans and work boots were already caked in the clay-colored dirt of a fresh project.

Josh let out his breath. Aside from the shorter hair and the extra two inches of height, looking at his younger brother was like looking in a mirror. "Inappropriate on so many levels, Jay. Why don't *you* sleep with her?"

"Sleep with who?" Jason glanced behind him.

"Melissa."

"Hmm. Nope, Melissa doesn't sound like a girl I'd sleep with. Melinda, maybe. Madonna, definitely. Melissa is so... girl next door."

"Glad you have such high standards. But do you really think we need her? I mean, I'm never one to pass up coffee, but..." He scanned his surroundings. Where had he set his coffee? He was always carrying coffee around with him, then forgetting where he set it down. He probably went through a half dozen partially-consumed cups a day. He sighed. "That's weird."

"You're weird," Jason said. "Quit wasting time and come on. Dad wants to see you."

Josh shrugged and followed Jason out of the trailer. They were greeted by the grinding sound of bulldozers. Bob waved his arms, guiding a cement mixer as it backed up to a gaping hole in the earth, his yellow hard hat bouncing on his head. It wasn't just Bob's substantial girth that made him seem larger than life. He didn't do anything in a small way.

Josh tapped him on the shoulder. "Dad," he shouted, "why did you—"

"Josh!" Bob practically threw the clipboard at him. "Take a look at this. This project is huge, son. This is a breakthrough! Look at all these stories. Can you believe it!" He gestured toward the sky before clapping Josh on the back so hard he almost knocked the clipboard out of his hand.

Josh smiled. It was good to see his dad so excited. He needed this project. They all did. Josh glanced at the plans. It *was* complex. But the payout . . .

"Was there something you wanted to ask me, son?"

Bob's ruddy cheeks were flushed with excitement. Josh didn't have the heart to ruin the moment. After all, it was still Bob's company. If he felt the need to hire a secretary, that was his prerogative.

"It can wait, Dad." Josh handed back the clipboard. "This is amazing."

The rest of the day was busy, filled with planning, hauling, and working alongside his dad and brother. They were too busy to talk, and they couldn't have heard each other over the machinery anyway. Josh didn't see Melissa again. By the time he got in his truck the sky had darkened and rain had begun to fall, cooling the air. His back and shoulders ached from the hours of physical labor, but he was grateful for the work.

If the traffic didn't hold him up, he'd get home in time to tuck Caleb in. Josh couldn't stand not seeing him in the evening. His heart swelled at the memory of Caleb saying, "Dada". He didn't let himself think about the other voice he'd heard.

The rain progressed from a shower to a downpour. He turned the wipers up and braced himself for the boring twenty-minute drive down the desolate roads. Few cars were braving the weather. The windshield wipers groaned with the effort of keeping up. He squinted out the window. Something was in the road. A deer? A dog?

To Josh's horror, an old man stood directly in the path of his truck. The man was illuminated by the truck's headlights. Dressed in overalls, his long gray hair hung in wet ropes down around his beard. He looked like he'd stepped out of the beginning of the century. What in the hell was he doing in the middle of the road? In a rainstorm?

All of this flew across Josh's mind in an instant as he slammed on his brakes. They squealed in protest as the truck fishtailed wildly on the wet pavement. His heart pounded as he laid on the horn. "Get the hell out of the road!" he screamed, pumping his brakes.

The man stood frozen, staring straight at Josh. In the sickening moment their eyes locked, Josh knew he wouldn't be able to stop. At the last second, he jerked the wheel in a desperate attempt to avoid collision.

The truck bounced off the road and went careening into the ditch. The wheel wrenched from his hands. Metal screeched. His head jerked to the side.

Did I hit him? It was the last thought Josh had before his temple slammed against the driver's side window and everything went black.

Chapter 3

By the time she put Caleb to bed, Amy had worked herself into a panic. Every muscle in her body made its tension painfully known. Where was he? Josh always tried to make it home before Caleb went down, if not by dinner. When he got held up at work he made it a point to call her from the job site. Josh had been working himself ragged now that the summer days were lengthening. But they couldn't work in the dark, in this weather.

She paced the first floor, circling from the linoleum in the kitchen to the worn wood and shag rug of the family room and back again, pausing to peer out the foggy squares of glass in the door leading outside from the kitchen.

The thick blackness interlaced with violent torrents of rain. Hail battered the roof. Where was he? Amy bolted back to the family room and turned on the black and white television mounted on a wooden stand Josh had constructed and painted a cool green. It was impossible to walk five feet in the house without seeing Josh's handiwork. Though it was close to one hundred years old, every day the house felt new to Amy. Every day it made her proud of Josh. While she adjusted the sensitive antennae, she distracted herself with the memory of the first time they'd seen the house.

They'd looked at too many houses outside of their meager budget. Amy wanted a cozy home in contrast to the lavish one in which she'd grown up, and Josh was dead set against the reminders of inadequacy wrapped in offers of financial aid from Amy's father. The house was all peeling paint, scuffed floors, and old water stains.

"What do you think?" Amy asked Josh.

Josh spun to survey the compact first floor, studying the little family room and adjacent kitchen like a kid surveying Christmas gifts. "It's perfect. What do *you* think?"

Still unaccustomed to being asked for her input Amy cradled her growing belly and contemplated the question. "I don't know. I like it, but it seems like it's been through a lot . . ."

"I know," he'd said, taking her in his arms. "That's what makes it perfect."

Amy squinted at the blurry picture on the screen, holding her breath through the accident reports. She should call Bob and see if he knew where Josh was. Just as she returned to the kitchen and lifted the phone of its cradle, she heard a key in the lock. She rushed to the door and yanked it opened to a soaking-wet Josh.

"Oh my God," she breathed, tears of relief filling her eyes. "Are you okay?" She pulled him into the house. He spun abruptly and latched the door before turning back to her.

She embraced him, gasping as his icy wet clothing contacted her skin. Josh stiffened. She pulled back and held him at arm's length, fresh worry filling her stomach. A purple-yellow bruise covered his left temple. He held his body rigid.

"You're hurt." She pushed his dripping hair off his forehead.

Josh rubbed the back of his neck. "I'm sorry I worried you. There was some old guy in the road. I almost hit him. I swerved and the truck went into the ditch. I walked home."

"In this?" She trailed him to the family room where he

collapsed on the couch. She sat next to him, reaching to knead the cement muscles in his shoulders.

"A man in the road? In this weather?" Amy felt a flash of anger at this crazy stranger. He could've gotten Josh killed!

"I know, it was the weirdest thing. He looked like a farmer from early nineteen hundred. I blacked out, and when I came to he was gone."

Alarmed, Amy sat bolt upright. "You passed out?" The Rolodex in her head of random information flipped. Wasn't losing consciousness a sign of concussion?

Josh waved his hand. "Blacked out, not passed out."

She cocked her head. "What exactly is the difference?"

He offered her a smile. "One's shorter and less serious."

"This isn't funny, Josh. You should see a doctor. What if you have a concussion?"

"I don't have a concussion. I'm fine."

She searched her brain for more facts. *Loss of consciousness, confusion, nausea . . .* "Are you going to throw up?"

He smiled. "Why? What did you put in my sandwich?"

"Josh, I'm serious."

He touched her cheek. "I'm fine, Amy." He straightened up. "God, do you think I hit him? I searched the road, but I didn't see him anywhere. It was like he disappeared."

She rubbed his bicep. "You would've known if you hit him. What was he doing in the middle of the road, anyway?"

Josh shrugged, then winced. "Who knows? Poor guy must've been out of his head." He looked at his lap. "I'm getting the couch all wet."

Amy thought of the red velvet couches in the Richards' home. "Doesn't matter. All that matters is you're safe. Do you think you can eat something?"

"Actually, I'm starving."

She breathed a sigh of relief. It was a good sign, wasn't it, that he had an appetite? "I'll warm you up some meatloaf."

"You don't have to warm it."

"I want to."

"You're so good to me." They returned to the kitchen and he eased into the wicker chair at the small card table that served as a kitchen table.

Amy studied his bruised face and the dark circles under his eyes. "I'm worried about you. You've been so stressed with work, and now this. Why don't you take tomorrow and rest?"

He shook his head. "Can't. This project needs all of us working at one hundred percent if were gonna meet our deadlines. Rick's already skeptical. I'll call Jason for a ride in the morning. He can come with the hitch. Hopefully the truck's not damaged badly." He caught her frown. "I promise, I'm okay. Just a little sore."

She sighed. "Okay." She turned to the oven, willing herself to believe him.

Chapter 4

Every clean-cut rugby-playing son of Amy's parents' friends was a cookie-cutter of the last, and Michael was no different. He arrived at her door at exactly six o'clock wearing a ridiculous tweed jacket. He called her father "sir" and took her to dinner in his parents' red Mustang convertible. He was the perfect cliché; just what her parents wanted.

"Stop moving," her mother said. "Your hair is impossible."

Amy frowned at her reflection in the vanity mirror. Unlike her friend Gwen who turned heads with a swipe of mascara, Amy was plain-looking. Her dull brown hair was pin-straight and never seemed to lie smoothly. Her skin was pale even with a smattering of rogue, and her glasses hid her green eyes.

"Do I have to go out with Michael tonight? I'd rather just stay home. I have a headache."

Her mother's impeccably made-up face frowned behind her. Amy doubted her father had even seen her mother without makeup. Amy would never be able to keep up with the Eileens and Gwens of the world. She'd rather not waste the time, energy, and heartache trying.

Eileen wound a long strand of her hair in a curler, breaking her out of her thoughts. "Honestly, Amy, if you just had a better attitude you might get a second date with one of these young men. You're halfway pretty with your hair done up and a little color in your cheeks."

"I didn't want a second date with any of them." Amy's voice sounded whiny even to her own ears. Her parents always seemed to bring out the immaturity in her. She mediated her tone before continuing. "They're all the same. Everything's Yale this and Mercedes that."

"You'd rather we set you up with a dead beat?"

"I'd rather you didn't set me up with anyone. It's 1975. I can find my own boyfriend."

"But you won't. I don't understand you. You don't want to go to college. You don't want to get married. What do you plan to do, live in our guest quarters with several cats?" She smiled cruelly.

"Mom, please. I'm only sixteen. I think you're being a little dramatic."

"That's the problem with women nowadays. Always think they have *time*. *Time* to do *what*? Women have more choices now than ever before. And instead of being grateful, instead of planning for those opportunities, you bide your time. Let me tell you something, Amy. A man will not work for you. A man won't chase you unless you give him a glimpse of something worth pursuing. And then? You'd better keep his interest and not get lazy."

"I'm sorry, Mom," Amy said. As usual, she wasn't sure what she was sorry for, but the familiar edge of guilt gnawed her stomach anyway.

The doorbell rang. Eileen gave Amy's hair one last tug and then turned her around, surveying her. "Never mind. Michael's here. Don't keep him waiting. Wear your heels. Remember, beauty must suffer."

Amy descended the winding staircase, gripping the bannister the whole way. Her father stood in the foyer, the intrusive light from the overhead chandelier making the white marble floor gleam under his feet. Facing him was a short boy with slicked-back red hair. His stubby arms dangled at his sides as he talked easily with her father. Her stomach flipped with a dread she couldn't quite place as she hesitated just out of their line of vision.

It'll be fine, she told herself. *Gwen and Todd will be meeting us.* Hopefully having her best friend there would diffuse some of the tension, although it was just as likely Gwen would be too busy making eyes with her boyfriend.

Swallowing, hard, Amy forced her feet to carry her the rest of the way.

"There she is," her father said. "Amy, I would like you to meet the Newmans' son, Michael. Michael is headed for Yale next year, isn't that right, young man?"

"Yes, sir." Michael turned to Amy and stuck out his hand. "It's nice to meet you, Amy."

"Nice to meet you." Hopefully he didn't notice how sweaty her hand was. Had she imagined the flicker of disappointment in his eyes when he looked her over?

The sense of impending doom weighed on her shoulders like a thick blanket as Michael led her out to a fire-engine-red Mustang convertible, one hand possessively on the small of her back, maybe a little too low considering they'd just met. He opened the passenger door and she tried to relax into the cool white leather. *Give him a chance, Amy.*

Michael started the engine. He lit a Marlboro before offering the pack to Amy.

She shook her head, trying not to wrinkle her nose. "Thank you, but I don't smoke."

He let out a sound that was somewhere between a laugh and a scoff, still holding the cigarettes out to her. "Everyone smokes."

Amy shrugged, shifting away as though one would jump out of the pack at her. "I guess I just don't like the smell."

"Suit yourself." He revved the engine.

Amy watched her stately home grow smaller in the review mirror until it disappeared completely. This was what her parents wanted, so she'd try. She'd give Michael a chance and attempt to have a positive attitude.

That night would turn out to be a pivotal one in her life, but not in a way she could possibly imagine, and certainly not in the way her parents had hoped.

Chapter 5

Amy stared through the window of the bus, breathing through her mouth to avoid the stench of the other passengers' cigarette smoke. Her reliance on public transportation sometimes made her wish she'd learned to drive. Josh had tried to teach her, but she'd panicked, not trusting herself to control a potential weapon.

Josh. Something was off with him and she couldn't place it. He was stressed about the pressure from the project and deadlines, but it felt like more than that. He'd been uncharacteristically irritable and jumpy for the past two months. He seemed—what was it? Distracted?

"Wain." Caleb pointed his chubby finger at the drops beginning to streak the scratched window.

Maybe it was burnout. The Everetts were working on the largest project they'd ever been tasked with and Josh was running himself ragged. *That's all it is.*

Fortunately, it had stopped raining by the time the bus pulled up to the stop four blocks from the Richards' home. Though she'd grown up there since middle school, it had never felt like home. She unfolded the tattered navy umbrella stroller and strapped Caleb in in record time. She took off down the sidewalk at a good clip.

"Mimi, Poppy!" Caleb squealed as the red brick mansion came into view. Landscapers were scraping the stubborn ivy off the red bricks. Sweat beaded at her temples as she made her way up the circular driveway. The gold lion knocker swung away from her before she could grab it. Maria clapped her hands and looked up at Amy.

"Come, come," she said in her melodic accent. "Getting so big." She pinched Caleb's thigh and he giggled.

More mother than cook, Maria was her consolation during these visits.

"Maria?" Walt's authoritarian voice rang out from somewhere in the belly of the house. Amy almost looked up to make sure the chandelier wasn't vibrating. "Is lunch prepared yet?"

Maria's almond eyes widened. "Almost, Mr. Walt."

"Kindly show Amy to the sitting room and finish up," her father's voice said, as though the house's excessive size had wiped clean her memory of the sitting room's location.

Maria raised her dark eyebrows at Amy like a conspiring sister. "I will show you to the sitting room now, senorita," she whispered. Amy stifled a laugh.

Walt and Eileen were sitting in their respective suede wing chairs, the oriental rug surrounding them like an ocean. Walt adjusted his tie as though running a business meeting. Amy took her place on the red velvet couch facing them. Caleb rummaged in the diaper bag, knocking it over and dumping the contents on the rug. Cracker crumbs, diapers, a stuffed bear, and a wooden fire truck with three wheels tumbled to the rug. Her parents flinched simultaneously, as though Caleb had pulled the pin from a grenade. Heat rose to her cheeks. Amy leaned over and shoveled everything back into the cavernous bag, hoping her mother hadn't spotted the rip in the lining.

"Tuck," Caleb drove his truck around the perimeter of the rug.

"He's talking more," Eileen commented.

Amy sat up straighter. "Yes. On the bus, he said—"

"Gemma Ward, with whom I play tennis, said her two-year old grandson has been speaking in sentences for a year already. You remember the Wards, Amy? You went to high school with their son, Julian? He's in medical school now." She smiled.

Amy's shoulders slumped. She'd long ago learned to recognize the reminders of disappointment disguised as nuggets of praise from her mother, but chose just as often not to, because maybe one day the praise would turn out to be authentic.

Walt studied his grandson. "Hmm. Still not pronouncing Rs?"

"Most kids don't do that until six, Dad."

"Don't shoot for average Amy. Speaking of average, how're the Everetts handling such a substantial project? I'm seeing a lot of these little mom and pop construction companies fold in this market. People are building bigger and they need bigger companies." His eyes bore into her. "How's Josh handling the extra pressure?"

"Josh is fine," Amy said, a picture of the crescents of exhaustion under his eyes crowding her mind before she could chase them away.

"Hmm. I'm willing to assist financially in the interim. I know they weathered a tough winter and a slow spring."

She jerked her head up. "How do you know that?"

"I'm a developer, Amy. We talk. It pays to know the most reliable, efficient builders with proper resources." He frowned. "I put in a good word for Everett and Sons."

"I'm sorry, you what?" Was her father trying to take credit for the Everetts winning the bid?

"How will it look for me if they can't measure up? I couldn't, in good conscience, recommend them again."

Amy's eyes ached with the desire to roll upward. She squirmed on the hot red velvet, suddenly hypervigilant about her second-hand bell bottoms and faded denim shirt.

"Aren't those clothes a little small on him?" Eileen nodded toward Caleb.

"They're play clothes." Amy watched her innocent son making large then smaller and smaller circles on the ornate rug.

"Lunch is ready," Maria called.

"Thank you, Maria," Amy said, abandoning the couch and lifting Caleb.

She eased Caleb into the wooden highchair, out of place at her parents' grand dining room table set with fine china. Ignoring her mother's frown, she transferred Caleb's pasta from the gold-rimmed plate to the high-chair tray. Eileen's frown would quickly turn into a gasp if Caleb got his hands on a plate that cost more than all his toys combined.

Over Maria's salmon and pasta, Amy half heard her parents' dialogue about the success of their friends' children, the going-ons at the country club, and her father's extensive development projects.

"Thank you for lunch," Amy said, pushing back her chair and gathering her plate. Her parents stared at her.

"Amy, we're all still seated. Maria will get that. Take your seat."

"It's just that Caleb's getting restless."

For the first time since they'd begun lunch. Walt and Eileen's head swiveled over to Caleb, who was studying his fingers contentedly. "Take your seat," Walt repeated.

Amy sat. She couldn't fault Walt for his surprise. Like one of Pavlov's naïvely loyal dogs, she followed Eileen's example and waited to rise until Walt declared the meal over. Today, her stomach churned, and her nerves were on end. Her cozy home called to her.

"What was that?" Amy looked at her father.

"I said you may be excused."

"Honestly, Amy, where's your head today?" Eileen said. She stared at her made-up face in the table's pristine glass top, a hand gently patting her chestnut curls.

Walt glared at his wife. "She's worried. Wouldn't you be? Her family is supported by the sweat off that boy's back and he has no backup plan."

Every muscle in Amy's body tightened, like her father had a screwdriver to her spine. "I'm not worried."

Caleb slammed his hands down on his highchair tray. "Not!"

"Don't lie to me, Amy." Walt said, ignoring Caleb. He rearranged his face. "I want to help."

"It's fine, Dad. We don't need help but thank you. I should probably let you get back to work, and I need to get Caleb home for his nap, so . . ." She continued babbling as she gathered her things, hardly noticing her father retreat to his office, giving her a chance to escape.

She found Maria washing dishes and gave her a hug, accepted a stiff kiss from Eileen, and headed for the door. "Tell Dad I said—"

"Don't leave without this."

Amy's hand slumped off the doorknob. She turned back toward Walt, who promptly shoved a check into her hand.

"Dad, no. Thank you, but no. I really appreciate this, but I can't accept it." She thrust it back at him.

He crossed his arms like a defiant child. "You will accept it and you'll be grateful. That stubborn streak won't put food in your son's body or proper clothes on his back."

"Dad, I think Josh—"

He held up his hand like a stop sign and her protests screeched to a halt. "I'm not doing this for Josh or even for you. This is for my grandson."

Caleb tugged at Walt's pants and let out something between a growl and a squeal. Amy sighed. He'd never make it home for nap, and a cat nap on the bus would leave him groggy and cranky.

"That's enough, Caleb," Walt said without looking down. "I'm talking to your mother."

Caleb wailed.

"I said that's enough!"

"All right. Thank you, Dad." Amy shouted over Caleb's shrieking, shoving the check in her bag. She'd rip it up as soon as she got home. Josh would never see it.

Once home, she fished the check out of her bag. The amount swam in front of her eyes, which cut over to the stack of bills on the breakfast bar. Josh was adamant about not borrowing a dime from the Richards. Typically, she agreed with him, but a project of this magnitude would take time, and bills wouldn't wait.

She held the check over the garbage, ready to tear it to pieces. They didn't need this money to float them. They always made it work. She only needed Josh.

The shrill ring of the phone interrupted her destruction of the check.

"Hello?"

"Amy."

The sound of his voice still transformed her into a love-sick teenager. But the way he said her name caused her heart to seize. "Josh, are you okay? Did something happen?" Her questions came out in a rush, willing him to rip the band aid off and tell her what happened.

Josh cleared his throat. "I'm so sorry Amy."

Chapter 6

The truck in the ditch was the least of Josh's problems. Jason helped him resurrect it; it was an easy fix. Upon returning to the scene of the accident, they found no sign of the man—no boot prints in the mud, no splash of blood in the road.

"Probably some kook," Jason said. "No harm, no foul."

Except Josh was fairly certain the old man from the road was still messing with him. As the weeks passed, Josh became increasingly convinced that the man—whomever he was—had been in the road on purpose. But why?

He couldn't prove the farmer's involvement or motivation; all he knew was since the accident, *if* he could call it that, there was a constant buzzing in his truck. Sometimes he heard strange whispers coming from the radio. The guy must've planted something in the truck while Josh was unconscious. Some kind of recording device. Maybe he'd even planted a chip in Josh's head. Almost daily, he felt around his skull for an unexplained bump under his skin but found nothing.

At work, he got the eerie feeling he was watched, and not only by the impatient project manager's critical eye. Something was going on with the project. People kept talking to him, warning him. But they never showed their faces and their voices were unfamiliar. None of it made sense.

Then there was Melissa. She constantly found reasons to be around him. Her pursuits intensified with his avoidance. He'd almost mentioned it to Bob several times, but his dad was stressed under the pressure of looming deadlines. He didn't need his grown son whining about a crush.

Josh rubbed the sweat from his forehead with the back of his hand. The rain had left the air hot and bloated with feverish moisture. When he finally retreated to the trailer to inhale his peanut butter sandwich and review the blueprint, Melissa was already seated at a small card table next to the desk. She nibbled on an apple, peering down at the blueprint. *His* blueprint. She jerked her head up when she noticed Josh.

"Where'd the table come from?" He snatched the blueprint and folded it on the desk.

Melissa's face turned the same shade of red as her hair. "I set it up. I thought it would be a nice little nook to have lunch and get out of the heat. I didn't mean to pry." She nodded toward the blueprint. "Those things are so fascinating, like art gestating to become a three-dimensional building." She looked up at Josh, her long eyelashes brushing her speckled cheeks. "Does that sound weird?"

Despite his busy morning and painfully empty stomach, Josh laughed. "Yes. But I know exactly what you mean." He gestured to the folding chair next to her. "Mind if I join you? I'm starving."

She pushed it out with her foot. "I'd love that. It's weird, nobody around here talks to me. It's like I'm invisible or something. Do you ever feel like that?"

Josh took a generous bite of his sandwich and chewed thoughtfully before answering.

"I can't say that I do. Amy, though, she's mentioned that. The way she grew up—"

Melissa's expression darkened. "You talk about her a lot."

"She's my wife."

Melissa made a strange sound, like an aborted scoff. "Right, but do you talk to her? Does she listen *to you*?"

Josh frowned. "Well, sure. She's my best friend."

"Ugh! God, Josh, you sound brainwashed." She fired her apple core at the trashcan in the corner. It ricocheted off the metal filing cabinet and bounced into the bin with enough force to tip it over.

Josh glared at her. "What's your deal?"

She closed her eyes, took a few deep breaths, then opened them and smiled at him. "God, sorry. This is none of my business. It's... well... it seems like you have something on your mind. Maybe something you can't tell even Amy?" She put a hand on his arm, sending an involuntary shiver through him.

"Someone's messing with me," Josh blurted, "and maybe even the company." He rubbed the back of his neck. "I didn't mean to say that out loud."

"Josh, it's okay. It's not good to keep things bottled up. I'm a good listener. Plus, I'm your secretary. If something's threatening the company, maybe I can help."

"Not something, some*one*." He shook his head. "It sounds crazy."

"Try me."

Despite his resolve to keep his theories to himself, it all came rushing out, his relief at having an ear palpable. Melissa listened intently, nodding and offering the occasional, "hmm" as he told her about the strange man in the road, the accident, the threatening voices, and his fear that someone had placed a recording device in his truck. She didn't laugh or look at him like he was crazy.

Melissa's hand trailed down his arm to his hand. She wrapped her fingers around his. "I'm so sorry you've been alone with all this. We'll get to the bottom of it."

"You believe me?"

She leaned back in her chair and gave him a pointed look. "I have every reason to believe you."

"What do you mean?"

"Look, this is just between us, okay? The owner, Rick? We used to date. He's still kinda obsessed with me." She smiled.

"Melissa," he said, pulling his hand away, "I don't want to hear about your dating history, okay?"

Melissa crossed her arms. "You should."

Josh sighed. "How's that?"

"Rick and I, we still, umm, *talk* and stuff. He blabs his fat mouth to me all the time. I know everything. I can help you. It's in your best interest if we work together. What do you say we give each other what we need?" She brushed his knuckles with her thumb.

"I need to get back to work. I'm being paranoid." He vacated his chair.

"You're not."

"She's right," a scratchy male voice whispered. "Like I said, watch your back."

Melissa bolted to her feet. Josh watched her. "Did you . . . did you hear that?"

"I think you can guess what I want from you, and I know what you need." She stared at him so intently that Josh had to look down. "Let me know when you change your mind." She squeezed his bicep, her nails branding his skin.

Josh spun around and watched her exit the trailer, nearly colliding with Bob in the doorway. He brushed past her. Josh shook himself like a dog. What was wrong with him? Why had he opened up to Melissa, of all people? He wanted to speed home and take Amy straight upstairs.

"Dad, about Melissa—" His complaint dissolved when he caught Bob's expression. His heart plummeted.

"What is it? What's wrong?"

Bob's face matched the gray-white linoleum. "We lost the project, son." He stared down at his work boots, caked with red clay.

Josh shook his head to clear it. A chill went through him despite the muggy trailer. He wasn't paranoid. He was right. Melissa was right.

Josh shifted gears to fix-it mode. "They signed a contract. I'll talk to Rick. We'll figure this out."

Anger tightened Bob's ruddy face and a knot formed in Josh's stomach. A deep laugh rumbled through the trailer. Josh stared at his dad.

"What's so funny?"

Bob's frown deepened. "Funny? Not a damn thing. Rick doesn't trust that we'll make the deadline, and he wants to build higher, bigger, sleeker. He's going with a larger builder. I'm sorry, Josh."

"Why are you apologizing to me?"

"You've got a family to support. You were counting on this pay out more than any of us."

Josh's mind flashed to the bills piling up on the counter; he'd promised Amy everything would be okay with this project in the works. And now?

"There has to be something we can do."

Bob shrugged. "Rick's got a lot of clout and an expensive legal team. I can probably secure the first installment but as far as the contract goes, they'll find a loophole." Shoulders drooping, he approached the toothpick model and studied it. Then with one swift motion of his hand, he knocked the structure and sent it flying. The Plexiglas top popped off. Toothpicks scattered across the floor. "Dammit! I never should've put all my eggs in this corporate basket."

"Dad, it's okay. I'll take care of it."

Bob was only forty, but the stress wasn't good for him. With two kids to raise and a business to keep afloat on his own, he'd never stopped to take a breath. "I'll take care of it," Josh said again.

Bob shook his head. "What can you do? Jason's out there, tearing Rick a new one. He thinks he's helping, but that temper only makes things worse."

"It's going to be okay, Dad," he said again, clapping his dad on the shoulder. Bob hardly seemed to notice.

Jason's venom-filled voice reached Josh the minute he opened the door. He followed the noise a few feet away from the trailer.

"We had an agreement, Rick! A fucking *contract*. Does that mean nothing to you? You can't deny the integrity of our work." Jason towered over Rick, a stout man with a halo of dark hair circling a shiny bald spot. It was hard to picture Melissa with him.

"He's still obsessed with me. I could talk to him."

Rick spread his stubby fingers. "It's business, Jason. It's not personal. We've decided to go a different route."

Jason took a step closer and Rick shrunk back. Josh almost felt sorry for him. "You *decided* to go a different route? You up and fucking *decided?*"

Josh came up behind Jason and put a firm hand on his shoulder. The relief on Rick's face was unmistakable.

"Josh, you understand, right?"

"Not really. You'll be hard pressed to find a more dedicated builder."

"You better think about what you're doing." Jason's fists clenched at his sides, his body vibrating with rage.

This wouldn't be the first time Josh had intervened in the split second it took his brother to go from zero to three hundred. "Leave it alone, Jay."

Jason turned to him, his eyes flashing a dark emerald. "How can you say that? He's screwing us!"

"Assaulting him won't help."

Jason opened his mouth then snapped it shut, glaring at Josh.

"Look, guys, I wish this had worked out. Your father's a nice guy, but—"

"Save it." Josh didn't want excuses, and he couldn't afford to burn any bridges. "Come on, Jason. It's been a long day. I'll buy you a beer." He all but dragged his brother across the jobsite to his truck before he imploded. The silence created a pall as jack saws stopped hammering and engines died, leaving only exhaust.

"That's the smell of failure," a scratchy voice said.

"Not helpful, Jason."

Jason glared at him. "Oh, I'm not helpful? What about you, Mr. 'Oh, let it go. Live and let live?' Where'd your hero complex go?"

"Grow up."

Jason flopped in the passenger seat of Josh's truck, kicking at a half empty Gatorade bottle on the floorboards. "Doesn't anything bother you?" The rage leaked out of his voice, leaving weariness in its wake.

"Yes, it bothers me, but starting a schoolyard fight won't help." Josh leaned into the driver's side. "Were you really gonna clean Rick's clock?"

The corners of Jason's mouth turned up. "Nah. It would've been too easy."

"You want a challenge, wait until we get to the bar and I'll arm wrestle you."

"Who says that'd be a challenge?" His grin didn't reach his eyes. "So ya gonna get in or what?"

Josh patted the top of the truck. "Yeah, I'll be right back. Just gotta talk to someone really quick."

"Rick?"

Josh leaned into the car to look at Jason. "No. But don't worry. I'm gonna fix this."

Leaving a bewildered Jason in his truck, he went in search of Melissa.

Chapter 7

Josh wound his way through dormant machinery and discarded hard hats. "Has anyone seen Melissa?" He asked the guys, some of them standing around grumbling while others half-heartedly collected debris. He was met with blank looks. How could he blame them? They'd been counting on Everett and Sons for their livelihood.

He found Melissa leaning against the side of the trailer, smoking a cigarette. She inhaled and blew several perfect smoke rings in his direction. The corners of her blood-red lips turned up.

"Rick's afraid of your little brother." She let out a harsh laugh. "Guess he never did grow those balls." She took another drag of her cigarette, then stubbed it out in the dirt with the leather toe of her boot.

"Everyone's counting on you to fix this."

Josh whipped around in the direction of the scratchy voice. He peered around the corner of the trailer. Nothing. The jobsite was as silent as a cemetery, void of its usual sounds of life. A breeze kicked up miniature tornados of red dirt.

"What's going on here?" Josh yelled into the wind. "Who are you and what do you want?"

Only the wind rattling the aluminum sides of the trailer answered him.

He turned to Melissa. "Am I crazy?"

She pushed herself off the side of the trailer and took a step toward him, penetrating him with her intense gaze. "No, you're not crazy, but he'll make you look like it."

"Who? Rick?"

She shrugged. "Him, too."

Josh lowered his voice, unable to shake the eerie feeling they were being watched. Monitored. "Who else is involved? What are we talking about here?"

"I shouldn't say."

"Dammit, Melissa. Why are you being so evasive? How can I save this project? What am I saving it *from*?

His thoughts swirled, too frenzied for him to catch. His mind grappled for a solution. If he could just think.... The crackle of static filled his skull and the world lost its definitive edges. Josh threw his hand against the trailer to steady himself.

"Josh?" Melissa's voice reached him underwater. Invisible walls closed in on him and he swore he could hear the finite clang of an iron door closing. It was a sound he still heard from time to time, in his dreams. A sound he'd never forget, despite his best efforts. The sound that said *there's no way out*.

He swayed on his feet, struggling to force air into his lungs. Melissa's hands on his shoulders broke him from his stupor. He blinked heavily.

"Josh? Hello? Can you hear me?" She snapped her fingers in front of his face.

He shook his head to erase the floaters from his vision. "Sorry. I feel . . . a little weird."

"That's understandable." Her eyes darted around. She stood on her tiptoes and whispered in his ear. Her breath was hot against his already clammy skin. "I don't want you to go to jail again, but you could if you won't accept my help. Bob and Jason too. Your brother's tough guy act won't last long in the slammer."

Josh jerked back. Despite the humidity, his body went ice cold. "How did you—"

"I told you, I know things."

"Is that why Rick pulled the plug?"

Melissa rolled her eyes. "Rick doesn't give a shit about your criminal record. He's much more concerned with your dad's crimes."

"I'm sorry, my dad?"

Josh strained to decipher something solid through the fog. Bob had never so much as stepped foot on an abandoned property without a permit. What the hell was Melissa talking about?

"Look, Walt's been snapping up all the big developments. Rick turned up the heat on your dad. Bob cut corners to save time and money. Do you really think anyone will believe you didn't know what your pops did?"

Josh laughed. "Didn't know what, exactly? Dad would never do anything unethical. He's fair."

Melissa's eyes narrowed. "I have proof. Proof you don't want leaked." She wrapped her fingers around his wrist.

Dazed, Josh let her lead him inside the trailer. She latched the flimsy door behind them. Instantly, sweat beaded at his temples.

"Relax. I don't bite." She winked. "Unless you want me to."

His stomach ached. He hovered near the door as Melissa went over to the desk. She lifted the rotary phone, removed the bottom and grasped a small black object.

"When Rick added more floors to the building plan, Bob eliminated some of the shores from the second level to save money."

Josh's face burned. "You're lying."

"Thought you might say that." She stalked back to him with the blueprint she'd been studying at lunch. A lifetime ago.

Josh reached for the familiar blueprint like it was a grenade.

To his relief, the structure was mapped out meticulously, Bob's pencil marks allowing for the added stories. Of course, it was. Josh had every drop of ink memorized.

The steel beams between the stories were outlined in the blueprint. The shoring process of placing them had been completed on three stories before the concrete was poured, which was as far as the project had gotten. He looked up.

"I don't under—"

Melissa held up the small black rectangle. A tape recorder. She hit a button and Bob's voice filled the space, the evidence garbled but damning just the same.

"Look, we can't fund it. No, he'll balk if I charge.... And the timing. I know I know. God, I don't want anyone to get hurt, but.... Yeah, can we eliminate a few of the shores without compromising the safety? Okay, tonight. You have my word. Don't involve my boys..."

She punched the stop button with a triumphant smile.

Josh shook his head. "No."

Her smile morphed into an expression of sympathy. She touched Josh's arm. "He meant well. He wanted to protect you. He has a lot of guilt, you know, about how fast you had to grow up, without your mom. Working at such a young age. Taking care of your brother. Giving up school."

"How the hell do you know so much about my life? Who *are* you?"

"I can be your best friend or your worst nightmare. Up to you."

She pulled the tape from the device. Josh reached for it letting the blueprint fall from his hand. She yanked it out of his reach. Ice filled his veins as a wicked smile broke through her façade, turning her face into something grotesque.

"Rick cries on my shoulder all the time. It's totally annoying. I told him I'd do some sleuthing and make sure your little mom and—ahem, sorry, pop and sons' business was up to the task. Turns out I uncovered something more *illegal* than incompetence.

"Melissa, please" It didn't matter how she knew what she knew or that he couldn't make sense of this alternate reality. His mind screamed one phrase: *fix this.* "My dad can't go to jail. He's a good man. He had to be really desperate to do something like this."

Josh swallowed hard. Why hadn't his dad come to him like he always had in the past? "And I... I can't go back there. I won't."

A wave of vertigo hit him as his own words answered his question. Bob hadn't discussed the problems with the financing and time crunch because he'd already solved them. Illegally. People could have been killed! How could he?

He held out his hand. "Give me the tape, Melissa."

She slipped the tape under the plunging V-neck of her yellow shirt and into her bra. "Come and get it."

Josh closed his eyes. His real life, his life with Amy, played like a movie reel in technicolor behind his eyelids. Maybe a man's love story flashes through his mind when he's about to destroy it in the same way life is said to flash before the eyes of the dying. His chest ached as he relived that beautiful night on the beach when he'd begun the painstaking process of earning the invaluable gem of Amy's trust. He snapped his eyes open.

"I love my wife. I promised her I'd never hurt her, and I won't. I can't." He took a step toward Melissa. "Give me the tape."

She rubbed his arm. "She'll never know. Then we destroy the tape, and no one knows anything. Josh, think about it. At the very least, you'll be named an accessory."

"Rick will still press charges," he said, not believing he was considering what he was considering. He was removed from his body, or maybe his mind. Detached.

"He won't. I can promise you."

Amy. Bob. Jason. Rick. Jail. *Melissa.*

Melissa grabbed his hand and placed it on her breast, the outline of the tape under his palm. "And don't even think about wrestling it away from me. I've got a whole box of them. I tell you where they're hidden, or I tell the police. Your choice. The metallic taste of entrapment flooded Josh's mouth. *No way out.*

Melissa reached for him, and, God help him, he let her.

Chapter 8

Amy fidgeted in front of the stove, staring at the tea kettle when the door creaked open and Josh shuffled into the kitchen.

"Making tea?" His voice sounded weary.

She shrugged. It had been a while since tea bags had made the grocery list, but the act of boiling water and pouring it into a cup and adding a squeeze of lemon if available offered a kind of ritualistic comfort. "It's hot water."

Josh stared into space. His expression remained blank. The worry reignited in her chest. His apology on the phone had made it sound like he'd done something terrible. Instead he was apologizing to her about losing the project, as though he'd sabotaged it himself. Apologizing about the bills. He was too hard on himself. Which was why she couldn't take her father's money. Walt used his money to make statements—currently his view of Josh as less than.

"Josh?"

He shook his head. "What?"

Amy frowned. Was he okay? "You asked if I was making tea. We're out of tea bags, so just hot water."

"Oh," he said. "Shit."

He looked so stricken over stupid tea. She didn't care about tea. She'd subsist on dry cereal and water forever to be with Josh, rather than return to her previous life. Despite her parents' opinion, Josh was enough. The thought reminded her of the check. She flinched inwardly. Her father's gifts always had strings attached—translucent as gossamer but damning just the same.

Josh's humiliated expression the day her father had dangled the keys of a shiny new station wagon toward him flashed into her mind. *"You're a father now, kid. I won't have you driving my daughter and grandbaby around in that rattletrap truck."*

Amy went to him and reached out to pull his rigid body into her arms. "It doesn't matter."

He took a shuddering breath and backed away from her.

Amy frowned, dropping her arms to her sides. "What's wrong?"

He fixed his eyes on hers, but when she tried to stare into their depths they darted away, bobbing left and right, unfocused. "Nothing. I'm dusty and sweaty. I need a shower"

A chill went through Amy. Something wasn't right. Was this only stress? Sleep deprivation? Something worse? Had he sustained a more serious injury in the accident? Was he sick?

"Are you okay?" she asked him.

He almost managed a smile, his face contorted with the effort. He rubbed the back of his neck. "I don't know. I don't know what I am."

"We'll be okay. You and me against the world, right?" If only she could erase the sadness in his eyes.

He looked at her intently. "Amy, you know I love you, right?"

She studied him, her anxiety sprouting like a weed. He jumped, jerking his head around like he'd heard something.

"I love you too." She took his hands. "Baby, what's going on?"

"We lost the project," he said to a spot above her shoulder.

She squeezed his hands. "Yes, I know that. But you seem—I don't know. Not yourself."

Finally, he looked at her. His expression darkened. "This project was a big deal, Amy. We were all counting on it."

She dropped his hands and stepped back, stunned by his harsh tone. "I know that. I was worried you were sick or something."

He sighed, running a hand through his hair. "God, I'm sorry. I don't know what's wrong with me."

"You're stressed."

He approached the breakfast bar, zeroing in on the stack of bills in various threatening shades of yellow and red. Amy's stomach dropped.

"Josh, we need to talk—"

"Let's see how many of these we can defer until—" He stopped, his fingers closing around the check on top of the pile. This time he stared right into her eyes. "What the fuck is this?"

She jerked back as though he'd hit her. Josh didn't talk to her like that. Josh didn't talk to *anyone* like that. "It's not what it looks like," she managed.

"Really? Because it looks like your dad's money is where it doesn't belong."

"Josh, please." She spread her hands out in front of her. "I can explain."

He shook his head. "Let me guess. He *forced* you to take it?"

She closed her eyes, replaying the visit. "Well, kind of. We were—"

"Dammit, Amy!" He slammed his hand on the counter. "When are you going to stand up to them?"

She stared at him. Who was she talking to? She'd expected irritation, but this? Josh was so rarely angry. "That's not fair! I told him we didn't need help, you were doing fine, but he kept pushing. Caleb was getting fussy and I . . . I wanted to get out of there. I was about to rip it up when you called about the project. I thought—"

"You know what? Allow me." He tore the check into tiny

pieces and fired them at the floor. The scrapes floated to the linoleum gently, in contrast with his force. "Shut up!" he screamed.

Amy tensed. "I didn't say anything," she whispered.

"I wasn't talking to you."

Amy glanced behind her, but they were alone. Worry solidified into cold, hard fear. "Then who are you talking to?"

"I bet your dad is in on this. Don't think I don't know what's going on here."

She took a step closer to him. "Do you? Because if so, please enlighten me. You're scaring me."

A growl escaped his throat. In one smooth motion, he sent the bills flying.

Amy gasped. She resented how quickly the tears clouded her vision. Josh was her safe place. Her only safe place. "What's wrong with you?" she cried.

His shoulders dropped. The fog dissipated from his striking green eyes. The sudden and drastic flip of his mood startled her almost as much as his outburst.

"God, I'm sorry. I'm so sorry, Amy. I don't know what came over me." He bent and began gathering the bills into a pile. He came to her and she took a step back. His face crumpled along with her own anger. He held his arms open. "Come here. Please."

She walked into his arms and buried his head in his chest, inhaling the earthy smell of sweat, sawdust, and cologne. He held her close and stroked her hair, repeating his apology over and over. She was safe again.

"I was trying to help," she said into his chest. "You push yourself so hard. You haven't been sleeping. You don't have to fight everything alone."

"I know. I know. I just wanted to give you everything. You and Caleb. It's all I want."

"You do give us everything. We're a family. We're in this together."

"You're too good to me Amy. I don't deserve you."

Self-flagellation; another new thing. "Don't be silly."

He sighed. "You have no idea."

He was right about that. She had no idea what to make of his erratic behavior and uncharacteristic outbursts. No matter how many times she tried to convince herself he was only exhausted and stressed, a deep sense of foreboding clung to her.

Josh's arms tightened around her. She squirmed. Her face smashed into his chest. "Josh, you're hurting me."

He dropped his arms and took a step back, looking her over. He brought a hand to his mouth. "I didn't mean to. I swear I didn't mean to."

Amy's brain drew a blank. The exhaustion of worrying, of trying to decode the unnatural cadence in his mood, barreled into her. She reached for his hand. "Why don't we get some sleep?"

He nodded. His eyes were on her, but they were somewhere else. The vacantness of his expression was so jarring she had to look away. At the top of the stairs he stopped, studying the wooden name sign hanging on Caleb's bedroom door. He'd carved and painted it while she was still in the hospital. He reached out to touch the blue "C".

"I didn't get to see him today. I should've come home earlier. I didn't get to see him, and now . . ."

He inched the door open and she followed him into the room the soft glow of the rocket nightlight creating a path to the crib. Caleb was sound asleep on his back in what they'd dubbed the "touchdown pose", his arms flung straight above his head. Josh placed a hand on Caleb's chest and sucked in a breath.

"Love you, buddy," he whispered.

He looked so sad, like he was saying good night to Caleb for the last time. She shivered. *Stop it, Amy.*

Back in their own room, they prepared for bed in silence.

Josh tossed and turned, finally flopping on his back and staring at the ceiling.

"I should get up," he said to it. "I'm keeping you awake."

Amy grabbed his arm before he could rise. "Stay. You know I can't sleep without you anyway."

He rolled toward her and searched her eyes. "Talk to me."

She traced his strong jawline with her fingertip. "About what?"

"Anything. Something happy."

His vulnerability tugged her heart, but the story was already in her head. "How about our first date?"

Chapter 9

Amy watched the mansion disappear in the truck's rear-view mirror. Her usual anxiety was replaced by an unfamiliar feeling. The whole scenario was unfamiliar to the point of being surreal. In sixteen years, she'd never lied to her parents, and here she was sneaking out with a boy she barely knew.

"Have you ever been to 5 Mile Point Lighthouse?" Josh asked.

"Once, when I was really little."

"It's my favorite place. There's tons of history."

"What kind of history?" she asked, wanting to hear the cadence of his baritone voice more than she wanted to hear the actual history.

"It dates back to the Revolutionary War. The keeper, Amos Morris, tricked the British into retreating. He saw them approaching from the lighthouse and he got on his horse, shouting orders to nonexistent soldiers."

"How do you know all this?"

He shrugged. "I love history. I like to know the how of things, but also the why. Why was a building designed and constructed? How do some buildings last for centuries, especially on a rocky foundation vulnerable to high tides? You have a better chance of understanding something if you're tuned in to its history."

He stopped the truck in an empty parking lot. The sound of waves gently lapping against the rocks floated through the open window. She filled her lungs with salty air. Why didn't she ever come to the beach? She spent her summers in her pool or at Gwen's house, where an almost identical replica of her own pool existed in a backyard with cement instead of grass. Josh was staring pensively out the window.

"Eventually, complaints that the lights weren't bright enough increased. This one is more than twice the height of the original."

"Wow," she breathed. History was mind numbing, but she could listen to Josh talk about the lighthouse all night. He described the time as though he'd been there. "You're kind of an old soul."

Josh smiled. "I get that a lot. Let's go see it before I talk you to death." He came around to her side of the truck to help her down. She caught the curious look on his face.

"What?"

"Nothing I—I can't believe you came with me."

"Me neither. I've never done anything like this before."

He turned his back to her and rummaged in the back of the truck. The flash of nervousness hit her then. What was she doing? No one knew where she was or who she was with. Did *she* know who she was with? She was completely at his mercy.

She took an unsteady step away from him. When he turned around he held a thick blanket over his arm and a wicker basket in his hand. "Midnight snack. When were kids, my brother and I thought we were such rebels, sneaking into the kitchen for ginger snaps at twelve on the dot. Turns out, Dad only pretended not to hear us."

Amy let out her breath. The wind whipped her hair into

her face as he led her onto the beach. The lighthouse came into view, even more majestic than she remembered it. How did it stay so white amidst all the sand? Her eyes followed the brilliant light casting a path out onto the water.

"I've never seen all the stars so clearly," she breathed.

"Yeah, you can't once you get closer to downtown New Haven. Here, they're amazing."

"Do you come here a lot?"

He nodded. "Especially when I can't sleep, or I need some quiet to think."

"Your dad—he doesn't mind?"

Josh scuffed his shoe in the sand. "As long as we do our work and stay out of trouble, we come and go as we please."

What would it be like to have that freedom? You could feel claustrophobic and imprisoned in a mansion. Especially in a mansion. Josh offered her his hand and guided her over the rocky ground onto the spit of land surrounding the light house. Though it was cheesy of her, she took a mental note of how perfectly her hand fit into his like a missing puzzle piece. *Maybe I watch too many movies.*

She helped him spread the fuzzy blue blanket. He dropped down onto it, patting the spot next to him. He pulled out a box of ginger snaps, a bag of sour dough pretzels, and a carton of plump strawberries. He frowned at the spread.

"Not exactly fine dining."

Tentatively, she touched his arm. "It's perfect." Before she asked him what she wanted to ask, she took a ginger snap, savoring the burst of spice in her mouth. "Josh?"

"Hmm?" he popped a strawberry into his mouth.

"Why did you bring me here?"

He looked at her, his gaze intense. "It's a symbol, the light house."

"A symbol?"

He leaned back on his elbows, his dark hair almost brushing

her shoulder. "Well, historically they've been used to keep sailors safe. To protect them and guide them to where they need to be. It's a symbol of protection and safety."

For a moment, she lost herself in the depths of his eyes, deep green with flecks of gold.

"I brought you here because I thought you needed to feel safe."

Amy swallowed hard, the cookie sticking in her throat. It was quite possibly the sweetest thing anyone had ever said to her, and oddly, she did feel safe with Josh. If only it were that simple. If only she could stay here forever.

"What else does it symbolize?"

"Strength. Hope that there's a light at the end of the darkness. Resilience. That's why it made me think of you."

"But, I'm not resilient."

"Sure, you are."

She shook her head. "I'm not. I'm weak."

"Being not okay doesn't make you weak. You're not okay, are you?"

"I'm—" She tried to choke out the word "fine". To her horror, Amy felt the tears hot on her cheeks. She tried to wipe them away, but Josh saw them anyway.

Josh put his arm around her shoulders. Instinctively, she stiffened, but then she relaxed into him. His chest was solid and strong. She listened to his heartbeat through his shirt. His arms encircled her. Safety. Protection. Strength.

"You're going to be all right," he said, pulling her closer like it was the most natural thing in the world. "Is this okay?"

She nodded, surprised to find that it was. He didn't feel like a stranger anymore. He didn't seem like a kid either. He was so different from the boys shoving each other into lockers in the hallways, talking about who scored.

No one had ever simply held her. Oh, her parents must have, when she was little. This was different. This was a boy.

"Amy? Do you think I could see you again?" His chest vibrated against her ear.

"I hope so," she sighed.

"But your parents," he said, as though reading her thoughts. "Do you think I could convince them to let me take you on a real date? Like, someplace with tablecloths or at least tables?"

"Josh, this is a real date. It's the first real date I've been on. Anyway, if you don't give a shit about makeup then I don't give a shit about tablecloths." The forbidden word was candy on her tongue.

"Well, okay. You're parents, though. They might give a shit."

"We'll figure something out."

There had to be a way. She'd had a taste of something real and she couldn't go back. She'd never just been Amy. She'd spent her life leading up to that night surrounded by people who'd known her forever yet didn't really know her at all. Staring out at the water from the shelter of Josh's arms, she was finally able to place the sensation she'd been feeling since they pulled away from the mansion.

For the first time in her life, Amy Richards felt free.

Chapter 10

It had taken all of Josh's strength to drag himself away from Amy once she'd dropped into a serene sleep. He'd checked in on Caleb again, unable to shake the eerie feeling that he was doing so for the last time. But that was ridiculous. He'd go to the jobsite under the cover of darkness, travel to the northwest corner of the building, dig up the tapes, and return home before anyone knew he was gone. The shores. He had to find a way to replace them before anyone got hurt. But how could he without implicating anyone else?

Josh pulled to the edge of the jobsite and cut his engine. The eerie quiet was accentuated by the inky darkness of a starless night. He drummed his fingers on the steering wheel. He brought his hand to his mouth, quelling a sudden urge to be sick.

Exhaustion and fear weighed him down like concrete. If only he could confide in someone. He couldn't. He'd confided in Melissa and look where that had gotten him. Another wave of nausea overtook him. He was going to fix this, and he was going to fix it alone.

The crunch of gravel under his tires, like the splintering of bones, shattered the night air. Josh shivered. Gripping the trusty old truck for support, he dragged himself to the bed and retrieved his flashlight and shovel. The beam bobbed in front of him, cutting through the darkness. He was a small child again, afraid of the dark. His body stiffened with every step closer to the building as though rigor mortis was settling in while his blood still flowed.

Or *was* he dead? Everything appeared surreal. God, he was tired. Sleep deprivation could do strange things. When was the last time he'd slept? Despite the flashlight, he stumbled several times.

Suddenly, his light was drowned out by other, brighter lights; the red and blue lights he'd never forget. Josh squinted. An officer was approaching him, badge glinting. The man was tall, even taller than Josh, with buzzed hair and eyes so dark they looked almost red.

"Whatcha doin with that shovel, son?"

Josh opened his mouth, but nothing came out. The air was in short supply.

"You wouldn't be tryin to remove evidence, would ya?"

"No, sir, I . . . I work here. I mean, I used to. Our company was on the project."

"I need to see some ID."

Josh's hands shook so badly he could barely remove his chain wallet from his jeans pocket.

The officer snatched it from him and flipped it open, holding it under the beam of his flashlight. Without warning, he flicked the blinding beam into Josh's eyes. Josh brought his arm up to shield his eyes, but the officer grabbed it and squeezed until Josh lost feeling in his fingertips. He jerked Josh's near-catatonic body toward him and hissed in his ear.

"Josh Everett, I'm Deputy Shane West. I remember your sorry ass crowding my jail. What was it, three years ago, now?" He gave a short laugh. "If I had my way they'd let the violent perps rot in there so they couldn't go out and hurt anyone else."

"I—I wouldn't hurt anyone," Josh managed.

He forced himself to scan the man's face. His memories of his time in lock-up didn't include this guy. But there was something recognizable about his voice . . .

"I know what's going on here. Daddy can't save you now. Hope ya liked jail, cuz I gotta feelin it'll be a one-way stop this time," Deputy Shane growled.

Josh jerked away from Deputy Shane, doubled over, and retched. He spat bile in the clay dirt. Deputy Shane's voice was yelling something. Screaming. Key words reaching Josh in his fugue.

"*Missing Shores . . . Reckless endangerment . . . You have the right to remain silent . . .*"

Those final words snapped Josh to attention. He jerked his head up in time to see Deputy Shane whip out shiny handcuffs. Josh jerked away and ran. Voices and footsteps pursued him. He broke through the brush bordering the jobsite, lunging for his truck, and hitting the locks as his tires spit gravel. As if that would save him. As if anything could save him now. His worst fear, the fear he'd carried behind his sternum seemingly since birth, was realized. He'd failed to protect his family. He'd let everybody down.

His home came into view, dark and asleep. He cut his headlights. Josh smacked his forehead, the pain spreading to his temples. What the hell was he doing? The fuzz had his driver's license. They knew where he lived and what he'd done. They had to be right behind him! He turned off the engine on the one-way dirt road in front of his house and sat like a statue, listening. Only the erratic pounding of his heart betrayed his existence. The night was silent.

Josh opened the door and listened again. The cool night breeze caressed his face and he thought of Amy, his sweet, pure wife asleep inside. He didn't deserve her. He had to be in shock, because everything felt dream-like.

Suddenly, Josh laughed out loud, slapping his thighs.

"That's it!" he called into the night. A chorus of crickets answered him. Dream crickets.

Of course! That was it! He was dreaming. When he was a kid, Josh started having vivid night terrors. Each time it seemed he survived an entire freaky day trapped in his nightmare. He'd wake up screaming. For months he feared sleep; resisted it at all costs. In a rare role reversal, he'd taken to cramming his long body into Jason's twin bed.

He laughed again, flooded with relief. This *entire freaky day* had been a dream! Of course! Amy was right; he'd been stressed and overtired. Like when he was a kid, it was coming out in his dreams.

Josh's jubilation faded as he looked around at his fuzzy surroundings. He hadn't had a dream like this since childhood, but he typically awoke once he realized he was dreaming. Now he was trapped. *Just a dream.*

"Amy?" he called out. He'd been known to talk in his sleep. Maybe he could wake her and get her to wake him. She was right there in bed next to him. His dream-self reached out and tried to touch her. His dream eyes strained to detect her outline. "Amy?"

He threw his hands up. He tried pinching himself, then slapping himself. He punched the truck's door. So much for the theory that you couldn't feel pain in dreams. Then he remembered another theory: you didn't dream your own death. You woke right before the impact. All he had to do was kill his dream-self and he'd wake on his too-hard mattress next to his wife in his beautifully mundane life.

Josh breathed a sigh of relief. He looked down at the keys in his hand. Just like in real life, his lighthouse keychain held both the truck and station wagon keys since he was the only driver in the family. Real or not, he couldn't kill himself in the family car. Besides, he was more comfortable in his truck.

Anxious for this nightmare to be over, he pulled open the

garage door, dented from when he'd attempted to teach Amy to drive. He maneuvered the station wagon down the gravel drive and parked it on the lawn.

He returned to the truck. The engine roared to life. He pulled it into the garage. In just a few minutes he'd wake up next to Amy and tell her about this his bizarre dream. Or maybe she'd still be asleep, and he could get up before her and make coffee.

His eyes scanned the dim garage, lit only by the truck's headlights. The hose coiled up on a rack on the wall came into view. His eyes watered. Grabbing the hose, he wedged it into the truck's tail pipe. It wasn't quite wide enough, but it would have to do. He didn't want to take the time to find the duct tape. The rust bled ominously into the dusty white paint on the bottom of the truck's door. What a place to die.

Not die, he reminded himself. It was a dream no matter how real it felt. He'd go to sleep in the truck, in this dream, and wake up next to Amy. He'd tell her about the creepy dream, and she'd shake her head, frowning at him in that concerned way. She'd put the back of her hand to his forehead.

"I'm not sick," he'd assure her. "I'm all right now."

"You've been working too hard," she'd say. "What you need is a good breakfast."

He imagined the smell of fresh ground coffee beans. But when he applied force to the chipped bronze window crank, cracked the driver's window, and wound the other end of the hose through the crack in the window, all he could smell was exhaust.

His arms felt weak as he pulled down the garage door with a crash. He eased into the driver's seat and reclined it a little, inhaling the smell of acrid coffee mixed with exhaust. He glanced at the cup holder where his stainless-steel mug sat, *World's best DADA* stenciled on the side in blocky, childish print. Funny that he remembered that in his dream. A few water bottles and candy wrappers littered the passenger floor, partially obscuring the torn carpet. It would save a lot of time if you could clean in dreams. His eyelids fluttered. Funny you could be tired in a dream. Exhausted, really.

He couldn't keep his eyes open any longer, so he closed them and leaned back. Breathing in deeply through his nose, he tried to smell the coffee. Vertigo overtook him, and he felt his body slump forward. He must be waking up, but he couldn't open his eyes.

He felt himself losing consciousness, or coming to? Josh swore he could hear Amy's voice calling him. An unexpected bolt of panic shot through his paralyzed body. He tried to reach the key in the ignition, but it was too late. The last thought he had was this was no dream and Amy and Caleb would never know he hadn't intended to kill himself. Bob and Jason would go to jail, never knowing he'd tried to protect him. This was real. He needed to . . . Call . . . Tapes . . .

His hand dropped to his lap. His head lolled forward. His body went numb.

At last, Josh fell asleep.

Chapter 11

Amy would never be sure what woke her up that night. She sensed Josh's absence before she reached over and found his pillow vacant and cool. The house screamed of it. She pulled a robe on over her nightgown, tucked the baby monitor into the deep pocket, and descended the stairs.

"Josh?" she called to the emptiness as she turned on the lights. Panic slapped her. After quickly dashing upstairs to check on Caleb, she grabbed her keys and slipped into her tennis shoes, locking the door behind her as she stepped out into the night.

The heat of the day had given way to a cool night, but the chill she felt had no correlation to the weather. Her eyes slowly adjusted to the darkness, landing on the garage a mere ten feet away. It was the only other place he could be. Maybe he'd gone out to tool around or pour over a blueprint when he couldn't sleep. She had only a moment to hold on to this deniability. As she approached the garage the sound was unmistakable. The deadly sound of an engine running behind the closed door.

"Josh!" she screamed in a voice not her own. Pebbles sprayed up under her feet as she ran, nearly losing her footing on the uneven ground. This was a dream. A nightmare. It couldn't be real. He wouldn't. How could she have missed *that*?

In seconds she was yanking the garage door up with the force of pure adrenaline. The overpowering smell of fumes assaulted her, making her eyes water. The garden hose was out of place there in the dim light from the single lightbulb, running from the truck's rusty tailpipe through a crack in the driver's side window. The hose was meant for watering the peppers and tomatoes and pumpkins; it was meant for spraying Caleb as he ran barefoot through the hot grass. She screamed again, the sound melting into the roar of the engine. How long?

Coughing, she yanked the truck's door open. Josh was slumped over the steering wheel, unmoving, his hair obscuring his face. Tearing the keys from the ignition, she let them drop. The engine died. It was quiet. Too quiet.

"Josh!" His head lolled to the side as she pushed him upright. The whites of his eyes were slightly visible under his lids. His lips were tinged blue. He wasn't breathing.

He's dead.

Choking on fumes and sobs, she hauled him out of the truck, half falling to the garage floor under the burden of his weight. Stumbling blindly, she dragged him to the door of the garage and pulled him into the fresh air of the shattered night. His neck was cold under her searching hand. The pulse was there. Faint, but there. She had no time.

Flipping the Rolodex in her head, she recalled everything she'd learned in the CPR class she'd taken to prepare for Caleb; for choking or drowning. Not for this. Nothing could've prepared her for this. She put her hands in the center of his chest and pumped rapidly as hard as she could, keeping count in her head.

"Come on, Josh, breathe," she pleaded as she lowered her face to his, her tears wetting his cheeks like they were his own.

Tilting his head back, she pinched his nose and breathed air into his lungs. His chest rose and fell artificially. She was doing it right. Over and over she breathed life into his lungs and forced his blood to keep pumping. Even when the world began to spin and her arms burned with fatigue, she didn't stop. If she stopped, he would die.

Just when she thought she'd collapse, his body convulsed, a gasp rattling through his chest. He coughed and choked, his head thrashing. She rolled him onto his side in case he threw up. How was she remembering all this? His lids fluttered and then stilled again.

Amy pulled him into her arms and rocked him as though he was a child instead of a two-hundred-pound man. "Breathe," she sobbed. "Breathe."

His chest rose and fell. He was unconscious, but he was alive. He was breathing. Amy's head ached from lack of oxygen. Her stupidity slapped her in the face. She had to call for help! But, she had to leave him to get to the phone. Gently, she rolled him onto the gravel driveway and got to her knees.

"I love you," she said. "Don't you dare let go."

She bolted for the house. Caleb's baby monitor remained silent in her robe pocket. Caleb. What would she tell him if Josh died? No. He wouldn't die. He was young, strong, and healthy.

"How could you do this?" she asked the empty kitchen as she lunged for the phone. Her fingers fumbled over the 9-1-1.

"Nine-one-one, what is your emergency?"

"I need an ambulance. It's my husband. He's unconscious. He stopped breathing. Please hurry." Amy couldn't talk fast enough; she had to get back to Josh. What if he stopped breathing again?

"Miss, please calm down."

That was the most ridiculous thing anyone had ever said to her. She may never calm down again.

"Is your husband still unresponsive?"

"I did CPR. He's unconscious but he started breathing

again. He's out by the garage." She recited her address, surprised she could even remember it.

"Okay, miss, I've dispatched an ambulance. Can you tell me what happened?"

"He was in the truck. It was running. The garage was closed. He—he tried to kill himself." Her own words were sharp and impossible in her ears.

"I see. And how old is your husband?"

"Twenty-one. Oh, God, he's only twenty-one. He can't die. We're supposed to get old together. Our son's only one. Please, you can't let him die."

"Help is on the way. They'll take good care of him." The voice was kind. Soothing. Irrelevant.

The image of Josh lying on the cold hard ground alone haunted her. "I have to get back to him."

"Miss, I need you to stay on the line until—"

The phone fell from her hand, bouncing at the end of its cord. The dash back to the garage was a blur. Josh lay on his side on the gravel where she'd left him, unmoving. The stones skittered under her feet and assaulted her knees as she dropped down beside him. His shoulder rose and fell. Except for the gray pallor of his skin, he looked like he was only sleeping.

Weak with panic and exhaustion, she couldn't pull him back into her arms. Instead, she threw her body over his as though trying to protect him, even though it was too late for that. Her hand cradled his head, the gravel scraping her knuckles as she tried to shake him. She heard herself screaming.

"Josh, wake up! Please, Josh. Don't do this to me. I need you. Please, wake up!"

She screamed his name over and over again until her throat was raw. The whine of approaching sirens drowned out her wails.

The driveway was awash with red lights, the ambulance tires spitting gravel with an abrupt stop. Strong arms lifted her off Josh's motionless body.

"No!" she cried, trying to cling to him.

"It's all right, miss. We're here to help." The voice was deep and soothing. Amy's body went limp. She would've fallen if not for the EMT's firm grip on her arms. Two other men knelt beside Josh, swiftly rolling him on to a stretcher. One of them pinched his wrist.

"Pulse is thready. We gotta move."

"He won't wake up." Amy's voice was hoarse. "Make him wake up."

The men tightened straps across his chest and legs and loaded him into the ambulance. His face was a disturbing shade of gray. Amy peered after him. Would this be the last time she saw him alive?

"Amy!" a voice called. She turned. The paramedic let go of her arms. Mrs. Croftsky was hurrying over from next door, her snow-white hair matted.

"I heard the sirens. What happened?"

"It's Josh. He—" She couldn't say the words again. "Will you stay with Caleb so I can go with?"

"Of course, dear. Take all the time you need."

Relief and gratitude flooded through her. Mrs. Croftsky had always been kind. When this was all over they'd have to think of a way to repay her.

Amy handed her the key and monitor and headed for the back of the ambulance.

The EMT put a gentle hand on her shoulder. "You'll need to ride up front."

"Please, let me be with him."

His eyes were kind. "I would, but they need room to work on him."

She stared into the gaping mouth of the ambulance. An oxygen mask covered Josh's nose and mouth. One of the EMTs slid a needle into his hand.

Please, God, don't let him die. If he does, I will too.

Chapter 12

Josh hovered in some dark place suspended between life and death. It was hard to breathe, the air coming in reluctant fits. Maybe he'd already stopped breathing? Voices screamed at him so loudly he couldn't pick out a discernable word. The dark, dark terror was swift and consuming and unrelenting.

Oblivion punctuated by a familiar, soothing voice.

"Josh, I love you. Please don't leave me."

Amy? He tried to call her name but when he opened his mouth a pulse of air forced its way down his throat and into his lungs.

"Josh. Don't let go."

Let go of what?

Josh tried to reach out into the darkness. The air was cold. Something sharp and precise punctured his hand. A face morphed in front of him. Officer Shane. This time the blood-red color of his eyes was unmistakable.

"Boo!" spittle flew from his mouth, landing like frozen acid on Josh's face.

Josh flailed backward. "Where's Amy?"

The words came from Josh but not from his mouth, where air was being shoved inside him like a balloon being blown up.

The words came from somewhere in his mind. He thought them; he felt them.

"Shoulda thought of that before ya offed yourself."

"I didn't—that's not what I . . ."

Shane tapped his chin. "What do you think, should I tell Amy about your criminal negligence first, or about you screwing Melissa. Hmm. Tough call."

"Melissa means nothing to me. I love Amy. I need her. She needs me." His body convulsed with cold and dread.

"Don't worry. I'll explain for you. Seems you forfeited your chance to do it yourself."

Josh lunged but grabbed only air. Cold thick air everywhere. Pushing its way down his throat and into his chest. He coughed, choked, thrashed, fought. For life or death; anything but this.

Laughter echoed after Josh as he fell into blackness.

Amy!

"I'm right here, Josh. Please hold on."

Her voice was close, close enough to touch, to hold on to. It was all he had.

I'm sorry. I made a mistake. Don't let me die.

"Please, come back to me. Don't let go. Please don't let go."

He held on to the distraction of his wife's voice in the darkness.

Josh didn't let go.

Chapter 13

Josh was stable. His vitals were strong. But he hadn't regained consciousness and the team of doctors and nurses in the emergency room couldn't tell her why. They looked at each other, telling her in unspoken words the question was "if" and not "when". Amy stopped asking questions.

She answered plenty, though. Had Josh ever attempted suicide before? Did he have a history of insanity? Drug use? No, no, and no.

"Shouldn't he fill these out himself, when he's awake?" she asked when they handed her a stack of papers and a leaky black pen.

They looked at her with some mixture of pity and weary disdain. She oversaw Josh's affairs when he was incapacitated, they informed her. Incapacitated.

Mechanically, she filled out each sheet, answering the same repetitive questions and signing her name at the bottom. When she got to the sheet about advanced directives she froze. She didn't know Josh's end-of-life wishes. She hadn't realized he'd been thinking about the end of his life.

She brought the clipboard to the front desk in the ER waiting room, feeling like a schoolgirl unable to understand her homework. "I don't know my husband's end-of-life wishes."

The nurse or receptionist with the big hair nodded at her as she took the clipboard. "Then you'll be the one to make those decisions, should such a situation occur," she said robotically.

Amy could barely decide whether to spend extra grocery money on milk or cheese. She was trapped in some bizarre play where everyone had the script except her.

Amy called Bob's number from the front desk. When Jason's groggy voice answered, she forced herself to say, "Josh tried to kill himself," before she dropped the phone, bolted for the bathroom across the waiting area, and promptly threw up.

By the time she returned to the desk, the receptionist's expression had softened. "They're transferring your husband to the ICU. They'll take you back once he's settled." She regarded Amy. "For what it's worth, I've seen a lot of people come in here unconscious and walk back out those doors."

Amy turned in the direction of her gesture, half expecting to see Josh standing there. As hard as she tried to brace herself for the ICU, it was impossible. ICU. ER. DNR. GSC. So many letters. Cries and moans haunted the antiseptic-leaden air. Machines beeped in a maddening rhythm. Everything was cold, colorless, and sterile.

Josh was at the end of the hallway behind a gray curtain. His eyes were closed. The oxygen mask fogged with his breath. Tubes and wires snaked from his body. Amy had to collapse into the chair beside his bed to keep from falling. Reaching through the metal bars of the bedrail, she touched his arm. He felt like cold putty.

"Josh, can you hear me?"

They didn't know, they'd told Amy when she'd asked. But, survivors reported hearing family members even while in a deep coma. It couldn't hurt to talk to him.

Except part of Amy wanted to scream at him, to shake him awake and demand that he tell her why. But when she looked at him lying motionless under the burden of those tubes and wires keeping him breathing, it was hard to stay angry. She wanted to hold anger around her like a blanket. Angry was easier.

She stuck with telling him she loved him and begging him not to let go. Amy pictured him stuck in some in-between place, confused. Did he regret what he'd done? Would he still come back to her? Could he?

She stroked his arm and squeezed his hand. Nothing. Someone cleared his throat and she turned to see Bob standing right inside the curtain, shifting his weight from one foot to the other. His eyes darted to the floor, the ceiling, the heart monitor; looking anywhere but the bed. He cleared his throat again.

"How's he doing?"

"He's stable," was all she could offer.

"They told me you saved him." His voice barely rose above a whisper.

"I did CPR." Amy stared at Josh.

"Thank you, honey. I always knew you'd take care of him."

Amy swallowed the lump in her throat. Josh was the one who took care of her.

She'd done too little, too late. Josh never seemed to need taking care of. He was the lighthouse in the storm. Maybe if she'd looked closer, sooner, she could've seen the lights flickering in distress.

"Josh." Bob rubbed the back of his neck. "Why would you do this? You have responsibilities. A family."

Amy had the same question, and it was a fair one. Yet she was defensive. "He didn't want to, Bob."

He didn't answer.

"Why don't I give you a minute?"

He nodded. "Jason's out in the waiting room. They'd only let one of us back at a time. Someone needs to talk him off the ledge. Usually that's Josh's job." Amy winced at his choice of words, even though it was nothing more than a clichéd expression.

In the waiting room, Jason paced like a tiger in a pen. When he saw Amy, he came over to embrace her. She willed herself not to fall apart at the gesture. She pulled away and looked at him, momentarily startled by his striking resemblance to Josh.

"Are you okay?" he asked.

"Not really."

"Yeah, me either. It doesn't look good, does it?" His voice cracked on the last word and he masked it with a cough.

"He's breathing," she offered lamely.

"Thanks to you, I hear."

Why did everyone keep saying that? What good would her interventions do if he didn't wake up? She'd have only prolonged whatever suffering had prompted him to drag the garden hose to the truck. The image popped into her head. The room swayed.

Jason grabbed her by the shoulders. "You should sit down." He led her to the bank of plastic chairs. "Here." He handed her a paper cup of water that seemed to materialize out of thin air. She swallowed the tepid liquid.

When she looked up, she realized the receptionist had been replaced by a younger woman, and the small T.V. mounted in the corner was displaying the 4:00 a.m. news. She had about two hours until Caleb woke up. He'd be upset if neither she nor Josh was there. She had to get home, but that meant leaving Josh in this harsh place that smelled of death.

Bob shuffled into the waiting room, watching the floor. "Take Amy home." He didn't look at anyone while he pulled a set of keys out of his pocket and dangled them toward Jason. "I'll take the bus to the job site and get a head start on the clean up."

Jason stared at him, a complex web of emotions playing across his face. "You're going to work?"

Bob held up his hands in a helpless gesture, finally looking at him. "What do you want me to do, Jason? There's nothing more we can do here."

Jason opened his mouth and closed it. Amy could feel the tension radiating off him. "Right." He got up and took the keys from his dad, slapping him on the back in the Everett way of showing affection.

Amy got up too. Never much of a hugger, Bob patted her arm. "Take care of yourself, honey. Call me." He shuffled away, a lost man.

Jason snorted. "Bob Everett running away from feelings. Shocking."

The sharpness of his tone surprised her. "He's taking it hard, though."

"We're all taking it hard." He looked at her. "Can I see him?"

"Of course." Amy lead Jason back down the long hallway, already jaded to the misery around her.

For one bizarre moment, she expected Josh to be sitting up in bed, eyes open, waiting for them. Of course, he was lying as she'd left him. Josh moaned softly. Jason flinched. "It's okay," she said, not sure to which brother she was speaking. She rubbed the crease in Josh's forehead. "Your brother's here to see you. I have to get home to Caleb, but I'll come back as soon as I can."

She stepped back to give Jason some space. He dropped heavily into the chair, reaching out to ruffle Josh's hair. He'd done it a million times, although never so gently. Together they were like rowdy children, punching each other, arguing about ridiculous things, and making up.

"Josh, you gotta wake up. I can't handle this shit without you." He waited. "Well, okay, I guess you can take off today, but let's not make this a regular thing, you hear me?" He nudged Josh's limp arm with his index finger. "Josh. Can you hear me?"

He looked at Amy, the pain in his eyes so potent she had to look away. "Can he hear me?"

"He can hear you," she answered, choosing to believe it was true.

Chapter 14

August 21, 1979

The sun was rising, turning the sky from black to gray to a more palatable pink. Josh was on a beach, though he had no idea how he'd gotten there. The old man from the road was there too, tossing stones and shells into the calm water.

Josh came alongside of him, the water gently lapping at his shoes. "Who are you?"

The man looked up, frowning, his white eyebrows knit together. "I'm no one." He tossed another stone and it skipped across the surface.

"Well, can I call you something other than 'the man from the road?'"

He gave a short laugh and wrote something in the sand with his finger. "How about Sam? Short and simple."

"Sam. Is Amy okay?"

"She misses you."

"And Caleb?"

"Doesn't know you're gone yet."

"I don't understand what's happening." Josh looked at the water. It was like him—calm on the surface; turmoil swirling just underneath.

Sam stood up, dusting his hands on his overalls. He was at

least a head shorter than Josh. His thick gray-white hair blew in the slight breeze. "The mind is a terrible thing to lose."

Josh nudged the sand with the toe of his shoe. They should take Caleb to the beach again soon. He loved feeling the sand between his bare toes. Would he have another chance?

"Am I dead?"

"Not yet. But you're close."

"Amy doesn't want me to let go. I made a mistake, Sam. I don't want this. I need to go back to her."

Sam shrugged. "It's too late, Josh."

"Please." Panic and desperation washed over him. Did Amy know how much he loved her? She needed to know he didn't want to leave her. And Caleb. Caleb wouldn't remember him at all. An unfamiliar pressure built behind his eyes begging to be released.

"You think I got control over life and death? I look like God to you, boy?"

Josh looked at him, but Sam was gone. He was alone.

"God," Josh called into the silence. "Please. I don't want to die. I need to go back. I need another chance."

He squeezed his eyes shut, hearing nothing but the waves lapping the shore and the sudden call of a seagull. His face was wet. Then he heard it; a familiar voice calling his name.

"Josh. Josh can you hear me?"

"Jason!" Josh ran along the shoreline, straining to detect the direction of his brother's voice. Jason would know how to get him out of this.

"Josh, can you hear me?"

"Jason! Jason, I'm right here! I can hear you. I made a mistake. Help me." He ran and screamed for his brother until his throat filled and he couldn't run anymore. He couldn't shout anymore. He was alone.

"Jason, take care of Amy and Caleb," he said with the last of his voice. Then he fell to his knees and he cried.

Chapter 15

Without Josh, Amy slowly fell apart. It'd been two weeks since she'd found him in the truck. She wore a mask for Caleb, even when it felt like her face would crack under the weight of her porcelain smile. Caleb looked for Josh morning and night. All Amy could tell him was that Daddy got sick and would be home soon. Each passing day chipped away at her hope that this was true.

The moment she closed the door to Caleb's room after his last bedtime story, the tears she'd held back all day broke through the worn floodgates. In the safety of her own room, she sobbed until she made herself sick. Sleep was elusive. She dragged Josh's pillow to Caleb's room and lay of the floor next to his crib, finally lulled by the sound of his steady breathing and the smell of saw dust and Old Spice that still clung to the fabric, rough from too many trips through the wash.

But it was fading. She was fading, doing what she had to do for Caleb, forgetting to shower or feed herself.

"Amy, you have to eat something," her mother told her, but Amy had forgotten what food was for. Still, she nestled into the unfamiliar maternal gestures, letting her mother drag her out of bed, feed Caleb breakfast, and wash the clothes.

Eileen stayed with Caleb while Walt dropped her at the

hospital and waited in his gold Bentley. Without a word, he wrote checks for the bills stacking up on the breakfast bar. Amy didn't have the energy to contemplate her parents' uncharacteristic behavior. She figured she must be really scaring them.

Unless she was at the hospital, Amy rarely left the house for fear they'd need to reach her. Caleb grew restless. Jason came over after work and took him to the park or out back to throw his foam football. Her house had become a prison instead of a home. Home was the place she shared with Josh. The reminders of him were in every room, simultaneously comforting and gut wrenching.

Amy existed in this bizarre world between hope and grief. Until one day she exited the hospital elevator to the terrified sound of Josh screaming her name.

Chapter 16

Josh was close, but to what? If only he could get out of this dark room to the light beyond it. Life? Heaven? He coughed, something forcing its way out of his throat. He thrashed. The walls were closing in. He panicked, striking out with his arms and legs. His wrists were caught on something. Handcuffs? He was in jail! The unthinkable events hadn't been a dream. By now, whenever *now* was, everyone who counted on him must think he'd tried to escape. Caleb. Jason. Bob. Amy.

"Let me explain," Josh said. "Forgive me." An incessant beeping filled his ears.

"Josh, calm down," someone said. A cop?

"I never meant for any of this to happen."

"Heart rate's spiking. We need to give him something to calm him down."

"No, wait, you have to believe me. The building's not safe. Please."

"Tube's out. He's coming to." This was a woman's voice.

"Amy?" Josh called. He tried to push aside the remaining darkness. "Amy! I need to talk to Amy!"

"Have someone call the wife."

"The tapes . . ."

"What tapes, Josh?"

He clamped his mouth shut. He had to talk to Amy. And Bob and Jason.

"What tapes. Josh?"

Josh opened his eyes.

Chapter 17

It sounded like him, but it didn't. His voice was raw and petrified as he screamed her name repeatedly. Her heart seized in her chest and she ran, almost flying to his room.

Josh thrashed violently, his wrists bound by soft restraints snaking from the bedrails. His eyes were opened but clouded with panic. Sweat poured down his face. A doctor and a nurse turned when Amy burst into the room.

"Josh!" She rushed toward him, but the doctor stopped her.

"What's that?" She nodded at the foreboding syringe in the nurse's hand.

"It's a sedative."

"A sedative? But he's finally waking up!"

"Amy!" Josh saw her and began flailing harder. "Amy, please help me. Amy, please! I can explain!" Sweat ran into his eyes and he blinked rapidly.

"Oh, Josh." She struggled against the doctor's grip.

"I'm going to have to ask you to step back for your own safety."

"My—my safety? He's my husband. He would never hurt me."

"Not in his right mind, maybe. He's having a psychotic episode."

Amy tried to process the words, but they were devoid of meaning. She'd been waiting for Josh to wake up, begging him to come back to her.

"Let go of her!" Josh screamed. "Don't hurt her!"

He was scared and confused. He'd awakened in a strange place. A wave of fierce protectiveness filled her. "If you're worried about getting sued I'll sign whatever you want. But if you touch him with that—" she nodded toward the syringe, "Then you'll have to worry about getting sued." She almost turned around to see who had questioned the doctor's authority. "Please let me talk to him," she said in a softer voice.

The doctor sighed. He signaled to the nurse. "We'll be right outside the door."

The moment they crossed the threshold Amy went to Josh. He tried to reach for her, but the restraints stopped him. He growled with frustration.

"Here." Amy undid the Velcro and freed his hands, rubbing his wrists where they'd already become raw. He was shaking all over, his arm jerking as he reached to touch her cheek. He was awake. He was alive. She needed to make him better.

Amy lowered the bedrail, raised the head, and scooted onto the bed next to him. She pulled him into her arms and held him tightly until the shaking stopped. He clung to her, burying his face against her shoulder. She stroked his hair.

"I'm right here," she told him. "You're okay. Breathe."

"Amy. Amy. Amy."

"Shh-shh. It's okay. I'm not going anywhere."

His body stilled in his arms.

"I thought I'd never hear your voice again," she whispered into his tangled hair.

He raised his head and his eyes searched hers. The roller coaster of emotions spun a rapid loop from relief to anger to worry to protectiveness and back again.

"Amy, what is this place?" His voice was raw from screaming.

"You're in the hospital, Josh. Do you—do you remember what happened?"

The lines on his forehead deepened. "The last thing I remember is getting in the truck and pulling it into the garage."

"You tried to kill yourself." Her stomach dropped as the roller coaster sped into a freefall. She wasn't ready to have this conversation.

He grabbed her hand. "No, no. I wasn't trying to kill myself. I would never do that."

The sound of the running engine. The overpowering smell of fumes. Josh slumped over the steering wheel, lifeless. These were things she'd never forget.

"But Josh, you ran the garden hose from the tail pipe into the window. The garage was closed. You weren't breathing. Do you know what that was like for me? I thought you were dead."

He looked stricken. "Oh, God, Amy, I'm so sorry. Can you forgive me?"

"Of course, I forgive you, but you can't bail on me, Josh. You promised me. For better or for worse. In sickness and in health. Us against the world."

"I swear, I wasn't trying to kill myself."

"Then what were you trying to do?"

"I was trying to wake up. I must've been in shock. I thought it was a dream, but it wasn't. I couldn't think. I need to think." He wrapped his knuckles against his forehead.

Amy's blood went cold. She tightened her arms around him. "Josh, slow down. You're not making sense."

"He's having a psychotic episode."

None of this made sense. People didn't go crazy overnight. *Did they?*

Josh jerked his head up. "Amy, the things they told you about me . . . I can explain.

"You don't have to explain anything. Not now. You're alive. That's all that matters. Focus on getting better."

He shook his head vehemently, then whispered in her ear. "My dad? Jason? Are they okay? Are they in jail? I need to talk to them!"

"Jail?" *He's confused. He just woke up. He's fine.* "Of course not. They're at the jobsite doing some clean up."

Instead of relieving him, this information agitated Josh further. He emitted a wail of despair.

She gripped his chin and tilted his head back to look in his eyes. He had beautiful eyes, green with brilliant flecks of gold. But the colors were dim, his eyes glassy. "It's okay. Everything's okay. Jason will be by after work, and, Oh! Wait until I call him and tell him you're awake!"

"Tell him I tried to stop it. Tell Dad I... I don't blame him."

Amy tried not to blame Bob either. He called daily for updates, but he hadn't returned to the hospital since the night Josh was admitted.

"You tried to stop what?"

"Oh, God, the tapes! It might be too late, but the cops can't hear them."

"Tapes?" Amy scrambled to keep up. It was like they were having two separate conversations. "What did you try to stop, Josh?"

Josh's body stiffened. His head whipped around. His eyes fixed on the corner of the room. Amy followed his gaze to the empty nook.

"No. Get out of here! Stay away from her! She wasn't involved. We need more time!"

Amy stiffened. "Sweetie. No one's here. It's just us."

But Josh was somewhere else entirely, his eyes unfocused.

"No, you won't! Get out of here!" He grabbed the bedrail and tried to right himself, but his body trembled, weak from disuse. "The tapes. Where are the tapes?"

"What tapes, Josh?"

"Tell Jason! He needs to dig under the northwest corner of the—oh no! Did they find the box of tapes?"

What the hell is he talking about? "Josh!" Amy shook his shoulder. "Look at me! Listen to me! We're alone. I need you to stay with me. Please." Her voice broke.

He looked at her, his eyes wild with fear. "I won't let them get to you. Don't talk to them. Not until—"

"Josh, no one is—"

His body tensed. "Amy, get out of here! Now! Save yourself!" He pushed her shoulder.

Caught off guard, she lost her balance and tumbled off the narrow bed, the worn linoleum bruising her knees through the holes in her jeans. Before she could right herself, the doctor and nurse burst into the room. The doctor lifted her by the arms and pulled her away from the bed.

"He didn't mean to!" Amy struggled against the doctor's grip, trying to claw her way back to Josh. If she could talk to him. She needed more time.

"The tapes. Please!"

"What tapes, Josh?"

"He's out of his mind. He doesn't know what he's saying," the doctor said.

She broke from the doctor's grip as the nurse plunged a needle into Josh's arm and he was lost to her again.

Chapter 18

The familiar drive to the hospital gave Amy too much time to think.

"How do you feel about bringing him home?" Jason glanced at her out of the side of his sunglasses, one hand on the wheel.

Amy fiddled with the radio, then the cracked air vents. "Good."

"Yeah? You seem nervous."

She glared at him. "Why would I be nervous? He's my husband."

Jason sighed heavily. He'd been good to her, fixing things around the house, playing with Caleb. But right now, he was infuriating her.

"I don't know, Amy. Something's wrong. He tried to kill himself. He's talking to people who aren't there. He's ranting about fictitious tapes. That's not my brother. My brother's cool. Level-headed. The voice of reason."

Amy stared out the window at the passing trees and still pink morning sky. Each mile closer to the hospital stripped away at her certainty. "I need him home." She flushed at the selfish sound of her words. "He needs to be home with Caleb and me. Besides, what if he's really trying to tell us something? How do you know he's not right?"

Jason was uncharacteristically quiet as they pulled into Fairview Hospital's parking garage and circled, finally finding a parking spot on the fourth level. He cut the engine and turned to her. "How do I know there's not a box of tapes hidden under the northwest corner of the office building? I checked, okay? I had a hellava time explaining to Rick why I was digging around a project I no longer have claim to."

"What if they were moved?" Amy sounded crazy. Better her than Josh.

He shook his head. "What's on these supposed tapes anyway?"

She looked down at her hands, suddenly self-conscious. "I don't know. He keeps ranting about buildings, tapes, and jail."

Jason raised his eyebrows.

"Do you have any idea what he's talking about?" Her voice was almost a whisper.

"I told you, I don't."

She recoiled from the hard edge in his voice. "I'm sorry. I . . . He's trying to tell me something and I don't know what it is."

"Hey." Jason touched her shoulder. "Look at me."

She wiped her eyes and trained them on his face.

"I don't think *he* knows what he's trying to tell you. But I can tell you that the building is fine." He made a noise in the back of his throat. His eyes searched hers and his expression softened. "I didn't mean to upset you. We'll figure it out."

He came around and opened the door for her. She gave only cursory attention to the musty smell of old gasoline and the chipped white paint punctuated by red arrows leading the way. It would be nice to leave this place for the last time.

They made their way in silence through the now familiar halls. Amy stopped at the nurse's station.

The day nurse looked up from the binder in which she was writing. "Good morning, Amy."

"Hi. I'm here to take Josh home. Are his discharge papers ready?"

Her ever-present smile fell along with Amy's heart. Something wasn't right. "Wait right here, please."

Amy glanced behind her at Jason, who appeared overly interested in the motivational posters adorning the scuffed wall, a deep frown on his face.

"Amy." She jumped when she felt a hand on her shoulder. She spun around to face a short man with black hair tied back in a ponytail. The stark white of his lab coat contrasted against his caramel skin.

"Sorry. I didn't mean to startle you. Can we step into the office and talk for a moment?"

"Why?" She tried to monitor the shrillness in her voice. "Is something wrong?"

"I'd like a word."

She looked up at Jason with the queasy sensation of being called to the principal's office in her empty stomach.

The doctor led them down a long hallway, around the corner and down another hallway. The linoleum gave way to gray shag. Finally, he stopped in front of a heavy oak door with a gold name plate telling them they'd reached Doctor Jefferson's office. But who was *this* doctor?

Dr. Jefferson was stationed behind a worn wooden desk, his hands folded in wait.

The short doctor motioned to the tattered office chairs facing the desk. "Please."

Amy dropped into the hard chair and Jason sat beside her. The doctor pulled up a folding chair apparently brought in for this meeting. This couldn't be good.

"Forgive me," he said in a slight accent Amy hadn't noticed before, "I failed to introduce myself. I'm Dr. Patel. I'm a psychiatrist. Dr. Jefferson invited me to consult on Josh's case.

Acid spread to Amy's chest. Why were they wasting time?

Her parents would get restless after the whole morning with Caleb. Couldn't she sign the damn papers already? Why was everyone making this so complicated?

The two doctors exchanged a look. Had she spoken aloud? She clasped her shaking hands in her lap. Jason's knee was bouncing up and down the same way Josh's did when he was nervous. Amy felt like a child shrinking into the chair. Like *Alice In Wonderland*. Down the rabbit hole.

"We'll get right down to business." Dr. Jefferson opened a file on his desk. "As Dr. Patel said, I asked him to evaluate Josh. It's helpful to have a fresh set of eyes."

He leaned over the desk and held the file out to Dr. Patel. Amy had the strange urge to snatch it from the exchange and run out of the office. Dr. Patel flipped through a few pages; his black eyebrows knit together. The *tick tick* of the clock above Dr. Jefferson's head taunted her.

Dr. Patel looked up. "I'm going to cut to the chase. We don't believe he should be released."

There it was. The floor dropped out from under her. "But he's fine."

"Physically, yes. But he's still experiencing acute psychosis and he hasn't responded to the first line of antipsychotics."

"Antipsychotics?" The word tasted metallic in Amy's mouth. "I wasn't told anything about this." In her ears, she sounded like a whiny child. She was a whiny child. *No fair!*

Dr. Patel barely suppressed a sigh. He adjusted his glasses. "We are committed to keeping the lines of communications open, but sometimes for the safety of our patients and staff, we have to act quickly."

"Are you telling me Josh tried to hurt staff members?"

"Well, no. But he's extremely paranoid. He thinks we're prosecuting him for some crime. Yesterday we found him slamming his head against the wall. We had to sedate him for his own safety."

Amy winced. Her fairy tale life was turning into a Shakespearean tragedy. She needed Josh back.

She looked at Jason. His nostrils flared. He was gripping the arms of the chair so hard she wondered if the cheap wood would splinter. Dr. Patel turned to him.

"You must be Josh's brother. The resemblance is uncanny."

"Jason." He returned Dr. Patel's smile with a scowl.

"Right. Jason, has your brother experienced episodes such as these before? Perhaps during childhood?"

"No. Josh is the level-headed one in the family."

"I see." Pulling a pen from behind his ear, he made a note in the file. "What was your home life like growing up?"

Amy watched Jason. There was fire in his green eyes. *Josh's eyes.*

"Our home life? Fine. Good. I mean, our mom died when we were babies. We struggled to make ends meet, but we were always tight."

"How'd your mother pass?"

"Childbirth. But I don't see what that has to do with—"

"That must've been difficult, growing up without a mother."

"It wasn't." The defensive edge had crept back into his voice. "We never knew her. It's the way it was. Our dad was enough."

"And where is your father now?"

"At work. Look, where are you going with this?"

Dr. Patel continued, unaware or unconcerned that he'd lit a fuse. "Any abuse in the home?"

"That's it!" Jason slammed his hands on the armrests and shot to his feet. Amy shrunk down in her seat.

"I don't have to answer these asinine questions. I don't like what you're implying."

He towered over Dr. Patel, who held up his hands in surrender. Jason's temper had that effect on people. "I'm not implying anything. Just trying to get to the root cause."

Jason raked a hand through his dark hair. "It's not some hidden childhood trauma, Freud."

Dr. Patel's eyes widened.

"So, you have no explanation," Amy spoke up. "What you're doing isn't helping. He needs to be home in his familiar environment." She sounded like a broken record. *Records. Record player. Josh sitting in front of the record player, at home.* This was supposed to be a happy day. "If that's all." Amy vacated her chair.

Dr. Patel and Dr. Jefferson rose simultaneously. In another circumstance, their choreographed urgency would've been comical.

"Amy, please," Dr. Jefferson said. "We strongly insist that Josh be admitted to the mental ward for his own safety."

She'd heard enough. "He's safe with me." Amy wasn't used to battles, to questioning authority, but she wouldn't let Josh be locked up like a criminal. Not again.

"Allow me to be blunt."

Dr. Jefferson came around the desk, too close. She sidled closer to Jason, close enough to feel the heat radiating off his body.

"You have a young child, correct? Protecting him is your top priority, I'm sure."

Protect Caleb from his father? "I'll sign whatever you want. He's not going to hurt anyone."

"What about himself?" Dr. Jefferson interjected.

"Amy, this hospital can move to have him committed without your cooperation if we have reason to believe he's a danger to himself or others." Dr. Patel said. His words sent a chill through the cramped room.

Amy opened her mouth, but nothing came out. Josh, a danger? The two words didn't belong in the same sentence. Nothing made sense anymore. The room began to fade.

Jason's strong grip encircled her shoulders, steadying her. "You okay, Amy?"

She shook her head, clearing her vision. Her body sagged against his solid chest.

"Look, this is a lot. How about you let us see him? Give us a few minutes. We'll talk about it." He sounded calm now. In control. At least one of them was.

The doctors exchanged an entire conversation with a look. Wordlessly, Dr. Jefferson led them to Josh's room while Dr. Patel faded backstage in this demented play where everyone but her had a script. *Exit, stage right.*

Dr. Jefferson took out his key ring, as if Amy's heart could sink any lower. They'd locked him in.

"You know where to find me. Please call the nurse if you need help."

Exit, stage left.

At least Josh wasn't restrained to the bed. He was standing at the barred window, staring out. When had the light gone out of his eyes and why? And how could she get it back? Reflexively, she put a hand to her chest. Her heart hurt so badly the pain was physical. She cleared her throat.

"Josh." He didn't turn, even when she approached him.

She embraced him from behind, burying her face in the hollow beneath his shoulder blades. He was wearing his favorite Red Sox sweatshirt she'd brought him to ward off the hospital's artificial chill. To her disappointment, it smelled like antiseptic. It didn't smell like him. He didn't smell like him.

She squeezed him. He'd lost weight. He felt less solid. "You feeling okay, sweetie? Ready to go home?"

He tapped his forehead against the window. "Is this the eighth floor?"

"Yeah. Come on, let's get your stuff."

"Eight stories. That's how high it has to be to do you in. Otherwise you risk ending up a cripple. It's gotta be eight floors, at least."

The robotic monotone of his voice made Amy go cold.

"Josh, look at me."

It took force to spin him around to face her. She reached up with both hands and gripped his face, the unfamiliar stubble rough against her palms. The vacant look in his eyes terrified her to the core.

"Josh, look at me." This time it was a command. He smiled at her, but it didn't put the light back in his eyes. It was like someone had snuffed out a match.

Gripping his arms, she shook him hard. "For God's sake, listen to me! Don't you want to go home? Stop talking like that. Just stop it. They'll lock you up."

He shrugged one shoulder. "They won't let me out, anyway. They said I'm in here for life."

"No one said that. Will you stop it?" Amy felt herself unraveling like a spool of thread tossed haphazardly down a staircase.

Jason approached from his station in the doorway. She'd forgotten he was there. Amy backed up to give him space. Maybe he could talk sense into Josh.

"Hey, buddy. Do you know where you are?"

"Of course he knows where he is."

Jason held up a hand to silence her.

Josh looked at his brother. "The slammer. I'll never be the same after this." He gripped his brother's arm. "Don't worry. I know you didn't know anything. I tell them. I tell them every day you didn't know. It wasn't your fault." He turned back to the window.

Amy examined the yellow-blue constellation of bruising on his forehead reflected in the thick glass. She grabbed his hand and tried to pull him away. If he'd stop this nonsense, they could go home already. "You're in the hospital, Josh. I'm taking you home. You can see Caleb."

Josh shook his head furiously, his hair falling into his face. Amy pushed it back, her fingers brushing over the swelling in his forehead. "They can't get to Caleb. I won't let them. It's all over for me. Save yourself." He tapped his forehead against the window. *Tap, tap, tap.*

Amy put her hand between his head and the glass, the way she did with Caleb when he was coming up under the table. "Josh, please."

"Amy," Jason said, "can I talk to you outside?"

She shook her head. Was no one on her side?

"Amy."

She rested a hand on Josh's back. "I'll be right back."

Jason led her to the hallway and eased the door shut. He looked at her with something dangerously close to pity in his eyes.

"What? What do you want? You're not helping. You're just standing there."

Jason looked up and down the hallway as though waiting to be rescued. He sighed, his broad shoulders dropping. "I didn't want to have to say this."

"Say it. Just say it."

"I don't think he should leave."

"You don't mean that." She was losing her only remaining comrade.

"It's not safe. On some level you must know that."

"You can't believe he'd hurt anyone."

"He hurt himself." His voice rose. "He'll do it again, Amy. Did you hear him in there? He'll try to kill himself again and this time—" his eyes filmed. "This time you might not be able to stop him." He took a deep, shuddering breath, his eyes filled with raw fear.

Amy stared at him. Everything froze. The air evaporated. "Are you honestly telling me to have your brother locked up in a mental ward?" She shivered.

"No." Jason took her small hands in his large, calloused ones and squeezed gently. "I'm asking you, begging you as his brother to have him locked up. Right now, it's the only way to save him." He dragged a sleeve across his eyes.

Amy turned away from him and cracked Josh's door open. He remained at the window muttering to himself, or to someone created by his mind.

There in the cold hospital hallway Amy Everett knew a heart could literally shatter, because hers did. "I swear to you," she whispered, "I'll find a way to bring you back to me."

Straightening her spine, she eased the door shut and turned back to Jason. She nodded, not trusting her voice. Somehow, she had to wait to break down. She'd need her strength when she told Caleb Daddy couldn't come home after all. It was her turn to be the strong one, no matter how impossible.

Jason took her hand and led her back to Dr. Jefferson's office. They didn't speak. There was nothing more to say. Amy raised her hand to knock but it was shaking too badly. Jason rapped on the door with his free hand.

"Enter." Dr. Jefferson looked up from whatever he was writing, an unmistakable shadow passing over his face.

"Okay," Amy said. "I'll do it. I'll sign Josh into the . . . into the mental ward. Please help him."

She sank into the chair facing the desk before her legs gave out. Jason sat next to her. His hand made circles on her back. She wished he'd stop. It was taking everything she had not to dissolve into a heaping pile of sobs.

Dr. Jefferson's face softened. "You're doing the right thing. We'll take good care of him." He pushed his chair back to a beige filing cabinet against the back wall and fumbled with his key ring. Everything was locked up. They might as well lock her up too. She didn't want to go back out into the world without Josh.

But she had to think of Caleb. How would she stay together for him? How could they survive without their family's foundation? Josh was the one who made her world make sense.

If his world didn't make sense, hers didn't either.

"Can I still come and see him?"

Dr. Jefferson pulled out a thick file folder. "Yes, of course. This isn't a prison, Amy."

Prison.

The doctor slid a pen and paper across the desk to her.

The words "involuntary commitment" blurred as tears, just as involuntary, filled her eyes and dripped onto the paper. Amy picked up the pen and scrawled her signature.

Chapter 19

September 1979

Escape was futile. They'd moved him. A man on each side of him gripped his arms and marched him down the hallway, to the elevator, down another hallway and through a set of heavy doors. He thought his throat might close when they locked behind him.

He tried to force opened the bolted windows with his bare hands. When that didn't work, he tried to punch through the glass to make the unfortunate discovery that it wasn't glass at all but some type of hard, unyielding plastic. His knuckles swelled up.

"You're wasting your time," the mangy old man in the other bed told him. "The only way outta here is do what they say. Take it from me. I'm a frequent flyer. I was like you the first time. About the same age, too."

Josh ignored him. When he refused pills, clamping his mouth shut like his toddler son when offered anything green, they stuck needles in his arms that made his vision fade and his bones buckle. Interchangeable people in white coats pressed cold fingers to his wrist, probably trying to shove a chip under his skin so they could record his thoughts. He tried to cut it out with the metal prong of a pen cap he'd swiped from one of the lab coat's pockets.

The mangy man started screaming when he saw the blood. The lab coats walked in and shook their heads.

"You're going to have to stop all this," a hard-faced woman in a paper hat said as she wove a threaded needle through his wound. "Now we'll have to put you back on suicide watch. Josh didn't flinch as the needle pulled at his skin, nor did he try to explain that he was only trying to get at the chip. He never did find it.

They searched his room. They took away his sheets and covered the stained mattress with clear, thin plastic that crinkled every time he moved. Paper Hat sat beside the bed, alternating between flipping through a magazine and glaring at Josh. She even followed him to the bathroom.

Exasperated, Josh held up his left hand. "I'm married," he said, but his wedding band was gone, his skin pale where it had been.

Paper Hat made a noise in the back of her throat. "Don't make me vomit."

"Who took my wedding band? Was it you?" The hammered metal wasn't worth much, but it meant everything to him.

If possible, Paper Hat's eyes grew darker. "I'm no thief. Your wife has all of your personal belongings."

Someone laughed. "She's leaving you. That's why it's gone." Josh raised his eyes to see Officer Shane crowding the doorway, that satisfied smile on his face. The guy had a special vendetta against Josh. Why else would he be in this confusing lab-prison? As if regular prison wasn't bad enough.

"Get away from me!" Josh shouted.

"You know I can't do that," Paper Hat said.

"I wasn't talking to you. I need to find it." He bolted out of bed so fast that he had to shake floaters from his vision. Paper Hat was right behind him. Why wouldn't she leave him the hell alone? All he wanted was to find Amy and make sure she had his ring. Make sure she still loved him. Paper Hat turned away from him to grab a phone mounted to the wall. Josh used the distraction to bolt past Shane and take off at a dead run down the hallway. "Amy!"

Somehow, Paper Hat was in front of him. Josh skidded to a halt. He could easily get past her, but he didn't want to hurt her. It wasn't her fault they were making her follow him around. He changed direction and began running the way he'd come. He didn't know where the exit was anyway.

He ignored the shouts behind him as he ran. "Amy?" he called, as he was tackled from behind. He went down hard, his face smashing into the linoleum. The metallic taste of blood filled his mouth. He tried to turn his head to spit when a knee was shoved into his back.

"No, please. I'm only trying to find my wedding band."

"For your own safety . . ."

"If you cooperate . . ."

They didn't understand. Spent, Josh went limp before they even put the needle in his arm.

They dragged him like excess baggage into an empty, closet-like room covered from floor to ceiling in blue mats. Josh heard the unmistakable click of the lock. He laid still on the mat, detached. Blood trickled from his lip. His wrist throbbed. There was nothing to see, so he closed his eyes.

Escape was futile.

Chapter 20

September 1979

"Where is he?" Amy stared at the empty bed. Its sheets had been replaced by a clear plastic covering.

"They hauled him off to the quiet room." Josh's roommate bounced on his mattress.

Amy turned to him. The poor man. She hadn't seen anyone visit him and he was always sitting on his bed. "I'm sorry, the what?"

He shrugged. "The quiet room. It's where they put you when you lose it. It's really a padded closet." He laughed, and then seemed to notice her look of horror. "Don't worry, sweetheart, it ain't so bad. I've been there."

"Why'd they put him there?"

He shrugged again. "He managed to get ahold of one of those pens the wardens carry around in their pockets. Broke the metal part of and sliced his wrist open." He made a slashing motion across his pale wrist with a bony index finger. "Then he accused Nurse Ratched of stealing some ring and went running outta here. I keep trying to tell him he's not gonna get anywhere, but—"

"He cut his wrist? Why?"

"He's going to hurt himself again."

"Don't ask me. I can't even figure this out," he tapped the side of his head.

"Why didn't anyone call me?" Amy demanded at the nurses' station. "I had to hear that Josh cut his wrist and was moved to something called the quiet room from another patient."

The nurse had the decency to look chagrined. "Yes, I'm sorry. Someone should've contacted you. We're spread rather thin around here. The wound was superficial. It only required four stitches."

Amy stared at her. Was that supposed to make her feel better? "Can I see him?"

"We don't let visitors in the quiet room. Isolation." She nodded, as if this was supposed to make sense to Amy.

"Please." Josh couldn't stand being confined. He wouldn't even close the bedroom door. "My parents are with my son. I can't stay long."

She looked at Amy for what seemed like a full minute. Finally, she sighed. "Follow me."

The nurse led Amy to a door that blended into the wall, the seams barely giving it away. "I could get into a world of trouble for this," she said as she located a small key.

"I won't say anything."

"You have five minutes. The room is soundproof, so I'll leave it cracked and wait right here. Yell if you need me."

Amy's stomach flipped. This must be awful for him after where he'd been. She pictured him screaming for help and no one able or willing to hear him.

True to the man's word, the room was the size of a large closet. The air smelled stale. The walls, floor, and even ceiling were covered with what looked like gym mats. Josh was lying on his side in the middle of the room, curled into himself. He was facing away from her and she couldn't tell if he was breathing. Jolted back to That Night, tears sprang into her eyes.

She fell to her knees beside him. He smelled of sweat and

neglect. Relief flooded her as she touched his shoulder and heard his sharp intake of breath. "Josh."

He rolled toward her. His eyes were red-rimmed, his face gaunt. His hair was matted to his forehead with sweat. Bruises in various stages of healing dotted his temples. Amy was almost knocked over by a fierce wave of protectiveness.

"Josh." She slid her arms under his shoulders. "Baby. Sit up."

She helped him into a sitting position. He leaned against her for a moment, his body like a furnace. Then he looked at her. Really looked at her. His hand brushed her cheek. "Don't cry. I'm all right."

It was so like Josh, her Josh, to worry about her when he was suffering. Her eyes were drawn to the white bandage on his wrist. "You cut your wrist. Why?"

He followed her gaze. "Oh, that. I thought they put a chip under my skin." He shrugged. "Guess not. Hey, I was looking for you. I think someone stole my wedding ring."

"No, I have it. It's at home."

He tilted his head to one side looking so much like a child. "Don't you love me anymore?"

She took his hands. "Don't be silly. Of course, I love you. I wanted it to be safe. I'll bring it to you if you want."

He shook his head. "No, you better keep it. Can't trust anyone around here." His eyes searched hers. "I know I deserve to pay, but that—"

"Josh, stop. You don't deserve any of this."

"How can you say that, after what I did? How can you forgive me?"

"You were hurting."

Josh was quiet for a moment. "Hey, you remember that old movie, *Gaslight*?"

She nodded. The reference brought her back to an ordinary rainy night. She could almost feel the scratchy fabric of the orange couch in Josh's childhood home, his arm around her as they shared a bowl of popcorn.

Her thoughts bounced to their wedding day, to the vows she'd spoken under Walt's glowering stare. She'd meant them, but had she really understood the implications? How could she? She was young and naïve, and she hadn't pictured a world in which her hero needed to be taken care of. Any moments of vulnerability had been so fleeting she wasn't sure they existed at all.

But now? Amy felt her marriage cascading toward a crossroad. Her parents were stepping back in and symptoms of her old life were bleeding through as she flailed in this bizarre parallel universe in which Josh was locked inside a padded room. Time was running out.

"What about the movie?" She asked him.

"That's what they're doing to me," he whispered. "Officer Shane, he must run the whole damn place. He's torturing me, Amy. The guy's sick. People talk to me, taunt me, make noises, all the damn time. Sometimes they show themselves, sometimes they don't." He gestured wildly. "They pretend they can't hear them. They act like I'm the only one who can. But obviously everyone can. It's so fucking loud. They dress like doctors, all standing around in their white coats with their fucking clipboards like, 'no one's there, Josh. No one said anything,' trying to make me think I'm crazy." A trail of sweat ran down his temple. "I know what you're doing," he yelled at the wall.

A chill went through Amy despite the acrid room. "Hey." She turned his face toward her.

As his eyes softened, she saw past the mysterious storm in his mind. Tenderly, he traced her face with his fingertip, tucking a strand of hair behind her ear.

"You look so sad."

"I'm worried about you."

"I don't want you to worry about me. How's Caleb?"

Amy adapted to the abrupt subject change. It was so Josh. "He's good. Really good."

"That's good. Tell him I—" He stopped abruptly, a shadow passing over his face as he stared over her shoulder, Amy turned her head to survey the empty space. The hair on her arms stood on end. It was like he was seeing a ghost.

"Yeah, you can hide all you want, Shane, but we can hear you. It's not gonna work. You won't get me to talk."

She touched his arm. "Josh, I didn't—" His stricken expression stopped the words.

"Not you, too," he whispered.

It was hell, not to trust anyone. She remembered that. He didn't trust the doctors or nurses. He couldn't trust his own mind. He needed to trust her. She needed him to trust her. If she broke his trust she could lose him completely.

There are times in life when you make a judgment call based on what you hope is intuition but could just as easily be reckless emotion.

"I didn't catch exactly what he said. Did you?"

He grabbed her arm, his relief palpable. "I knew I could count on you to tell me the truth. He's yelling. He's always yelling."

Amy nodded. "He's very loud."

"He's saying you'll leave me. He says it a lot."

Amy felt a pang. She leaned her head close to his. "He's lying," she whispered.

Josh gave her a conspirator smile. "I knew you wouldn't trick me."

That was, of course, precisely what she was doing. A wild idea occurred to her. "Josh, why not do what they say?"

"Who? The cops?"

Cops? "The people here. The people in the coats and the scrubs. Fighting them isn't working, right? Why not beat them at their own game. Make them think your submitting to them. Then maybe you'll get out of here."

He frowned thoughtfully. "But what about the pills?"

"One more minute," the nurse called. Josh's eyes widened with panic.

Amy squeezed his arm. "Placebos," she whispered.

He nodded slowly. "So, if I cooperate, you think that'll get my sentence reduced?" He made air quotes around the word "cooperate."

"I think so. We know the truth, right? I'm not going to let anyone hurt you."

"You and me against the world," he whispered.

Amy swallowed hard.

"If you think that's best, that's what I'll do."

She kissed his forehead. "It'll be okay, Josh."

"Do you have to leave?"

"I'll be back tomorrow. Remember our plan, okay?"

He nodded. "Okay. I love you."

"I love you, too. No matter what they say."

There were no instructions on what to do if your husband woke up one day and started hallucinating. But in a strange way it felt like she'd had a real conversation with him. Maybe if she found a window into his confusing world, she could find a way to bring him back.

Chapter 21

Josh shifted his weight from one foot to the other on the porch of the foreboding mansion.

"She doesn't want to see you." Walt stood in the doorway, an immovable roadblock.

"Please. Give me five minutes to talk to her."

Walt stepped out and closed the door behind him. He crossed his arms over his chest. Josh's head ached. He needed to see Amy, to explain.

"Look, kid, what you did really upset her. She's afraid of you, and quite frankly, I don't blame her."

Amy, afraid of him? That was the last thing he ever wanted. "But, that doesn't make sense."

Walt shook his head as though Josh was thick-skulled. "I thought maybe getting locked up would get this out of your system."

Josh didn't know what in the hell he was talking about. "I love her. I'll never hurt her."

"You're nineteen years old. What do you know about love?"

"Enough to know that I love Amy. I need to see her. If she tells me to go, I'll go. I need to hear it from her."

"You got a lot of nerve, kid. If you really love her you'll leave her be. Let her move on. You're not good enough for her. Deep down, you must know that."

Josh took as step back as though Walt had physically struck him. Maybe he *should* let Amy go. He was nothing more than a high school drop out with a criminal record. Without another word, he turned and walked back to his truck.

"You're doing the right thing," Walt called after him. "Get your life together," he added, as if he gave a shit what Josh did with his life.

Josh turned the radio up to drown out his thoughts. It had been a hell of a summer. Losing Amy was the worst thing that had happened to him. He wanted to crawl out of his skin.

Josh rolled the windows all the way down despite the chill that had crept into the air. Never having been claustrophobic, he found he could no longer tolerate enclosed spaces. The other night he'd dreamt of cement walls and iron doors; no way out. He'd woken himself up, screaming. Bob and Jason nearly fell over each other rushing into the room to see what was wrong.

"Only a dream," he assured them, but when Bob went to shut the door on his way out, Josh had practically shrieked at him to leave it open.

He got to the job site, a new general store, and sat in his truck. This was where it had all started. Josh slammed his hands against the steering wheel. There was nothing he could do. Somehow, he had to get out and help build this new two-story shop out of the rubble. How would he rebuild the rubble left of himself?

"Damn, you look like hell," Jason said as he grabbed his hard hat.

"Gee, thanks."

"Come on, man, I know it's been rough, but look at all the trouble you got into because of her. She was nice and all, but maybe she's not so good for you."

"What do you know about it? Your relationships expire faster than milk."

"I'm just looking out for you."

"Yeah, well, don't."

"What the hell happened to you?"

"You wouldn't understand."

"Whatever." Jason stalked off toward the trailer.

Josh pinched the bridge of his nose. It wasn't his brother's fault. He went to the single-wide trailer. Jason and Bob looked up from the blueprint when he entered.

"Jason, I—" a gust of wind blew the door shut behind him. Josh jumped. Spinning around, he tried to open the door again, jiggling the temperamental hinge.

"Take it easy." Bob came over and swung the door open. Josh bolted.

Outside, he put his hands on his knees and sucked in the cool air. How had everything gone so wrong? Bob came up behind him.

"Go home, son. It's a small project. We can manage without you for now. This is the last place you need to be."

"I'm fine, Dad."

"You're not fine. Go home. That's an order from your boss." He patted his arm.

The fight siphoned out of Josh. He turned to go. Something made him look back. Bob was still standing there, watching him carefully.

"Dad? I don't want you to worry about me, okay? I'll be all right."

"I know you will. Always are."

It didn't take Josh long to discover he couldn't be at home either. The walls were closing in. He'd never felt so alone. The idle time gave him too much room to think about Amy. To miss her so much it was hard to breathe.

Josh rummaged in the front closet until he found a pair of

gym shoes he hadn't worn in months. He laced them up and went for a run. He ran until the sweat soaked through his shirt; until his lungs burned and his mind could focus on nothing more than the pounding of his shoes on the asphalt.

Josh spent his newly found and unwanted free time—time he would be spending with Amy—running. Sometimes he ran around the neighborhood and sometimes on the beach, always trying to outpace the pain inside. His muscles grew taut, leaves shivered and fell from the trees, a fine frost coated the grass, and still he ached for Amy. Was she okay?

Josh might've gone on like that indefinitely, working and running and hurting. Then fate intervened in the form of a Guatemalan cook named Maria.

Josh pulled into the grassy overgrown driveway after work one cold night to find her bundled up and shivering on the sagging porch.

His stomach lurched. "Maria. What are you doing here? Are you okay? Is Amy okay?'

"You don't worry about me." Her familiar rich accent washed offer Josh, striking him with nostalgia. "It's Miss Amy."

"Come inside. You'll freeze."

She shook her head. "I cannot stay. Mr. Walt and Mrs. Eileen go to China for Mr. Walt's work while I look after Miss Amy."

"What's wrong with Amy, Maria? Is she sick?"

Maria shook her head, her eyes filming as she tapped her chest. "It's her heart. She's so sad. I never see her so sad. She won't eat. She don't sleep. I tell her to get up, but she won't. You have to come."

Josh's knees turned to jelly. "She doesn't want to see me, Maria. Walt said so."

To his surprise, Maria lurched forward and grabbed his arm, her grip almost painful. She shook her head furiously. "He lies. I know he's my boss, but he don't know his girl. I can't lose my job. I send money back to my mama in Guatemala, you understand? If Mr. Walt finds out I came to see you, he makes sure no one hires me, see? But I care about Miss Amy. She listens to you. Please come."

"I have a criminal record. I didn't graduate high school."

"You think I graduated high school, Mr. Josh?" Her dark eyes flashed. "You think Miss Amy cares about that? She's not like her parents. Don't choose for her. You let her choose. She's doing poorly. You care, no?"

"Of course, I care."

The truth was, Josh was a coward. He couldn't bear to see Amy only to lose her all over again. But, she was in trouble and Josh had to go to her.

"How did you get here?"

"The bus."

Maria wouldn't have spent the bus fair and risked her job if this wasn't serious. He helped her into the passenger seat of his truck and sped toward the mansion. Maria threaded rosary beads through her fingers.

"Mr. Walt can't know. I need work."

"He won't hear it from me."

His heart constricted as he pulled up to the rolling estate. Every curtain was pulled tight. It looked even colder against the sheen of frost. Remembering his manners, he opened Maria's door and offered his hand.

"You're good man. Not many good men left." She led him into the house. The darkness and silence hung like a pall.

Josh's mouth went dry. Maria gestured for him to follow her to a back sitting room he'd forgotten existed. A motionless form lay under a blanket on the couch. The T.V was on, but muted, some home improvement show, miming mindlessly.

"Miss Amy?"

"I'm not hungry, Maria." Her voice was flat. Lifeless.

Maria gave Josh a pleading look. "Do something," she whispered. "Please."

Josh tentatively approached the couch. He could see Amy's face, what wasn't covered by the blanket, in the flickering light of the television. Her skin was translucent, pulled tight over her gaunt face. Slight to begin with, she'd lost an alarming amount of weight. Her green eyes were swollen and red, the irises dull.

It was too much to take in. Everything he'd done had been to *help* her; protect her. Her pain crowded the room.

"Amy. It's me." He touched the blanket, feeling the sharp curve of her shoulder, the softness chiseled away.

She peeked up at him, her eyes widening. "Josh?" She pushed herself up to a sitting position, wrapping the blanket tightly around her. Her body swayed. He wanted to take her in his arms and make all the bad things go away.

"Can I sit?" he asked.

She nodded.

He sank into the couch next to her. Instinctively he pushed her tangled hair back. "Oh, Amy."

"Josh, I'm so, so sorry."

"Sorry for what?"

"What you had to go through. For me. It must've been awful for you. I don't blame you for hating me."

"Amy. I don't hate you. I could never hate you."

"But, my dad said he talked to you. He said you never wanted to see me again. That I was too much trouble." Her voice broke. "I am."

How had he fallen into Walt's trap so easily?

"He's been playing us."

"Who?"

"Walt. Your dad. I came here to see you. He wouldn't let me in. He told me you didn't want to see me. That I wasn't good for you. I wanted to argue, but I'm a high school drop out with a criminal record. What do I have to offer?"

She stared at him. "My dad said that?"

"In so many words. Amy, please don't be afraid of me."

"Afraid of you? Why would I be afraid of you?" Slowly, she reached out and touched him as if sure he'd disappear, "I can't believe this. I actually can't believe he did this." Her eyes filled with tears. "All this time, he's watched me sitting here *suffering*, and he said *nothing.*"

"He doesn't want to see you wind up with a criminal."

Her hand rested on his arm, warm and familiar. "You're not a criminal, Josh."

"Yeah, well, the state of Connecticut says different."

"If you'd told them why . . ."

"Doesn't matter. What matters is you. What's going on with you?"

Amy shrugged. "Nothing. I'm fine."

"Come, on, Amy. It's me. Don't do that."

She searched his eyes for a long moment, apparently finding what she was looking for. She tilted her head and smiled, inviting a glimmer back into her eyes. "Isn't it obvious? I'm a mess without you. I'm pathetic."

"If you're pathetic, so am I. I've been pretty lost myself."

"You hide it well."

"I've been running. You know, trying to outrun reality. It hasn't worked so far."

They smiled at each other. "It's not fair," Amy said. "You come over here looking like that." She looked down at her worn sweatshirt.

He tilted her chin toward him. "I've never loved seeing anything more." When he kissed her, it was like waking up from a bad dream.

"Where do we go from here?" she whispered.

"First thing's first. You need to eat something."

She groaned. "You sound like Maria. I'm not hungry."

He raked a hand through his hair. "Fine, but I am. How about I get us a pizza from Al's? You can't let me eat a whole pizza by myself."

She laughed, the sound like a salve. "Because you've never done that before."

"Come on, do me a solid. At least pretend you're going to help."

"I know what you're doing."

"I'm not doing anything."

She rested her head on his shoulder. "You're going to get tired of swooping in to rescue me."

"I doubt it. Besides, life's a circle. One day, I might need you to rescue me."

Chapter 22

"**M**ow! Mow!" Caleb pushed the wooden car into Amy's hand. "Mow wace, Mama."

Amy sighed, the exhaustion weighing her down like an anchor. The impulse to close her eyes felt irresistible. Josh had been gone over a month. Caleb was getting his molars and he'd been up countless times during the night, his piercing cries jangling her already unsteady nerves. He batted away Amy's offer of a frozen washcloth. Even rubbing whiskey on his gums hadn't helped.

She'd sat in the rocking chair taunted by the lullaby music, helpless to sooth her son. Her eyes were drawn to the bedroom door, waiting for Josh to come in, take Caleb from her arms, and shoo her back to bed. Josh could've gotten him to settle, too. These were the days and nights Amy felt altogether ill-equipped.

Pushing cars around for a solid hour made her weary and restless. Josh made playing look so effortless and, well, fun. Without the promise of Josh's arrival home at the end of each day, time slogged on, one day dragging unceremoniously into the next.

Jason was her saving grace. He dropped by after work and took Caleb out to play. She told him about gaining Josh's trust by colluding with his delusions, how the hospital staff accused her of enabling. Yet even they couldn't deny her effect on him. Often, she'd pick up the phone to an exasperated nurse on the other end. "Can you talk to him?"

Josh had lost a startling amount of weight fearing the hospital food was poisoned until Amy showed up and assured him it was safe. Amy, it seemed, was the only person he trusted.

They were having limited success with combinations of sedatives and antipsychotics, if success meant Josh was so out of it he didn't even know his own name. They tried different combinations; different doses. Some days he was entirely lucid, and she allowed the spark of hope to ignite. No one could tell her what invisible force was tormenting him. How could she save him from an adversary she couldn't see?

As much as possible, Amy stuck to their typical routine, including Wednesday lunches at her parents' house. Her bus pass was still nestled in the bottom of her diaper bag, but she accepted Walt's firm offer to send his driver, saving whatever money she could.

Slipping a few extra diapers into the tattered blue bag, she took the car from Caleb and forced a smile. She gulped the remainder of her coffee, wincing at the tepid temperature, before kneeling down to drive the car. Caleb grabbed another car off its side and crashed it into Amy's.

"Ouch." Amy forced inflection into her voice.

She swept a mess of blocks into a pile and began constructing a wall, noticing the dust that kicked up from the shag fibers. When had she last vacuumed? Laundry spilled off the couch. Was it clean or dirty? Did it matter?

Caleb propelled the car into the block wall. A horn sounded. Immediately, he abandoned his toys and ran for the door, his chubby toddler legs pumping to keep up with the momentum of his little body.

"Ca! Ca!" He jabbed his little finger at the already smudged storm door.

Amy gathered up the diaper bag, took Caleb's hand, and double-checked the locks. They settled in the back of Walt's town car, dubbed his "work car" as it was used to chauffeur clients.

"Good afternoon." The driver nodded at her in the rear-view mirror, his eyes obscured by dark sunglasses. He rubbed a finger over his thick mustache and lit a cigarette before pulling out of the driveway. Gravel crunched under the white-walled tires.

What was this driver's name? Dean? Dan? She rolled down her window and watched the tree-lined streets and small businesses pass by. If her father had his way, they'd all be bulldozed in favor of luxury houses and high-rise condos.

Amy's eyes closed of their own accord, and in what seemed like seconds the town car was rolling smoothly up the winding brick driveway. Workers were putting the finishing touches on a gaudy fountain where the driveway widened near the entrance to the mansion. Stone crayfish paralyzed mid-jump, spit at each other. They seemed to be rolling their painted white eyes at her. *You don't belong here.*

Thanking Dean or Dan, Amy pushed the door open, quickly snatching the sippy cup of juice Caleb was wrestling from the side of the diaper bag. "Not in the car," she hissed in response to his protests. Dean or Dan was likely glaring at her behind his sunglasses.

"Mom, Dad, I'm here," Amy called into the vastness as she pushed inside the marble foyer of her parents' fortress.

"Hola, Miss Amy. Hola, Caleb." Maria appeared in the front room, wearing her ever-present smile.

"Nice to see you again, Maria." Amy hugged her, breathing in the scent of spices and warmth from her childhood.

"I make tamales today. Mr. Walt and Mrs. Eileen are upstairs getting ready.

"What do they need to get ready for? I'm their daughter."

"Ah." Maria patted her arm. "You know how they are. "Come, come. I have a toy for Caleb." She gestured to a wooden duck on wheels, its cheery yellow paint and smiling orange beak a bright spot on the oriental rug in the middle of the front room.

Caleb ran to the duck and immediately began pulling it around the room.

"Caleb, say thank you to Auntie Maria."

"Dank a," Caleb said to the duck.

Maria clapped. "He talks so much now." She put her arm around Amy. "Good mama."

"Thank you." Amy feared she might cry. She needed so badly to hear she was doing something right.

"You go lie down. I watch him. I call you when lunch is ready."

Amy began to protest, but Maria pushed her toward the stairs. "Maybe I'll close my eyes for a few minutes." The offer was irresistible.

Voices floated through the closed door of her childhood bedroom. Last time she'd been up here it was like she'd never left, her four-poster bed still made up with the frilly duvet and her Beatles posters still adorning the walls. It was weird. Her parents hadn't exactly been sentimental about her leaving. Maybe they were finally ready to change it. They'd probably ask her to go through her stuff while she was here. Something made her freeze, her hand halfway to the doorknob.

"The lawyer said it should be pretty straightforward," Walt was saying. "It's not like he has any money. He can't even work, for Godsakes."

Amy covered her mouth to suppress a gasp. Her mother spoke next.

"But what will she do as a single mother? She'll end up a spinster! What will our friends say?"

"She's barely twenty, Eileen. She made a mistake. We knew

that. I'd say she's learned her lesson. We'll hire a nanny. She can go to college. Meet a nice educated boy from an upper-class family. Start over."

"It scares me, what Father Donovan said about the demon possession. What if it gets her, too? Or the baby. We'll have to have the room blessed. What if she's already under its spell?"

"Let me handle it. She's been malingering without him, but she'll be safe. She needs us to get her away from him. Once she's back home, we can take care of things."

Demon possession? Moving back into her old bedroom? She pushed the door open to face the absurdity of such suggestions. Her parents stared at her and she at them, the three of them momentarily frozen like actors who'd forgotten their lines. Amy wanted a stagehand to whisper-yell to her what to say next.

Walt was holding a drill in one hand, his other hand resting on a partially constructed white crib. The irony of it was almost comical. Amy couldn't remember him so much as putting together a doll house.

Eileen broke the silence. "Amy, good, you're here. Maria made tamales. Your favorite! Where's—"

Walt cleared his throat and silenced his wife with a look. Standing in this sterile, dainty room with her parents, Amy shrank, reduced to a submissive little girl. Her parents were suggesting she return to a bigger house but a smaller life.

"What's this?" She gestured toward the crib, hating the tremor in her voice.

Walt set the drill in the crib. "It's for Caleb."

"But Caleb doesn't live here."

Her parents exchanged a look. "Come sit." Eileen lowered herself to the bedspread and patted the spot next to her. The mattress felt harder than she remembered.

Walt remained standing, facing them. "Amy, I took the liberty of contacting a well-respected divorce attorney. He's expensive, but I'll take care of that."

Eileen assumed the role of supportive mother. "We'll take care of everything, honey. You and Caleb come home where we can protect you." She put an arm around Amy.

Amy stiffened. "Protect me from what, exactly?"

"We also met with Father Donovan. You remember, he did your confirmation. We explained Josh's visions and voices and he advised us that it sounds like demonic possession. Now, he's willing to initiate an exorcism, but you must get away from him, Amy. Before it gets you, too."

Amy laughed; the sound harsh with disbelief. She studied her mother. Not a curl was out of place. Then she looked at her father, his face lined with determination. Only the crinkles in the corners of his eyes and the silver shot through his black hair betrayed the fact that he, too was vulnerable to aging.

She found her voice. "They're called hallucinations, not visions. You can't actually believe Josh is possessed by a demon."

"You don't think that happens?" Eileen practically shrieked. "Read the Bible, Amy."

"I don't need to read the Bible, I don't need a priest, and I sure as hell don't need a divorce lawyer."

Eileen let out a dramatic whoosh of air. "Your husband's in a nut house."

Amy bristled. These people were her parents, but they were strangers. They'd never have her back. She was fighting the greatest battle of her life and she was fighting it alone.

"Mental ward. He's sick, but he'll be home soon."

"He's not sick, he's possessed! He can't take care of you. He never could. Do you really want to spend your life taking care of him?"

"We take care of each other. That's what marriage means."

Walt scoffed. "Amy, you're a child. It's time to stop playing house. Whether he's possessed or crazy, the show's over. The lawyer says there'll be no fight; no custody issue. You'll get everything. You may even be entitled to compensation for your pain and suffering."

"I can't believe this." A mounting pressure filled every cell in Amy's body. Her heart pounded in her ears.

"Divorce Josh," Walt said. "Come home. Fresh start."

Amy shot to her feet, fighting a wave of vertigo. "I have a home. I have a family."

Walt waved his hand dismissively. "Amy don't be stupid. Josh will be fine. They have places for people like him. Professionals equipped to handle these things."

People like him. These things. "Dad, I love him."

He frowned. "What does that have to do with it?"

"Please, be reasonable." Eileen got to her feet. She gripped Amy's arms; her blue eyes bored into her. "We know you love him, honey, but you can't fix him."

Amy held her gaze. "You're right," she said, "I'm not going to fix him."

Her mother dropped her hands to her sides. "I'm so relieved to hear you say that."

"We knew you'd come to your senses," Walt added.

Amy looked from one parent to the other. She hovered at a crossroad and she had to make a choice. Do what her parents asked or lose their support. She'd chosen option A every time. This time, their request was impossible to honor and unbearable to consider.

"I'm not going to fix him," she said, "because he's not broken."

"Amy—" Walt began, but she didn't hear what he said next.

For the first time in twenty years, Amy Everett turned and walked out on her parents.

Chapter 23

Between sitting in circles of other patients or prisoners or actors—whatever they were—and lining up for his paper cup of pills at a miniature drive-thru window at the nurses' station, Josh spent the endless hours in the "common room", which was a windowless space with cracked linoleum, plastic covered chairs, and an old black and white T. V. He recorded every thought, voice, and event in a black composition book and read it back to himself, making little notes in the margin. He was going to figure them out. The soothing motion of putting a pencil to paper filled his time between Amy's and Jason's visits.

"What are you writing so furiously? Is it about me?"

Josh jumped, the pencil flying from his hand and clattering to the scuffed floor.

"Here you go." A hand with long red fingernails held the pencil out to him.

Josh raised his eyes. "You! You can't be here."

Melissa smiled at him. "Poor Joshie. What did they do to you in here? You look like hell." She blew a strand of red hair away from her face.

Josh breathed deeply. He rubbed his eyes. She was perched on the arm of the chair kitty-corner.

"Close your mouth, you look like a nutter," Melissa said. The teenage boy slumped in front of the television glared at them. She shrugged. "No offense."

"I tried to take the blame for removing the shores, Josh said finally. "Why aren't they questioning me? Don't they want a confession?"

She leaned toward him and lowered her voice. "Sure, except they're all in on it. I never meant for you to end up in here. I tried to warn you. This is much bigger than a code violation."

"You think? I don't know how I thought I was going to fix it. I must've been out of my head."

Melissa leaned forward. "That's what they want you to think."

The memory he'd been fighting forced its way through the murky surface of his mind. "We slept together." The words were more bitter than the pills he'd been fed.

Melissa smiled. The smile was so familiar it sent a jolt through him. It was the same victorious smile she'd given him the moment she touched him. The moment he *let* her touch him.

"Don't tell Rick I said this, but you're the best I've had. I'm so glad you remember. I was worried with the pills and the brainwashing you'd forget." She touched his wrist. "Do you want to go find a supply closet?"

Josh jerked his arm away. "Stop! You and me—never again!"

She frowned. "You're upset."

"You're damn right, I'm upset."

"You're brainwashed."

"Why do you keep saying that?"

"Lower your voice! That's what I've been trying to tell you. I've been keeping a low profile at work, gleaning as much information as possible. This thing is way bigger than I realized. I'm sorry I threatened you, okay? I'm going to get you out of here. You don't belong here."

Josh stared at her, still hoping she'd dematerialize like a ghost; a figment of his imagination. She didn't. He leaned forward and rested his elbows on his knees.

"Tell me everything."

Chapter 24

"**H**e's been here over a month, and all these medications and everything, well, we don't have the money." Amy glanced over her shoulder as though Josh might be standing there.

Dr. Jefferson glanced up. "This is a state hospital. The cost of institutionalization is covered by the state of Connecticut. Beyond institutionalization, you'll need to apply for social security disability insurance. Assuming he's unable to return to work, you'll also need to apply for social security income." He rummaged in his file drawer and handed her a stack of forms. "Start the process now. I can't imagine you'll have an issue qualifying, but the government's not in a hurry." He offered her a wan smile and picked up the phone, dismissing her from his office.

Josh was sitting in the corner of the common room writing in a notebook. His hand jerked across the page. He was wearing a clean navy T-shirt and his damp hair was combed. Amy smiled.

"Hey, handsome." She dropped into the chair next to him, catching the familiar scent of baby shampoo. She ran her hand through his hair. "You smell like Caleb."

"Yeah, they only give you baby shampoo in here. Apparently, you can't off yourself by drinking it." He must've noticed her expression. "But you don't have to worry about that. I'll be out of here soon."

"I know."

He nodded, but he looked miles away. "How's Caleb? Where's Caleb?"

"Mrs. Croftsky's been watching him. She won't let me pay her. I've been trying to make up for it by helping in the garden, doing housework, that sort of thing."

"She probably likes it. I'm sure she's lonely."

When had she last had a real conversation with Josh? One that made sense?

He frowned, looking down at his hands. "Amy, I need to tell you something."

"Me first. I kind of got a job."

"A job?"

"Well, sort of. I drew a flyer for childcare and put it up at the library. Two moms answered. Caleb will have playmates and I'll be able to make a little money while still spending time with him."

Josh smiled, but it didn't quite reach his eyes. "That's great. You'll be perfect at that. When do you start?"

"This afternoon, actually. What was it you wanted to tell me?"

He sighed, his shoulders dropping. His knee began bouncing up and down. She put her hand on it. "Tell me."

He gazed at her for a long time. "I did something really terrible. I don't know if you'll be able to forgive me."

She swallowed hard, wracking her brain for what he could've done that was unforgiveable. "Okay."

"There's this woman, Melissa. My dad hired her back in August as a secretary."

"Okay," Amy said again. This couldn't possibly be going where it sounded like it was going.

He put his hand in hers. It was cold despite the stifling,

stale air. His face contorted in agony. Amy's heart sank. He'd been doing so well. She reached for him, wanting to pull the pain right out of him.

"I had to be crazy to sleep with her. Or desperate."

Amy dropped her hands to her lap. "What did you say?"

"I slept with Melissa, Amy. I'm so sorry."

She should feel something. Heartbreak, fury, at least disbelief. Her voice came out flat. "Why?"

"Because she had dirt on my dad. I was a fucking coward, okay? I was scared. She told me—"

"Stop." Amy held her hand up. "What are you saying?"

"She was here."

Amy couldn't get her brain to work. Time stopped. What was going on? "She came here to see you? Melissa?" The name tasted sour in her mouth. "When?"

"Right before you did. She's as real as you are." He flushed. "I mean . . . that's not what I . . ."

"Are you in love with her?" Amy blurted before she could stop herself.

"No! God, no. I don't even like her. I love you, Amy. You have to believe me." He reached for her, but she sprang to her feet.

"Don't *touch* me! She said, eliciting stares from the cluster of people around the television.

Josh looked stricken. "Amy, please!" He scrambled to his feet and then dropped to his knees. "Don't leave me."

She almost wavered. But whatever was going on in his head, a woman had been here with her husband. She might have passed Amy in the hall on her way out. That woman had sex with her husband. Had Josh attempted suicide out of guilt? Was all his ranting about tapes and shores him concocting some kind of outlandish excuse? Had he, as she'd always feared, grown weary of her reservations in bed?

"Get up, Josh."

He did, so fast he swayed on his feet.

"I'm going to figure out what's going on." She turned and headed for the exit. Josh was right behind her.

"Wait! Where are you going?"

Amy, who couldn't decide on how she preferred her coffee, knew exactly what she was going to do. "I'm going to talk to Melissa."

"Wait," Josh cried. "I'll tell you everything. Please, Amy don't get involved. She's crazy."

"I can handle crazy."

Amy watched her words hit him like a physical blow. He staggered backward. Her resolve weakened but didn't break.

She lowered her voice. "I have to do this."

The heavy steel doors locked behind her, leaving her husband trapped inside with his explanations.

Chapter 25

February 1977

It had taken a lot for Amy to learn to trust. Josh was the only person she trusted. How could he take that away? Suddenly the memory of that first time felt tainted.

Amy had followed Josh into the empty bungalow with its slightly earthy smell. You didn't tell me how you got the afternoon off."

Josh kicked aside a pair of muddy tennis shoes and grinned at her. "Jason owed me. I covered for him last week while he took his girlfriend to the half-price drive-in."

"I didn't know he had a girlfriend." Amy had seen Josh's impulsive little brother with several doe-eyed, giggly girls. The Everett brothers had no trouble turning female heads. Had she acted that giddy when she and Josh first got together? Probably.

Josh kicked off his shoes. "Yeah, well don't blink."

"You took me to the drive-in on our first date."

"Technically, that was our second date. It was the first one your parents knew about." He winked and she still felt the same fluttering in her stomach that she had that night.

"It was our first kiss, though." She linked her arms around his neck and stood on her tiptoes to kiss him. Funny how easy it was now.

He dropped her backpack to the floor with a thud and wrapped his arms around her waist.

She and Josh had been through a lot together; things that the couples walking down the hallways at school with their heads bent together seemed to deal with, but who knew? The time she'd spent without him had been unbearable.

Her parents were the one remaining catch in her fairytale romance, but they were gone increasingly. Walt was raking in developments and Eileen spent her time at the country club, or trailing him to various cities to shop, or mysteriously locking herself in her bedroom for days on end. Spells, her father said. They either didn't know where Amy spent her time, or they were too absorbed in their own lives to care.

Making out with Josh had evolved from scary to exhilarating, like the big drop on a roller coaster once you cleared the crest. Only once had his hand slipped between the buttons of her blouse. When she told him to stop, he'd yanked his hand away, apologizing so profusely Amy had to laugh.

She'd begun anticipating the tingling in her belly and the flush of her skin when they kissed.

Josh pulled away and looked at her, his eyes bright with hopeful anticipation. She closed her eyes and tilted her head toward him, a green light. They stumbled to the couch, never breaking contact.

All of Amy's senses were heightened. He was like a drug. The scuffed wood under her feet, the rough threads as they collapsed onto the couch, and Josh's mouth, warm and frenetic on hers, lit up her brain. His weight pressed against her and the unmistakable feeling of his arousal awakened a familiar panic inside of her. Panic and something else, something newer.

Josh pulled away from her and sat up on the couch, breathing hard. His face was flushed.

"So," he said, clearing his throat, "are you hungry? I think Dad got some eggs from the market."

Amy giggled. It was nice having someone to know her quirks, like her preference for sunny-side-up eggs as a snack no matter what time of the day. Even if his timing struck her funny.

He cocked his head to the side. "What's so funny about eggs? Could be pancakes. Chips?"

Her stomach rumbled. Maria's food was delectable, but it was Josh's simple food that she'd come to prefer. He'd even taught her a few tricks, like how to crack an egg without breaking a yolk and how to get the lumps out of the pancake batter.

Countless times over the years Amy had asked Eileen if they could bake together, or if her mother could teach her how to make a casserole.

"Why?" was always her response. "Marry smart, or at least go to college, and you'll have someone to cook or clean for you like you do now."

Her stomach growled again. The butterflies were akin to the first time Josh had kissed her.

"Is something wrong?" Josh asked.

She realized she'd been worrying a cuticle. Scooting closer to him, she rested her head on his shoulder. "Nothing's wrong. Actually, I feel like things have been really . . . right."

"Yeah, me too."

"Josh?"

"Hmm?"

"I think—I mean, I know I'm ready."

"Ready for what?" he asked innocently. "Eggs?"

She sat up and swatted his arm. "Can you stop thinking about food for a second?"

He smiled, the flecks of gold sparkling in his green eyes. "I'll try. I'm not making any promises." He rubbed her back. "I can feel your heart pounding. What's up?"

She tugged his sleeve and leaned close to his ear, which was silly considering they were alone. "I'm ready to make love with you."

Josh pulled his head back and stared at her. "Amy," he said, his voice thick with affection and bridled desire, "It's okay."

She'd anticipated this response. "I want to."

"Amy—"

"I'm a big girl, Josh. I'm ready. I want to." She traced the snake wrapped around his thick bicep. "I've been thinking about it for a while and I'm sure. You don't have to worry."

His muscle flexed under her hand. "You mean like, now?"

She smiled. "Well, yeah. I mean, unless you don't want to."

He laughed. "Don't be crazy. I think it's obvious what I want." He shifted his weight almost self-consciously. "You're sure?"

"I love you. I trust you. I want it to be with you."

"I love you too." He kissed her, tangling his hands in her hair. Her hands travelled up the back of his shirt. His skin felt hot under her palms.

Thoughts flew through her head as the kissing grew more frenetic. *What will it feel like? Will it hurt? Will I freak out in the middle of it?* She didn't have a sister or a girlfriend with whom to talk about this stuff. There'd be no one to call with excited whispers about losing her virginity as Gwen had done with her back when they told each other everything.

That was okay, though. Maybe this was better. She had Josh; she didn't need anyone else. He moaned, gently biting on her lower lip. The sound was raw and intoxicating. When he lifted his head, beads of perspiration dotted his forehead.

"Do you want to go to the bedroom?" he asked. Did he feel the same heady anticipation running through his veins?

Amy glanced at the front door. "Your dad or Jason won't come home?"

He shook his head, his hair falling into his eyes. "Not until the sun goes down." The sun shined permissibly through the window.

"Yes," she said.

He got up and offered her his hand. Staring at his unmade bed made it real. "I might be bad at it."

He smiled, kissing her tenderly before carrying her to the narrow twin bed, one hand cradling her head as he lay her down amid the tangled sheets.

One knee slid between her legs as he crawled over her, discarding his T-shirt. His confidence was warranted. She brought her hands to his solid chest as he began kissing her again. The waiting made her dizzy. Josh delicately peeled off her shirt. Her hands flew to her stomach, but he moved them.

"Don't," he whispered. "You're perfect."

Though she didn't quite believe him, she didn't protest when he undid her bra and lowered his head to kiss her. His hands shook slightly as they travelled down her body and latched on to her waist band. He searched her face. "Can I?"

She nodded mutely. The panic when he touched her was momentary. This was different. This was Josh. She was safe. It felt different, too. New and not unpleasant.

He hopped off the bed and undid his belt while she caught her breath. Amy couldn't take her eyes off him.

"Ready?"

"Wait." She held up her hand like a stop sign. "I—I'm not on birth control."

Josh smacked his forehead. "What an idiot!"

"What?"

"Not you. Me. Hang on, I'll be right back. Don't go anywhere."

Drawers on the other side of the wall opened and slammed shut. He returned with a foil packet.

Amy raised her eyebrows. "Do I want to know?"

He grinned. "Jason's room."

"Nope, don't want to know." She watched him.

He crawled over her and she lifted the sheet to give him access, pulling it back over them both. It was clumsy and awkward and not at all like the movies. It was perfect.

"Oh, God," he moaned, dropping his head to her shoulder, breathing hard.

The heat of his body, the rapid beat of his heart against hers was like coming home. She ran her fingertips over his back, imagining she could feel the ridges of his rising phoenix tattoo. Josh shivered and then stilled, his breathing slowly regulating.

"I love you, Josh Everett."

"Love you, too." His voice was muffled. He lifted his head, his expression morphing from contentment to horror when he looked at her face. He pushed himself off her. "You're crying! Did I hurt you?"

Amy reached for his arm, stilling him. She hadn't felt the tears. "You didn't hurt me. I'm happy."

Happy. The sensation was fresh and vulnerable. If only she could trap it in her hands and drink it in, like refreshing water from a spring. That's what she was with Josh. Happy.

He smiled. "Yeah? That was okay?"

She laughed, pushing his hair out of his face. "It was more than okay. I never knew it could be like that."

"That's the way it's supposed to be, when you trust someone." He flopped onto his back and pulled her against him.

She pulled the sheet up to her chin and rested her head on his chest. "I trust you."

Josh was the steady force in her life, the anchor that kept her from floating off into a mere hologram of herself; and ugly hodgepodge of her parents' expectations and disappointments.

"Can we do it again?"

He laughed. "You're gonna have to give me a minute."

She rolled her eyes. "I didn't mean right now."

The room was like a sauna. Josh nodded off, snoring softly. Running her fingertips through the course, dark hair on his chest, she watched him sleep.

In the weeks that followed, Amy was pleased to find that the happiness persisted, like a light that had been left on inside of her. The kids at school gave her a wide berth, and freed from the distraction of fear, her grades improved. For the most part, her parents ignored her when they weren't giving her disapproving looks or not so subtly mentioning so-and-so's handsome son.

Most of her time was spent at the Everett's modest bungalow, and it wasn't only Josh she enjoyed being around. Bob treated her like his own child, though more gently.

Jason made her laugh. He and Josh teased each other incessantly, sometimes falling on the floor in full-on wrestling matches, Bob yelling that he was too tired to take anyone to the emergency room today. As an only child, the dynamic fascinated Amy; the affection thinly veiled behind the banter. It was the only time Josh acted his age.

She slipped seamlessly into their lives. It felt more like a home than her own, with its shoes strew in the front hall, stuffing leaking out of one corner of the couch, laughter and good-natured ribbing.

"Josh has never really been a kid," Bob told her. "He's always stepped up and taken care of things. He's different with you. It's like he finally knows how to relax."

Things were too good to be true. A whole new life opened on the horizon. A life with Josh. She could have basked in the comfortable simplicity of their love story forever.

Then she missed her period.

Chapter 26

October 10, 1979

Amy crossed the dusty, barren lot, brought to life by the rumble of bulldozers. It was a much smaller project than the last one, a house from what she could tell. Melissa must be in the trailer.

She climbed the rickety steps and tried the door. It opened easily. The harsh artificial lighting assaulted her corneas. Jason was on his hands and knees on the grainy floor, making marks on a giant blueprint. He looked up, the carpenter pencil dropping from his hand. He tucked it behind his ear.

"Amy? Is everything okay?"

"Where's Melissa?"

He cocked his head to the side, adjusting the pencil. The gesture might have been humorous if the circumstances weren't so dire.

"Who?"

"Melissa." She tapped her tattered sneaker against the linoleum.

Jason's expression morphed from confusion to concern. He got to his feet and stared at her. "Amy, who the hell is Melissa?"

"Jason! Where is she? I need to talk to her. Now." An unwelcome possibility occurred to her. "Oh my God, did you know? Are you covering for him? Because I don't think—"

He held up his hands. "I have no idea what the hell you're talking about, but you're starting to wig me out."

Amy sucked in a deep breath and blew it out. "Melissa. The secretary your dad hired. Is she here today and did you know Josh was... did you know Josh was having...?" The words stuck in her throat. The air in the trailer evaporated.

"You're shaking. Sit down."

"I don't want to sit down," she said, but she let herself be led to the folding chair behind the desk. It's back wobbled as she leaned against it, unsteady like everything else in her life.

Jason hopped up on the desk facing her, his work boots swinging against the metal, kicking up mini clouds of reddish dust. Amy wrapped her arms around herself. Jason watched her. "You want to tell me what's going on?"

"You really don't know?"

He shook his head, his face earnest. The relief threatened to bring tears to her eyes. Who did she have left to trust? Who else was on her side? It had always been her and Josh against the world, but now . . .

"Josh admitted to having an affair with Melissa. He claims she was always hanging around him, and they—"

The look on Jason's face stopped her mid-monologue.

"Shit."

"I know. I need to talk to her. I won't make a scene or anything."

Jason shook his head. "Amy, you don't understand. There is no Melissa. There is no secretary. Dad has never and would never hire one. Trust me, I've raised the issue. My hand's about to fall off keeping the books." He held up his hand. I can show you our payroll if you don't believe me."

Like swimming upward through quicksand, realization slowly penetrated her. "So, you mean . . . Josh is hallucinating *entire people?*"

"I don't know what the hell he's doing, but I do know

there's no Melissa. Not here. I don't even know anyone named Melissa, and as far as I know, neither does Josh. And, let's be real, if there was a hot secretary, I'd be the one sleeping with her." He flashed his signature lopsided grin.

Amy couldn't manage a smile. "I never said she was hot."

"Don't get mad, but after he met you, I mean before I knew it was serious, I'd be all, 'Josh, look at that fox. She keeps staring at you,' and he'd be all like, 'what's it to me? She's not Amy.' And then I'd throw up a little."

Amy waited for the relief to envelop her. Josh wasn't cheating.

"You don't look relieved," Jason said, echoing her thoughts.

"I don't get it. How could he think he was with someone that doesn't even exist? I mean, how did he even get there, you know?"

"Yeah, it's fucked up. It's gotta be hell, not knowing what's real."

"I said things to him, Jason. Awful things. I wanted to hurt him."

"You're human, Amy. He told you he cheated on you. How were you supposed to react?"

"I should've put it together. It didn't make sense. He was so torn up about it and he didn't even do it." She straightened up in the chair, the back wobbling precariously. "It's not his fault."

"Are you always this hard on yourself?"

"You can find a way to blame yourself for the weather," Josh always told her.

"Yes."

"Look, can I be straight with you?"

"Always."

"Most people would've walked away by now. You've been dealt a shitty hand, and instead of running you've been taking care of everything. You're amazing."

Her eyes filmed, the words a salve for her self-doubt. "You're the only one I can count on anymore. I couldn't do it without you." She looked up at him. "You know, Josh sounded so sure ..."

Jason sighed. "Come with me."

"I don't want to disrupt your work anymore than I already have."

"Blueprint's not going anywhere. Besides, we're in this together." He slung his arm around her shoulders and led her out to his truck. She let herself indulge in the comfort of his proximity.

Amy winced as the truck lurched into oncoming traffic. A horn blared, and Jason flipped the finger out his window. Amy stared at the leaves changing from green to gold and orange. Josh loved the fall. Would he be able to pick out a pumpkin with Caleb? Take him trick-or-treating?

Caleb would get a kick out of Josh's dinosaur costume from the second-hand shop. He'd worn it all around the neighborhood last fall, giddy as a child, waving her off when she pointed out the absurdity of taking an infant trick-or-treating. Later, watching Josh pilfer the candy Caleb was obviously too young to have, she realized it had really been for him. Those were the moments she caught glimpses of Josh allowing himself to be young. What had Bob told her? *He's never really been a kid."*

"Here we are."

Amy realized they'd reached the Everett's previous jobsite. She'd only been there once, when they'd broken ground.

But now a four-story partial building stood on the plot of land, yellow hard hats buzzing around it like bees preparing a hive.

"The building was inspected thoroughly," Jason said. Not a beam—or a shore out of place. Rick's new crew even cut into the first two levels to make sure. You think he hated us before?" He scoffed.

Everything hit Amy at once. The silent tears felt cold sliding down her cheeks.

Jason cut the engine. "How can I help? What can I do?"

She turned her head away from the building and its proof of Josh's insanity. "What's happening to him?"

"I don't know. But we're going to figure it out. Together."

She managed a small smile. "Thanks, Jason." Grabbing his wrist, she squinted at his watch. "Mind dropping me home? I'm taking on some childcare this afternoon. I need to make some money before the lights get turned off again."

"Again? What about your parents?"

"They're not talking to me."

"Like, at all?"

"Not since they told me to divorce Josh and come home, and I refused."

"That's shitty." He was quiet for a moment. "Have you thought about it?"

"Thought about what?"

"You know. Leaving him."

"Of course not. I love him."

He nodded, reaching into the center counsel. He held a twenty-dollar bill out to her.

"You don't have to do that."

"Come on, take it. It's not much. I wish I could do more."

Reluctantly, she accepted the bill, holding it tightly in case it disappeared like the money from her father. She kicked at the empty soda cans and candy wrappers at her feet. "Jason? There is something I need you to do for me."

He glanced at her. "Anything."

Once she made the request she had to go through with it. It was time to grow up and rely on herself. "I need you to teach me to drive."

Chapter 27

Josh looked down at his hand intertwined with Amy's "What do you mean, there is no Melissa?" His eyes bounced over the peeling green wallpaper adorning Lab Coat's office and landed on the shiny paper in a cracked frame. He squinted at the calligraphy. 𝔐𝔞𝔱𝔱𝔥𝔢𝔴 𝔍𝔢𝔣𝔣𝔢𝔯𝔰𝔬𝔫, 𝔐.𝔇. 𝔇𝔬𝔠𝔱𝔬𝔯 𝔬𝔣 𝔓𝔰𝔶𝔠𝔥𝔦𝔞𝔱𝔯𝔶. He glared at Lab Coat. "Who the hell are you anyway? No more lies."

Lab Coat sighed, folding his hands on the desk. "Josh, we've been over this before. My name is Dr. Matthew Jefferson. I'm your psychiatrist. You're at Fairview State Hospital as you have been for the past month. You've had a psychotic break. We can help you, but you need to participate. You've been fighting us every step of the way.

Josh slouched in his chair like a chastened child, gripping the arm rests so hard his hands turned white. "Participate in what? Look, I know I'm in jail, okay? What I don't know is why you're trying to make me think I'm crazy. Did Officer Shane put you up to this?"

He shook his head "I don't know who that is. I'm not law enforcement, but I work with them often. I've never heard of an officer Shane. You're not in legal trouble, Josh. We only want to help you."

Josh stared at him. His dad always said a man couldn't hold your gaze if he was trying to pull one over on you. Dr. Jefferson, if that was his name, stared back, like the staring contests he and Jason would have as kids. As usual, Josh lost. Dr. Jefferson's eyes held determination and a hint of kindness.

Amy squeezed his hand. "He's telling the truth."

"But you said—"

Her thumb brushed his knuckles. "I know, I know. I'm sorry, sweetie. I don't know how to help you. But I talked to Jason. We were out at the old jobsite. The building's fine. Melissa doesn't exist, Josh. You didn't have an affair. It's not your fault."

"I want to believe that. But she was here. I saw her. I spoke to her. I . . . I . . ."

"Josh, all visitors are required to sign in at the front desk." Lab Coat rummaged in his drawer and slid a binder across the desk.

Josh studied each name. "You guys could've doctored this." His words lacked conviction. His certainty wavered. *Was* he in a hospital?

"I suppose. But why? What motivation would I have to trick you?"

Josh looked into Amy's pleading eyes. "It's okay." She whispered.

"Fine," Josh said to Lab Coat Jefferson. "I'll play. If I am in the hospital, am I heading to jail next?"

Dr. Jefferson folded his hands on the desk. "No, Josh, you're not going to jail. The goal is to get you back home as soon as it's safe to do so."

A hard lump formed in Josh's throat. "Is my dad in jail?"

Dr. Jefferson shook his head. "Not that I'm aware."

"You . . . you must know what I've done. I mean, I didn't mean for it to happen."

"I know you didn't, Josh. No one ever means for these things to happen. Let us help you."

"If I'm not going to jail then why am I here?" Josh asked in the small voice of a terrified child.

Dr. Jefferson exchanged a look with Amy. "Maybe he'd rather hear it from you?"

She searched his eyes. "You tried to kill yourself. Will you tell me why?"

"What? I didn't try to kill myself. I would never do that."

"I found you in the truck," Amy said, almost to herself. "You weren't breathing."

He gaped at her. "I wasn't trying to kill myself. You have to believe me."

Josh, you were in your truck in a closed garage with the engine running." Dr. Jefferson added. "Do you remember running the garden hose from the tailpipe in through the front window?"

Josh shook his head, but the memory flooded his brain, the force of it nearly knocking him out of his chair. Pulling the truck into the garage. Closing the door and starting the engine. Everything getting quiet, fading. Amy's voice screaming his name from somewhere far away. The sting of regret as he tried to lift his hand and pull the keys from the ignition. Too late.

"Josh? Are you with us?" Dr. Jefferson's face was impassive, but Josh caught a glimpse of compassion in his eyes. He had to trust someone. He was tired of fighting.

"I thought it was a dream," Josh said.

Dr. Jefferson straightened, folding his hands on the desk's warped surface. "You thought what was a dream, Josh?"

Josh glanced at the garbage can placed against the wall, wondering if he should grab it in case he was sick, though his stomach was empty. "The . . . everything. I tried to fix it, but it was too late."

He should demand a lawyer. But his memories of that day and night, pixelated though they were, spilled out onto Dr. Jefferson's desk. Both Amy and Dr. Jefferson remained silent until Josh had finished.

"I'm so sorry," Josh whispered. "It's all my fault. Dad would never have the shores removed. It had to have been me, I blocked it out or something. I don't know how I thought I'd fix it in time. I don't know..." His voice cracked. He wiped the sweat from his forehead. "I guess I couldn't face it, so I convinced myself it wasn't real."

Dr. Jefferson leaned back in his chair and regarded Josh. "What if I told you it *wasn't* real?"

"Look, I don't know what your game is, but it happened, okay? I take full responsibility."

"Josh, please! Listen to him!"

He studied Amy's beautiful face and earnest eyes. "You saved my life," he whispered. "That's why you had me put in here. So I couldn't hurt myself."

She nodded, swallowing hard. "Are you angry?"

"No. God, no. I owe you everything. I thought it was a dream," he said again, attempting to swim up through the murky confusion. But as he approached shore he flailed, desperate to sink back into the depths of uncertainty and denial. "If it wasn't a dream, then the rest wasn't either. The project. The tapes. The shores. I... I don't understand."

Dr. Jefferson picked up his phone and pressed a button. "Send him in now, please."

This was it. He was calling Officer Shane in to drag him away in handcuffs. They had his confession. Josh's shoulders slumped in resignation. He'd be a man and take what was coming to him, if Bob and Jason were protected. Would he go away for life? Would Caleb ever know him? Was his son better off without him?

Josh began to tremble uncontrollably.

Amy rubbed his back. "Shh," she whispered, the way she did to calm Caleb.

A hollow knock sounded on the door.

"Come in."

Josh rose to face his justice. But when he turned, he was face to face with Jason.

"Jason! There's so much I need to . . ." His surroundings grew fuzzy, sounds coming from underwater.

"Josh?" his brother's disembodied voice said. Strong hands gripped his shoulders and eased him back into the chair. "What the hell do you have him on? Is he okay?"

"He'll be all right. This is a lot. Give him a minute." Suddenly Dr. Jefferson was bent over him, shining a penlight in his eyes. "Listen, Josh, I need you to take deep breaths for me."

He felt firm pressure between his shoulder blades. "Breathe," Amy said.

Josh took a deep breath and shook his head. His vision cleared. He grabbed Jason's arm. "Please, you have to help me. Tell me what's going on."

For the first time he noticed the denim backpack slung on Jason's shoulder. Jason set it on the desk and rummaged through it, retrieving a familiar notebook and a handful of Polaroid photos, and an official-looking paper. "Since you're living in an episode of *Columbo* I brought evidence. He looked around the office. "Geez, I was trying to lighten the mood. Tough room."

"Jason," Amy spoke up, "Why don't you sit here? I need to take a walk."

"I'm sorry, Amy," Josh said. "I'm sorry for everything I put you through."

She offered him a smile, pained but still beautiful. "It's not your fault. I love you." She put her arms around his shoulders and kissed his cheek before exiting.

Once the door clicked shut behind her, Jason took her place. He handed the binder to Josh." Here's the payroll. There's no Melissa, in fact no woman, listed."

Josh flipped through the pages of familiar names. Jason handed him the photos along with the paper. Each photo was a different shot of Rick's building, including one in which the first two stories were exposed. It appeared the project was moving along steadily. Josh studied the final document. It was an additional safety inspection completed on October 7, a month after Josh had landed in the hospital. Every box was checked.

Josh looked up. "This doesn't make sense."

Jason studied him. "Come on, Josh, pull yourself together. It'll be okay. You didn't hurt anyone, okay? The new builder working on Rick's building had it inspected again. The shores are in place."

Josh let his breath out. "It was a dream. Thank God. But, wait, if it was all a dream, how'd I get in the truck? I thought—"

"It wasn't a dream, Josh." Dr. Jefferson said.

Josh wished he'd stop saying his name like that. He wished he'd go away. "You fucking presented this evidence to me and told me that the missing shores, Melissa, Officer Shane, the tapes—none of that was real. Now you're telling me it wasn't a dream?"

"You've been in a psychotic state. These events are hallucinations."

Josh laughed. He looked at his brother. Jason's face was serious.

"You were pretty wound up that day, but the way you talked to Rick and stepped up to take care of things like you always do . . . I thought you were fine. You were so busy talking me down and I—I thought you were fine." Jason rubbed his eyes.

Josh stared at him, then looked to Dr. Jefferson. "So you're telling me we lost the project *for real*, then I hallucinated the tapes, the shores Melissa, and the police after me? Then *in reality* I pulled my truck in the garage and tried to asphyxiate myself?"

Jason flinched, but Doctor Jefferson merely nodded. "When you lost the project, your mind created this outlandish scenario.

You most likely did drive to the jobsite. You believed the police were after you. But some part of your brain realized it wasn't real, so you concluded you were dreaming."

"And then I tried to wake up." Josh turned to Jason. "I was trying to wake up. I wasn't trying to die."

"But you almost did."

Josh swallowed hard. "What's happening to me?"

"We're going to get to the bottom of it," Dr. Jefferson said. "But we need you to work with us."

Josh's empty stomach flipped like he was on a rollercoaster. Who could he trust? What was real?

"Please, Josh," Jason said to the floor. His shoulders trembled. He pressed a fist to his mouth the way he had ever since some middle school bully had teased him for crying. That gesture broke Josh.

Resigned, he returned his focus to Dr. Jefferson. "What do you want me to do?"

Dr. Jefferson leaned back in his chair. "You're taking the pills. That's a start."

Josh scoffed. "How's that? I saw Melissa the other day."

"Visual hallucinations can be especially jarring. Melissa originated prior to treatment. She's part of your memory now, albeit a false one."

"What should I do if she comes back?"

"Dr. Jefferson smiled. "Tell her to leave."

"That's never worked before."

"You didn't know she wasn't real before." He flipped through a file on his desk. "We could try an injection of Thorazine if you're willing."

Josh couldn't make a decision. He used to be able to; he did it every day. He drew blueprints and put buildings together like jigsaw puzzles. He gave direction and people listened. Now he couldn't trust his judgment. He looked at Jason. Had he ever seen his brother's face so serious? Jason nodded.

"Okay."

"Head back to your room. I'll send a nurse."

"You catch the game?" Jason asked as they wandered down the hall to Josh's room.

Josh shook his head. Football existed in a world he was no longer a part of. He shuffled into his room. Jason surveyed the bare walls and plastic-wrapped stained mattress.

"I love what you've done with the place."

Josh flopped onto his bed. "I'm sorry, Jay."

Jason shrugged. His lack of reaction only served as further illustration that nothing was normal.

"You get to be pissed off," Josh said.

Jason smiled at him. "You know, I don't think you've ever said that to me before."

Josh's shoulders slumped. "I guess I can be kind of hard on you."

"We're brothers. That's what we do."

Josh opened his mouth to answer but stopped short when Officer Shane sauntered into the room. Sneering at Josh, he put his thumb and index finger to Jason's head and made shooting noises. Josh propelled himself off the bed and lunged at Shane.

"You! Get out of here!"

Jason intercepted him. He grabbed Josh by the shoulders. "Hey. Hey, it's just us. Stay with me, buddy." Jason half pushed half hauled Josh back to his bed.

It was the only wrestling match he'd ever lost to his brother. He let his legs give out. He landed heavily on the mattress. Shane was gone. Right. He buried his face in his hands.

Jason kept a hand on his shoulder. "You okay?"

Josh shook his head. He was having a . . . what had Lab Co—Dr. Jefferson called it? A psychotic episode. In front of his brother. "Don't look at me," he said into his hands.

"Josh, come on."

"Knock knock," a voice said.

Josh looked up. One of the paper hats appeared with a needle designed for a horse. Jason blanched the exact color of her uniform.

"That's my cue." To Josh's surprise, Jason crushed him in an awkward hug. "I'll stop by tomorrow. Stay strong. You got this."

Josh closed his eyes, allowing the hazy memories to filter through his fractured mind. Behind his lids he saw the dark, empty jobsite. He'd wandered around talking to the air. Ranting. Officer Shane wasn't there. He'd sped home, fleeing from phantom police cars. He could've killed someone! He could've killed himself.

Josh held out his arm to welcome the needle.

Chapter 28

"Papa!" Caleb shrieked, nearly colliding with the screen door in his haste to reach Bob.

Bob flashed a rare smile as Amy opened the door and Caleb launched himself at him.

"Somebody's excited." Bob swung Caleb up in the air and caught him. Caleb shrieked and giggled at the same time.

Amy smiled. "He's been waiting at the door all morning. Ever since I told him Papa was taking him to the park."

Bob chuckled. "I've got a rake in the truck. We're going to make a giant pile of leaves right at the bottom of the slide, and then . . ." He swung Caleb again.

"Oosh!" Caleb laughed.

Jason came up behind his dad wearing a bright green windbreaker that almost matched his eyes. His dark hair was tousled. It was getting longer. Amy felt lighter at the sight of him. Jason gave Caleb a fist bump and then opened his hand, making explosion noises.

"Boom!" Caleb said.

Jason laughed. "You ready for your driving pre-test, Amy?"

She groaned. "I don't know. Am I?" It had only been a few weeks, but the lessons had been daily. Jason was a persistent instructor.

He grinned. "We'll see."

Bob carried Caleb to the truck while Amy retrieved the keys to the station wagon. "Don't be too rough on her, son."

"Oh right, you're one to talk. 'Jason, break on left! Jason! Are you trying to kill us?'"

Amy laughed at Jason's uncanny impression.

"Your speeding tickets speak for themselves, kid."

He settled Caleb into the back of the truck and straightened up. "How's Josh doing?"

Amy looked down at the stoop. "He's okay. Better, I guess. The meds are working and he's participating in treatment. He might be home by the end of next week."

Bob nodded. "Good. I'll see you two in a bit."

When Amy looked up, Jason's expression had hardened. She touched his arm, desperate to recapture the lightness. It felt good to escape the seriousness temporarily. It felt good to escape the doom and gloom of Josh's world for a weekend. She wrestled with the guilt.

"I can spot you from a mile away in this jacket. Are you afraid I'll kidnap you?"

He trained his stormy eyes on her. "He could go to the hospital and see Josh for himself if he's so concerned."

Amy sighed, absently rubbing at the tension in his bicep. "I know, it doesn't make sense. He hasn't seen Josh since the night he was brought in. What is he so afraid of?" She paused, watching the orange and gold leaves tumble across the yard, scattered by the wind. "It's hard to go there."

"Don't defend him, Amy."

His sharp tone stung. "I'm not. I mean for me. Sometimes it's hard for me to go there. I want to see him, but I never know who I'm going to find. Sometimes I want to leave, to escape back into the monotony of normal life." She bit her lip. "Do you think I'm an awful person?"

She searched his eyes for judgement but found only

compassion. "I think you're human." He tucked a wayward strand of hair behind her ear. "You still go. That's what I love about you, Amy. You show up even when it's hard."

She dropped her gaze. "Not today."

"You get a day off."

"He doesn't."

Jason snapped his fingers. "Nope. I'm not gonna let you do that." He guided her to the station wagon waiting down by the road. "If you're feeling guilty, picture his face when you drive up to those hospital doors."

"Assuming I pass the test."

"If you can pass mine you can pass the state's"

Amy gripped the steering wheel with both hands. Jason made the sign of the cross. She swatted his arm. "Very funny."

"You hit like a girl. Drive like one, too."

"I'll take that as a compliment."

"Relax." He loosened her fingers on the steering wheel. "You've been doing great."

"Will I ever not be terrified of controlling this thing?" She put the station wagon in reverse, reminding herself to breathe as it rolled into the street. Even after all her lessons she couldn't shake the feeling that the car would take off on its own.

"You're in control," Jason said.

After a while, the turns and starts and stops felt smoother. Amy concentrated on nothing but the road in front of her and Jason's steady presence beside her. Before she knew it, she was pulling back into the driveway. She cut the engine and looked at Jason expectantly.

He nodded to himself. "Not bad. You've come a long way in a short time. But, you gotta stop panic breaking."

"Story of my life."

He smiled. "Well, my foot's always on the gas pedal."

"Combined, we make the perfect driver."

"Hmmm. The breaks are a little noisy."

Amy picked at a cuticle. "Josh was going to tighten them, but then . . ." Her voice trailed off as she fought the memory.

"I'll take care of it."

"Thanks."

"It's no big deal. I'll grab some tools." He headed for the garage.

Amy leaned against the hood of the car, relishing the quiet. She closed her eyes and listened to the leaves rustling in the wind. A strangled sound, almost a sob, broke into her trance. When she opened her eyes, Jason was standing in front of her, his face ashen.

She straightened abruptly. "Are you okay?"

He set Josh's rusty toolbox on the ground. His hands raked through his hair. "It's . . . I saw . . . The . . ."

"Jason!" She rushed to him. He blinked "What is it? What's wrong?"

"The hose." He cleared his throat. "He wasn't fooling around, was he?"

"Oh, God."

Amy hadn't gone near the garage since That Night. She'd assumed the paramedics or the police officer who'd arrived behind them removed it when they took pictures of the truck. It had never occurred to her that the grisly scene might still be set.

"I'm sorry. I should've . . . I didn't know it was still—"

He put his hands on her shoulders. "Stop apologizing. It caught me off guard. It makes it too real; how close he came."

"I know."

He looked at her. "I know you know. It must've been hell for you, finding him like that. We never talked about it."

She closed her eyes as the images played behind her lids like a horror movie stuck on repeat. "I keep seeing him like that. The whole night plays out in my mind over and over again. I can't make it stop." She looked up at Jason's stricken face. "You don't want to hear this."

"No, I do. We should talk about this stuff."

He was right. Last time she'd tried to keep traumatic memories to herself it had nearly killed her.

"I don't know what woke me. He hadn't been sleeping well. He'd go downstairs during the night to listen to records. But that night I knew. When I didn't find him in the house, I went outside, and I heard it. I heard the truck's engine. I don't even remember racing to the garage or lifting the door. The next thing I remember is the hose running from the tailpipe through a crack in the driver's window, spilling poison right into his face." She squeezed her eyes shut for a moment before continuing. *Don't cry.*

"I pulled the door open; grabbed the keys from the ignition. He—he was so still. I thought for sure he was dead. He was blue. That really happens, Jason. People really turn blue when they stop breathing. And he was cold. He was so, so cold." She choked on the words.

"Holy shit," Jason breathed.

"I didn't think I'd be able to get him out of there. I don't know how I did. I kept working on him until he started breathing again. Then I kept screaming at him to wake up, but he wouldn't. He wouldn't."

She held back a sob as the levies holding the memory of that horrible night broke and the pictures threatened to drown her. Jason's arms came around her, warm and safe. She clung to him, a buoy in an ocean of memories. He held her tightly and she buried her face in his chest, breathing in his scent, like freshly fallen leaves and comfort.

"God, Amy, what you've been through. You're even tougher than I thought."

What had Josh called her that first night at the lighthouse? Resilient? It wasn't true. She didn't want to be right now.

"I can't wrap my head around it." Jason's diaphragm vibrated against her ear. "It's killing me. I mean, he's got you. He's got a kid. How could he do that to you? To Caleb? To any of us?"

"I don't know." Her voice was muffled. "I don't think he meant to."

"I've been wrecked over this. I'm a mess."

A tremor went through him so violently that it shook her body too. He'd been putting on a brave face for her, but Josh almost dying had hit him harder than she'd realized.

"He's my brother, you know? He's always looked out for me. He... he takes care of things. Maybe I should've been looking out for him. I don't have anyone else."

"You have me." She tilted her head back to look at him. They didn't break their embrace. Their eyes locked.

He smiled, the color returning to his face. "Yeah, I do."

Amy Everett had spent her entire life being careful; thinking things through and then thinking them through again. She didn't think when Jason's eyes closed, his face hovering close to hers. She didn't think when her lips met his and stayed there.

It was impossible to know who initiated the kiss; maybe it didn't matter. The ache of loneliness, the visceral need to comfort and be comforted, and the intimacy of shared pain lit a spark.

The taste of urgency and the friction of intensity gained momentum. She parted her lips, her body flush against his, his hands hot on her back. Somewhere in her conscience, Amy was aware together they'd crossed a line that could never be uncrossed. Her mind screamed at her to pull away, but her body refused to comply.

He tasted like cinnamon and pain. Not like Josh. The thought of Josh finally broke the spell. Amy pulled back. Her eyes snapped open. Back to reality.

Breathing hard, Jason took a staggering step away from her, his expression unreadable. "Sorry. I... I shouldn't have done that."

But Amy couldn't escape the fact that she was equally

culpable. "It's not your fault. At least not entirely. I mean—"

She stopped. Jason wasn't looking at her anymore. Amy followed his gaze to Bob's truck idling in the driveway.

Chapter 29

October 31, 1979

"**I**'m not a cripple." Josh glared at the wheelchair.

The nurse adjusted her hat on her halo of blonde curls, an understanding smile on her face. "Hospital policy. It's not you; a lot of sue-happy people out there."

Amy touched his arm. "Don't be difficult. You're going home; that's what matters. You're going to see Caleb."

He sighed, dropping his weight into the chair. Home. Close to two months had gone by since he'd so much as breathed outside air. Before this, he'd never gone a day without seeing his son. He couldn't wait to see his face. Josh caught sight of a glossy calendar on the green wall in front of him. His heart sank as he looked up at Amy. He'd been trying not to notice the pathetic, torn paper ghosts, witches, and jack-o-lanterns placed randomly throughout the otherwise bare halls. Those decorations served as a reminder that the outside world plodded along without him.

"It's Halloween. You should be with Caleb. Taking him trick-or-treating. *We* should be taking him trick-or-treating." He swallowed hard.

"It doesn't matter. He won't remember missing out. You coming home is more important." Amy squeezed his shoulder. "I have a surprise for you." She hurried out of the room.

"Is she being weird today, or is it just me?" The hardest part about challenging his own perceptions was knowing when to challenge them. Amy could barely make eye contact with him, busying herself with signing papers. She'd seemed fine last time she visited.

"This is a big day," the nurse said. "She wants to make it perfect."

He gripped the arms of the chair to resist the urge to bolt when she unlocked the heavy doors of the ward. The hallways and elevator whizzed by until they reached the hospital's main doors. A feeling of awe hit him with the cool, fresh air. He lifted his face to the bright sun. Crimson and gold leaves not yet succumbing to fall clung to the skinny trees standing sentry in front of the hospital. Many of them already blanketing the ground. The garden was bare besides a few haphazardly arranged pumpkins. He'd completely missed the passing of the seasons.

A station wagon pulled up to the circle drive. Was that *his* station wagon? He shielded his eyes from the sun and saw Amy behind the wheel. He tilted his head back to try and see the nurse's expression. She was smiling.

"Are you seeing what I'm seeing?"

"Sure am." She wheeled him around to the passenger side. "Don't take this the wrong way, but I hope I never see you again." She closed the door and he was alone with his wife at last.

He turned to her. "Am I hallucinating, or are you driving?"

She rolled her eyes. "That's not funny." A shadow passed over her face. "I asked Jason to teach me." She wouldn't look at him.

"She doesn't want to be with you. There's someone else." Shane leaned in from the backseat. Josh ignored him.

She's nervous. He'd attempted to teach Amy to drive. It bothered her that she'd never learned. But she was so terrified that once she'd squeezed her eyes shut when a car pulled out in front of her. He grabbed the wheel, narrowly avoiding a collision.

It had taken her all day to stop shaking and he hadn't been able to get her to try again.

Now, her deep frown and pensive features were the only indications she wasn't comfortable behind the wheel. Josh stared out the window at the trees in their various stages of shedding. Was she just concentrating on the driving? Was his paranoia getting the best of him? Or, did she not want him to come home?

"Are you okay?" she said finally.

He rubbed his forehead where a headache was forming. He'd expected to feel a sense of freedom when he left the hospital. "I'm scared, Amy."

"I know. You're not alone, Josh."

"For now. How long do you think she'll put up with you? You can't take care of her anymore."

Josh still didn't rise to Shane's bait. "Thanks for sticking by me."

She bit her lip, staring straight ahead. "You don't have to thank me."

"Amy is something wrong?"

"I want you to be happy."

Tentatively, he rested his hand on her thigh. "I am happy."

"You are?"

"I'm happy to be coming home. I can't wait to see Caleb." He twisted a loose thread on his sweatshirt. "Are you okay with me coming home?"

"Of course, I am. Why wouldn't I be?"

"There you go. Piss her off before you even get there."

His head pounded with the effort of ignoring Shane's voice. "I'm sorry, it's . . . You seem . . . I don't want you to worry about me."

"I don't think that's possible." She punched the heater. "Josh?"

"Hmm?"

"You get why I had to do what I did, right? Why I had to sign you in to the locked ward?"

"I do now. You saved my life, Amy."

"Barely." Her eyes were dark, nearly matching the half-moons of exhaustion below them. "I knew something was wrong, but I couldn't figure it out. That night—you weren't yourself. You weren't making sense. I should've paid more attention."

That was it. If he hadn't been so busy questioning his observations, he would've easily recognized the shade of guilt she'd worn so many times before.

"Don't think that. Not for a second. You couldn't have known what I was going to do. *I* didn't know what I was going to do."

She said nothing, and he let the silence persist. His lids felt heavy; his head lulled against the window. The damn pills made him so, so tired. The next thing he knew, Amy was gently shaking his shoulder.

"Josh, we're home."

He rubbed his eyes and stared at the house, thinking of the first time they'd glimpsed it in all its fixer-upper glory. "I wasn't sure I'd ever see this place again."

"I wasn't going to let them keep you, you know."

Finally, she offered him a smile and the unease lifted. He followed her to the door like he was a visitor. It felt like he'd been gone a decade. What if he'd forgotten how to live in the outside world? What if he was no longer capable of it? Could he expect her to live life as his caretaker?

Amy unlocked the door and he inhaled, the sharp scent of pine stinging his nostrils. *"She wants to make it perfect for you."*

Josh touched the walls, the wallpaper tacky under his fingertips. He ran his hands over the breakfast bar he'd constructed with some damaged wood rescued from a job sight. He wandered through the living room, touching the record player, the rough fabric of the couch, and the framed pictures on the wall. His clear eyes stared back at him. The house was too quiet. He circled back to the kitchen. Amy was at the counter reading the papers from the hospital.

"Is Caleb next door?"

She nodded. "Will you be okay here while I go get him? I'll only be a minute."

Josh slid onto the bar stool. "I'm not going to try to off myself while you're gone," he said more harshly than he'd intended to.

"That's not what I meant," she said.

They both knew she'd meant exactly that. Deep down, he didn't blame her. He watched her go, hating the way they were tiptoeing around each other. It wasn't supposed to be this way. He watched the door anxiously. Caleb would tie them all back together. Josh closed his eyes and pictured the smile that lit up Caleb's whole face, his belly laugh, his voice proclaiming, "Dada!"

He'd nearly dozed off again when the door creaked open. Caleb bounded in before Amy, chattering about something or nothing. Josh's breath caught. The emotion thickened in his throat. His little boy. He'd gotten bigger; his face was already losing the chubbiness of babyhood and hinting at the boy he'd become. His gait was steady. And he was talking! Josh's arms ached to hold him.

He came around the breakfast bar and squatted down, spreading his arms to catch his son. Caleb noticed Josh. He stopped mid-chatter.

"Hey, little buddy," Josh whispered.

Caleb's eyes widened; the unmistakable look of fear filled his little face. He began to cry. Shriek. Retreating from Josh's waiting arms, he ran back to Amy and buried his face in her leg. "Mama! Want Mama!"

Josh straightened up, defeated. "He doesn't remember me." The pain crushed his chest, filled his cells. It was too much. He couldn't hold it all and he had no place to put it.

Amy lifted Caleb onto her hip. He hid his face in her shoulder. She bounced him. "Of course, he remembers you. He needs a minute to warm up, that's all."

"I'm his father," Josh said. "I should've never been gone long enough for him to have to warm up to me."

She pried Caleb's hands away from his face. "Come, on, Caleb, what's gotten into you? It's Daddy. You wanted to see Daddy, remember?"

She carried him over to Josh and he lifted his tear-streaked face. Josh reached out a tentative finger. Caleb shrieked and contorted his body away, clinging to Amy. Josh dropped his hand.

"He's afraid of me. He's afraid of me like everyone else." His voice broke. Caleb's cries of fear hit him like daggers.

"Josh, he's not afraid of you." Amy tried to pry Caleb away from her body. "Come on, Caleb. Say hi to Daddy."

"No!" He wrapped his arms around Amy's neck.

His distress was too much. "It's okay," Josh said. "Don't force him." An unbearable pressure built behind his eyes. "I need to lie down."

"Sweetie—" Amy tried again, unsuccessfully, to disengage Caleb. The matching fear in her own eyes was more than Josh could handle, except Amy wasn't afraid of him. She was afraid *for* him.

"Look what you're doing to the people you love." This time he couldn't tell if it was the voice tormenting him or his own thoughts. Was there a difference anymore?

"I'm okay, Amy. I need to be alone right now, okay?"

She nodded, her hair caught in Caleb's grip. He headed for the stairs, retreating from his son's cries.

"Everything's going to be okay," he heard Amy say, unsure if she was speaking to him or to Caleb.

The neatly made bed invited him. First, he went into the bathroom. Resting his hands on the counter, he stared hard into the mirror. It had been weeks since he'd looked in a mirror. They didn't have them in the mental ward. It made sense, for safety, but Josh wondered if it was also to spare the poor souls the shock of seeing the haunted vacantness in their own eyes.

Making sure the door wasn't closed all the way, he peeled off his sweatshirt and T-shirt and crawled under the comforter, pulling it over his head. The sheets were cool and fresh against his bare skin. Never again would he take for granted the luxury of sleeping on sheets; of having a blanket to cover himself instead of lying on cold plastic, shivering. The blanket was as soft as Caleb's cheek. Mercifully, misery gave way to sleep.

Chapter 30

"What's gotten into you?" Amy wiped Caleb's nose. "Don't you want to see Daddy?"

Her back protested as she bent to set him on the floor. He wandered to the pictures crowding the wall in the family room and shoved a finger at a shot she'd taken over the summer. Caleb was wearing his neon green swim trunks, his hair wet from the sprinkler. Josh crouched behind him, smiling.

"Dada," Caleb said.

Amy sighed, flipping on the T.V. and flipped through the four channels, landing on *Sesame Street.* She didn't have it in her to play today. While Caleb was absorbed in the antics of Cookie Monster, Amy stretched out on the couch resisting the urge to check on Josh and replaying her conversation with Jason that morning.

The phone had rung while she was on her hands and knees scrubbing the kitchen floor, Caleb "helping" by sliding his cars on the wet surface. She straightened up abruptly, whacking her head on the solid wood of the breakfast bar. Cursing under her breath, she grabbed the phone.

"Amy, it's me."

Amy closed her eyes, flooded with guilt at the sound of Jason's voice.

"Can I come with you to get him?" he asked. "We could bring Caleb. I could wait in the car with him while you—"

"I don't think that's a good idea, Jason."

"I'll behave myself."

She rubbed the back of her head where a lump was forming. "If he sees us together, he'll know."

"How?"

"He'll just know."

In many ways, Josh was even more perceptive since getting sick. Only, now he didn't trust himself. She was a rat for having this secret.

"It's not like we'll never all be in the same room together again."

"Do you really not see the problem?"

"We got caught up in the moment, okay? It won't happen again. It doesn't mean we can't still be friends."

"Doesn't it, though?" The sick feeling returned to stomach. "What about your dad? Did he say anything? Was he being weird?"

"He didn't say anything and he's always weird. If he saw, don't you think he would've said something?"

"How should I know? He's *your* dad."

There was a long pause. "Why are you so mad at me?"

"I'm mad at myself, okay?"

"Amy, please."

"I have to go."

It was too tempting to let herself lean on Jason; to confide in him about her fears. The only way to stop herself was to put the phone down and continue attacking the floor.

If she kept busy enough she could almost forget; until it inevitably hit her like a truck. *I kissed my husband's brother.* She replayed the moment before Jason's mouth was on hers. How had she let it happen?

She loved Josh; that hadn't changed. What weakness inside

her had allowed her to commit such a betrayal? She had to tell him. But not now. He was just getting home. She'd wait until things went back to normal. Except, seeing Caleb's reaction to Josh jolted her to the reality that they'd need to find a new normal. In the meantime, Amy would carry the heavy weight of her secret like a penance.

Caleb laughed at something on the screen, engrossed. He started to rub his eyes. Amy made him a quick lunch and settled him down for his nap. Maybe he'd be more receptive to Josh when he woke up. The wounded look in Josh's eyes when Caleb ran from him haunted her. What would it do to him when he learned of her betrayal? What if Bob *had* seen? Would he tell Josh? But, wasn't Jason right? If he'd seen, wouldn't he confront them?

She eased Caleb's door shut and stood still, listening for sounds from down the hall. How could she be sure he wouldn't hurt himself? Bracing herself, she tiptoed down the hallway and slipped through the partially opened door.

The comforter rose and fell evenly. Amy shivered. He'd been denied even that simple comfort for too long. Gently, she pulled it down enough to see his face. His eyes were shut tightly. She eased onto the bed and smoothed his hair. "I'm sorry," she whispered.

She was sorry for so many things. What she'd done with Jason, her inability to protect him, the hell he was going through. For a long time, she watched him sleep, hoping his dreams were free of the torment that pursued him while he was awake.

A knock on the front door disrupted the quiet. *Go away*, she thought. The knocking persisted. Her anger overflowed, the pressure of a frozen pipe bursting in the dead of winter. Kissing Josh's temple, she hurried downstairs, remembering not to shut the bedroom door all the way. She wrenched open the door.

A tall, rail thin stranger in a suit looked down at her, his hand raised to knock again. He was probably going to try to convert her or sell her something. She wasn't in the mood.

He cleared his throat and adjusted his tie. "Amy Everett?"

"Can I help you?"

"Are you Mrs. Amy Everett?"

She nodded, a coil of dread unraveling in the pit of her stomach.

He reached into his billfold, producing a thick manila envelope with a flourish. He thrust it at her.

"You've been served."

PART TWO

Chapter 31

Josh shifted his weight in the hard wooden chair. It creaked in protest. Wood. Everything in the courtroom was made of wood, save the popcorn ceiling. Unlike the rustic distressed wood with which he worked, this wood was polished, shiny, and harsh. The artificial lighting glinted off the paneled walls. Coughs and creaks seemed amplified. Even the cage-like box surrounding him reeked of lacquer.

"Please state your full name, for the record."

Josh willed his eyes to stop bouncing around long enough to land on the Richards' lawyer. The guy had at least two decades on Josh, all slicked-back sandy hair, pressed gray suit, and the smile of a shark circling its prey. *You can do this,* Josh told himself. *You have to. For Caleb.*

He sucked air past his tight diaphragm "Joshua Robert Everett."

"Josh—is it okay if I call you Josh?"

Josh nodded.

"Son, you need to speak out loud for the court reporter," the white-haired judge to his left said. Josh stole a look at him, focusing on his eyes. Not unkind.

"Yes, you can call me Josh."

"All right, then, Josh. Do you know why you're here?"

"It's a trap! Get out of here! Run!"

It took all of his will power to ignore the voice hissing from the radiator. He'd resolved to only respond to the judge and the lawyer. It was the only way he'd get through this.

"I'm here because my wife's parents want custody of our son." His eyes landed on Walt and Eileen on the other side of the courtroom. Eileen looked down but Walt held his gaze, defiant.

"Your in-laws are Walt and Eileen Richards?"

"Yes."

"How old is your son?"

"He'll be two in December." They already had this information.

"They'll take you down! You have to get out, now!"

The invisible shouting was painful in his ears. The disembodied voices were almost more disturbing than the phantoms following him around. He took a deep breath and closed his eyes.

"Are you okay?" Shark asked, clearly relishing his prey's discomfort.

"Fine." Josh met his eyes and held his steely gaze.

"Help me understand." He rubbed his pale chin in mock curiosity. "Why would Walt and Eileen Richards want to take your son away from you?"

"Don't you already know all of this?"

His smile was patronizing. "I want to make sure you understand the nature of these proceedings, Josh."

Josh stiffened. *I'm crazy, not stupid*, he thought bitterly. He looked at the judge.

The elderly man nodded. "Answer the question."

"You're screwed. Done for."

"What prompted Walt and Eileen Richards to file for custody of your son, Caleb?" He enunciated each word slowly, as though Josh was dense.

"They want my wife to leave me. They never wanted us to be together."

"Now you sound like a petulant child."

"And yet, you and your wife have been married for two years. Your son's been around almost that long. In fact, Walt and Eileen Richards planned and financed the entire wedding, isn't that correct?"

"Oh man! He's good."

"Yes, but only because—"

"Why now?" His voice was shrapnel. He was zeroing in. "What prompted the Richards to take such a drastic move now?"

Sweat soaked the back of Josh's button-down shirt. He swallowed bile. *Don't make me say it.* "They said I shouldn't be around Caleb. They claim I'm dangerous."

"And are you? Dangerous?"

"Yes. Too bad you didn't die in that truck." Shane stood next to Shark, mimicking his stance and motions.

"No. I'm not dangerous."

Shark sauntered over to his bench and riffled through some papers. "On the night of August 20, you were rushed to Fairview State Hospital by ambulance, unresponsive." He waved a paper at Josh. "You attempted suicide, correct?"

It was a trap. He couldn't see his was around it. The only path went straight down. "I wasn't trying to kill myself."

"Really?" His eyes narrowed. "It says here that your wife reported finding you in your truck inside your closed garage with the engine running. When paramedics arrived on the scene, they observed a garden hose running from the tailpipe through the front window. Do you remember doing that?"

His stomach lurched as the grainy memory elbowed its way into his unwilling mind. "Yes," he managed.

"So, you mean to tell me you were unaware that carbon monoxide poisoning causes death? Remember, you're under oath."

Josh bristled. "I know that. But I didn't want to die."

The lawyer shrugged. "Okay, then please explain what you were trying to do when you pulled the truck into the garage, attached the hose to the tailpipe, closed the garage door, got in the driver's seat, and started the engine."

The memories were dream-like. He could see himself dragging the hose to the truck. He could smell the fumes; feel his extremities go numb. And then blackness. Confusion. Fractured memories, only some of them real.

"Answer the question."

Josh hadn't looked at Amy once since the questions had started, afraid he'd fall apart. Now he looked at her to stay together. She nodded, pain shimmering in her eyes. Pain he'd put there. Trauma he'd etched in permanent ink.

"I was trying to make it quiet."

"Make what quiet?"

He took a deep breath. "The noise."

"The voices, you mean."

Josh nodded.

"You'll need to speak up."

"Yes."

"You've been hearing voices?"

How many times did he have to say it? "Yes."

Have you been seeing things, maybe even people, that aren't real?"

"Yes."

"Would it be fair to say you didn't understand the ramifications of your actions on the night of August 20?"

Josh let out his breath. "I didn't know what I was doing."

"You didn't intend to hurt yourself."

"No."

"Isn't it possible, then, that you might hurt Caleb without intending to? Without knowing what you were doing?"

The room spun, the floor falling away. Laughter. Josh reached deep inside himself to a place even the voices couldn't go. "A lot of parents hurt their children." He looked at the Richards. "Sometimes it is intentional."

"So, that's okay, then?"

"Of course, it's not okay," Josh snapped. He adjusted his tone. All he needed was to prove this bastard's point that he couldn't control himself. "It's not okay. But you'll be hard-pressed to find a perfect parent. I'm not a perfect father. But I love my son. I want to do right by him. I would never, ever hurt him."

"True, parents make mistakes. What I'm referring to is abuse. As I'm sure you're aware, it's the responsibility of this court to act in the best interest of the child."

"Don't do my job, counselor," the judge warned.

"My apologies, your honor."

But the words were already out there. They could take Caleb. Were they already breaking down Mrs. Croftsky's door? Caleb would be so scared! He had to get to him. He tried to get up, but his legs had turned to jelly. He gripped the arms of the chair.

"To Mr. Davis's point, this court is in the business of terminating parental rights if and only if the child's safety and well-being is compromised. Therefore, I'm ordering that Josh Everett be evaluated by a state-appointed psychiatrist before we reconvene."

"They're going to take your son."

"I know this is hard," Davis said, not even having the decency to plaster on a solemn expression. "But could you live with yourself if you were having an . . . um . . . *episode* and you hurt Caleb? Dropped him? Smothered him with a pillow?"

Shane rubbed his chin. "Yeah, you might do that."

Josh willed himself not to be sick right there in the front of the courtroom. "That would never happen! I'd never hurt Caleb! I'd never let anyone hurt him. I love him."

"No one's questioning that you love your son. No one's suggesting you'd intentionally bring harm to him, in your right mind. But what if the voices tell you to?"

"They don't!"

"But what if they do?"

"It wouldn't matter. I'd never hurt him, no matter what anyone said."

"But how do we know that? Are you aware of the term predictive neglect?"

"Yes," Josh said, although he wasn't.

It was clear how this would work. Guilty until proven innocent. A gavel crashed. Josh jumped, his head whipping in the judge's direction. His hands were still. Phantom, maniacal laughter tormented him.

"Josh? Are you still with us?"

His head snapped back to Davis. "I've never been violent in my life. I've never hurt anyone."

The lawyer's triumphant smile threatened to crack his stone face. He marched back to his bench and retrieved another file, this one's pages graying at the edges.

"It's not true that you've never acted out violently, is it? That you've never physically harmed a child?" He looked at the paper in his hand, nodding to himself.

"I don't know what you're talking about."

"On May 17, 1976, you pled guilty to assault and battery of a minor, is that correct?"

All the air was sucked out of the room. They found out. Of course, they found out.

"Josh, did you commit assault and battery of a minor? Did you, with your bare hands, put a boy in the hospital?"

"Yes," Josh said. "I did."

"Why?"

He looked at Amy. The haunted look he hadn't seen in years invaded her eyes. His fists clenched. He wasn't going to apologize because he wasn't sorry. He wouldn't betray her, either. He hadn't then, and he wouldn't now.

"It's complicated," Josh said.

Davis shrugged. "Seems pretty straightforward to me." He turned to the judge. "No further questions."

Chapter 32

The details of that day were etched into Josh's brain, a blueprint of his trajectory to being branded a criminal. He'd parked his truck outside the wrought-iron gates. His hands tightened on the steering wheel as he stared at the stately red brick building. His plan shifted his perception of the school as though he was seeing it for the first time. The lavender and pink hydrangeas peppered the unnatural emerald lawn. A nun pushed opened the gate and passed right in front of his truck, her black habit flapping in the spring breeze. She didn't glance in his direction.

He strode purposefully to the parking lot nestled between the church and school. *In front of God and everyone.* Josh remembered the phrase his dad used to use to chastise them when he and Jason fought in public. Those childhood scrapes with Jason were the closest he'd come to a fight, but Amy was worth fighting for.

He trekked through the rows of Mercedes Benz and Rolls Royce's until he found the red mustang.

He turned his back on the car and waited for its owner. Red hot rage pulsed too fast through his veins. Bob maintained that Jason was the one with the fiery temper, but Josh could be pushed.

The bell rang. The double doors vomited students onto the asphalt. Today he wasn't watching for Amy. She was at home, sick. Scared. Who could blame her? Josh felt sick himself every time he dropped her off at this prestigious penitentiary to face *him*. If she missed any more school she'd need to repeat her junior year. Once he left her alone, that wouldn't be a problem.

Josh's target sauntered into view, a denim backpack slung haphazardly over his shoulder, his red hair gelled in the front, an unlit cigarette dangling from his mouth. He was somehow managing to laugh at something his buddy said without dropping the cigarette.

"Catch you on the flip side, dude," the other guy said, lazily waving a leather-clad arm.

Josh stepped forward as he reached the car.

He looked at Josh, or rather looked through him, his face impressively devoid of recognition. He took the cigarette out of his mouth and tucked it behind his ear. "Can I help you? You lost or something?"

"I'm in exactly the right place." He stepped closer, staring down at beady eyes. For a fraction of a second, fear flickered in his eyes before the shroud of arrogance returned.

"Dude, I don't know what your deal is, but you need to get out of my way."

Other students glanced in their direction as they passed. Josh was close enough to smell the cigarettes on the other boy's breath. "I warned you once. Maybe you didn't take me seriously. Consider this a courtesy call. Stay the hell away from Amy. That goes for you and all your pathetic minions." His own voice sounded unfamiliar.

Josh's adversary had the nerve to snort. He raked a hand through his stiff hair. "She's only with you to spite her parents. It's all over town. Walt Richards' daughter running around with a high school drop-out." He laughed, looking around for an audience, but the students were thinning out.

"Local gossip goes both ways. You bother her again, and I'll know about it. Are we kosher?"

He took a step toward Josh. "What did she tell you?"

His fists clenched. "I was there."

Another fleeting look of uncertainty. "Then you should know she had it coming."

Josh swung, landing a clean blow to Michael's jaw. A sharp, satisfying pain radiated through his knuckles. Michael went down like a bag of cement. Scrambling to his feet, he rubbed his jaw and inspected the blood he came away with.

"You son of a bitch." He lunged at Josh, shoving him hard in the chest. Josh swung again. By this time, a small crowd had gathered.

"Fight!" some idiot announced.

Josh was distracted long enough for his opponent to land an uppercut below his left eye. Fueled by the pain, he swung again, dropping him back to the pavement. Thinking of Amy, Josh delivered a swift kick to his ribs and another to his kidneys.

Michael lifted his face from the asphalt. Blood trickled from his nose and dripped down his chin. He gave Josh a twisted smile. "Dude, you are so going to jail."

Josh crouched down in front of him, gripping his shirt collar. He could talk tough all he wanted, but the fear in his eyes was unbridled now. He'd gotten the message. "You know what, asshole?" Josh pulled his face inches from his own. "It'll be so worth it." Josh let go abruptly and Michael flopped back to the pavement like a fish out of water. He rolled to his side and curled into a fetal position.

"You're not half as tough as you think you are, and now everyone knows it. Stay away from her. He turned on his heal and retreated to his truck, wiping his bloodied knuckles on his jeans.

"Call the fuzz!"

Josh opened the passenger door and reached into the glove, his fingers closing around the small velvet box that'd cost months of salary. Today was a blip on the radar. Amy would be okay. Together, they could face anything. If she wanted a future with him, she'd have it.

Fear of consequence couldn't break through his resolve, nor his hope. He'd replaced the box, leaned against the truck, and waited for the fuzz to show up.

Chapter 33

The court proceedings exhausted Josh. He dreaded going back.

Unaccustomed to not working, he spent his days wandering the house, checking locks and pulling curtains tight. He only left to go to court-ordered evaluations with Dr. Sai, who seemed okay.

Josh solved childish puzzles, answered countless questions, and stared at ink blots. The ink blots were the hardest. The task itself wasn't hard. Before his eyes, the random shapes morphed into buildings, faces, plans. They reminded him of the promise of a fresh blueprint; the magic when a series of lines became a three-dimensional structure.

The loss of his work, the questioning of his integrity, the erosion of his identity plagued him like a physical ache. What was he good for now?

What he'd told Amy and the court was true; he hadn't been trying to kill himself. He'd been out of his mind. But these idle days he spent pacing and sleeping and swallowing pills invited unwelcomed thoughts of death. How much easier would it be to be done?

But then he thought of Caleb and Amy. He couldn't reconcile what he'd put her through, and he wouldn't do it again. He equally appreciated and resented the way she looked at him now, like he was made of glass that would shatter at any moment. Today, Caleb had been so restless, Josh convinced her to take him to the library.

"Are you sure you don't want to come with us?" she'd asked. He shook his head.

All morning, he'd stretched out on the floor, mutely constructing train tracks. He couldn't be caught talking to the voices, so he rarely talked at all. They were monitoring him. He wouldn't give them any more evidence against him, more reason to take his child.

He savored every moment with Caleb, but it had taken all his energy to keep a smile plastered to his face while making the required train noises and stretching an elaborate constellation of tracks across the family room. This at least he could do.

But he couldn't risk going out with his family. Not yet. Not until the case was over. He was under scrutiny. Anyone could be a spy.

Josh didn't like the quiet much either, though. The voices were too loud. He carefully navigated through the train tracks and turned on the record player. Too loud. He turned it off. He circled back to the kitchen to take his pills. He should eat something first, but his stomach turned at the thought. A knock on the door nearly made him drop his water.

For a full minute, Josh stood still, willing whoever it was to go away. Maybe it wasn't even a real person. How could he tell?

Knock knock knock!

With a shaking hand, he set the glass in the sink and crept to the door. The curtain was pulled tight over the small window. He moved it just enough to see out. Half of Bob's face was visible from his vantage point. He was raising his hand to knock again.

Josh fumbled with the lock, leaving the chain latched. He cracked the door open. "Are you alone? Did anyone follow you?"

Bob looked behind him. "Follow me? Who would follow me?"

"The government. Get in here." He undid the chain and pulled his dad in by the arm, promptly securing the locks and curtain. When he turned, Bob wore the look to which he'd grown accustomed—a concoction of confusion, concern, and pity.

"What are you doing here? Did Amy send you?"

"Amy? No. Why?" He shuffled his weight from one foot to the other, hands shoved in his pockets.

Josh shrugged. "She took Caleb to his program at the library. She doesn't like to leave me alone. I thought maybe she called you to babysit."

Bob winched. "She's worried about you, Josh."

Josh sighed. "I know."

They stared at each other, the thick tension forming an invisible wall between them. Usually, Josh was the bridge. Everyone shuffled around the role reversal.

"They're out there, watching you. He might work for them."

Josh shook himself, squirming under his father's scrutiny. "Um, do you want some coffee?"

Bob nodded, rubbing the stubble on his chin as though mulling the question over. "That'd be great."

Josh moved across the kitchen to the coffee pot, grateful to have a task, however simple. He tried to conceal the tremor in his hand while he poured, but some of the coffee missed the mug. Bob watched him.

"You okay?"

"Fine. Side effect of the pills. Do you want to sit?"

They picked their way through the tributaries of train tracks. Bob sank onto the worn couch while Josh took the chair. He crossed one leg over the other knee pulling some stuffing from a crack in the arm.

"To what do I owe this visit in the middle of the workday?"

Bob stared hard into his coffee as though the answer was hidden in the dark roast. "Look, Josh, I know you're mad at me. You have every right to be."

"I'm not mad."

"I should've come to see you in the hospital. I mean, after that night." He still didn't meet Josh's eyes.

"Then why didn't you?"

"After seeing you the night you were brought in—you were in bad shape, kid." He cleared his throat. "I couldn't go back there. I . . . I . . . couldn't."

Josh shrugged. "Okay." He let a beat of silence pass. "Are you afraid of me?"

At that, Bob looked up. "Of course I'm not afraid of you."

"You are. I can tell by the way you look at me. The way everyone looks at me now. Like I'm a bomb about to go off."

"No one thinks that, Josh."

"Did you come here to see the freak show for yourself?"

"That's enough." His sharp tone was grounding. Reassuring. "I wanted to see how you were holding up."

"Not great, Dad."

Bob rubbed his eyes. "Look, for what it's worth, this whole custody thing's asinine."

Josh jerked his head up. "You know about that? Who told you?"

"I own a construction company. Walt's a bigwig developer. Word trickles down the pipeline."

"Great."

"He doesn't have a leg to stand on."

"Sure, he does. I hear voices. I interact with people who don't exist. That sound like a stable parent to you?"

Bob closed his eyes for a moment. When he opened them, they were far away. "It's not that simple. Don't let them get to you. It doesn't change who you are as a father."

Josh shifted his weight. "Thanks, but I'm going to have a

hell of a time convincing a judge of that. The Richards have a really slick, really *expensive* attorney."

"That's the other reason I'm here." Bob set his coffee on the floor, stood up, and picked his wallet out of his back pocket. He handed Josh a glossy card. "I want to help with a lawyer."

Josh studied the card in his hand. JULIAN STEIN, FAMILY LAW.

"It's the least I can do."

"But how? You don't have any more money than I do."

"Well, you don't have to be a jerk." For the first time since he'd arrived, the hint of a smile played across Bob's face.

"Sorry."

"He owes me a favor. Back when he was fresh out of law school, not much older than you are now, I built him and his wife a house. They were expecting their first baby and law school had drained him dry. I only charged him for the materials. He's moved on to bigger and better things. Tried to pay me back several times over the years, but I told him he'd have a chance to do for me at some point."

"They told us they'd appoint a lawyer, but I don't trust him."

Bob snorted. "You shouldn't. Remember that tool who represented you on the assault charges? If Stein practiced criminal law, I'd have cashed in my favor back then."

"He's good?"

"He's known as the lawyer that doesn't lose. Not very original, but yeah, he's good. Call him."

Josh turned the card over in his hand. "I, uh . . . I don't really use the phone anymore."

"Oh. Well, how about I call him? I could give him the cliff notes and set up a meeting for you and Amy."

In that moment Josh was a little boy with blind faith that his big strong dad could make the monsters go away. "That'd be great, Dad. Thanks."

He slapped his hands against his thighs. "Well, I'd better get back."

"Right." Josh followed him back through the kitchen, suddenly desperate for him to stay.

"It'll be okay," Bob said, reaching for the doorknob. He paused, turning back around.

"Oh, and Josh?" He placed his hands on Josh's shoulders. Strong. Steady. His dad looked him straight in the eyes.

"Don't ever scare me like that again."

Chapter 34

Mark Sai was a slight man with a dark mustache, world-weary eyes, and an unfortunate preference for cashmere sweaters. His conservatively adorned office seemed almost comfortable now; Amy had begun to see him as an ally.

Dr. Sai waited patiently with his hands folded in his lap while Josh paced the room. Amy took his lead even though every muscle in her body screamed at her to intervene; to grab Josh and hold him tightly. The ticking clock punctuated his muttering. After what seemed like hours, but must have been only minutes, he dropped into the faded leather chair next to her and took her hand. He looked at Dr. Sai.

"Sorry."

The doctor waved off the apology. "Not at all. I know this is stressful. I want to start by saying it's been a pleasure to work with you."

"I seriously doubt that," Josh said darkly.

"Josh!" Amy flushed.

"It's all right. Listen, Josh, I know you don't believe me, but just because this is court ordered and the typical patient-doctor confidentiality is compromised doesn't mean I'm the enemy. It's my duty to be objective. Believe it or not I got into this profession to help people. I don't expect you to trust me, but do you feel I've been fair?"

"Yes. You've been fair."

With a nod, he pushed a pair of glasses onto his nose and opened the file in his lap. A thick file. Josh's file. Beside her, Josh started to shake, his knee bouncing rapidly. She brushed her thumb across his knuckles. The fear radiated off him like the heat spitting from the old unit in the corner of the office.

"Josh, we've completed an extensive evaluation process together. After reviewing your results along with your records from the hospital, I consulted with a colleague who specializes in psychotic disorders, leaving out any identifying information, of course."

Amy focused on Josh. She could read his thoughts. He was a *case study*. His face was dead white, his body frozen in the final moment of *before*. How many times could her heart break for him? He'd suffered enough. He deserved better than this. He deserved better than her, though he didn't yet know it.

She squeezed his hand again, harder, and he squeezed back, an entire conversation passing between them in a single gesture.

"You meet the full criteria for paranoid schizophrenia."

The clock continued to tick. The floor didn't fall away. The heater continued to spit. But everything changed. The words *paranoid schizophrenia* floated through the stuffy air. Amy wanted to snatch them and stuff them back into that file that didn't even tell a fraction of story. She watched the words hit Josh like bullets; his body jerked, the blow shattering him.

Paranoid schizophrenia.

That file left out so much. Like how Josh showed up in her darkest hours again and again. It left out the chapter when Josh asked before he kissed her for the first time in the bed of the truck. Or the chapter when he'd proposed to her on the beach. The file had forgotten the scenes of him holding tiny baby Caleb in his large, capable arms, or dragging himself through the door at the end of a workday and going straight to the toy box.

Her entire life with Josh flashed before her eyes. He'd never let her down. She'd let him down, though. She had to tell him, but how could she now? How could she wound him further? No, she had to wait. Telling him to relieve her guilt would be selfish, and God knew she'd been selfish enough. She put her arm around Josh's rigid shoulders. Shoulders that consistently carried the weight of the world without complaint. Finally, he spoke.

"I'm sorry, what's that now?"

"Paranoid schizophrenia is a mental disturbance categorized by hallucinations affecting multiple senses, paranoid delusions, disturbances in—"

"Okay, I get it. I just . . . You mean like the homeless people ranting and raving on street corners? The newspaper headlines of people snapping and going on a shooting spree?" His voice cracked. "That's not me."

"Schizophrenics are statistically far more likely to be victims of violent crimes than perpetrators."

Amy wished he'd stop saying "schizophrenics". But she latched on to the message he was sending. "Are you saying you don't think Josh is violent? You think Caleb is safe around him? You'll tell the court?"

Dr. Sai trained his eyes on her. "I'm not supposed to divulge that to you, but no, I haven't seen any indication that Josh is a danger to others, and my testimony will reflect that."

The tension drained from Amy's body. She smiled at Josh, but he was somewhere else entirely.

"How does this happen?" he asked.

"Could be genetic. We don't really know. There's no cure, but it's treatable. Some patients do achieve remission."

"Genetic?"

"Sometimes. Do you know of anyone in your immediate family that's exhibited similar symptoms?

Josh shook his head. "Just me." He looked up a Dr. Sai, his eyes wide with shock. "Does that mean it could happen to Caleb?"

"Only around thirteen percent of children with one schizophrenic parent develop the disorder themselves."

Josh looked at Amy. She offered him a sympathetic smile.

"The truth is," Dr. Sai continued, "there's still a lot we don't know about the brain. But new medications and treatments are being researched all the time. More resources exist now than ever before. And with the formation of the National Alliance for the Mentally Ill, well, attitudes toward mental illness are shifting."

"So, I went crazy at the right time," Josh said. "My timing is impeccable."

"I know this isn't what you wanted to hear today. But with consistent treatment, you could live a fairly normal—"

"I'm sorry." Josh got to his feet. "I know you're trying to help, and I appreciate it, I do. But I need to get out of here." He bolted for the door.

Amy got up.

"Let him go," Dr. Sai said. "It's a lot to process." His face was etched with sympathy. "You need support, too. Do you have support, Amy?"

"Yes," Amy lied, barring Jason from her mind. She sank back into the leather. "What's going to happen to him?"

Dr. Sai folded his hands. "You know, in my experience love and support make all the difference. I can see he has that with you. However, I have to tell you, this type of illness can shake even the strongest of relationships."

Amy had been shaken, all right. Right into the arms of Josh's brother. Josh's illness didn't give her absolution; it only made what she'd done more heinous. She clung to her determination like a lifeline. They'd come too far to break now. "Odds have been against us from the beginning."

"Yes, well, don't neglect yourself. You can help him, but only if he participates in his treatment."

"He's trying. It's not his fault, you know?"

Dr. Sai nodded.

"One more thing? You know Josh tried to kill himself. I mean, he didn't mean to, but he did almost die. How do I know he won't try it again?"

"You don't. You can't put that on yourself. The best thing you can do if you're worried he's thinking about it is to ask him. Ask whether he has a plan."

"But won't that put the idea in his head?"

"Not if it's not already there, no. "

"Thank you, Doctor. You've been immensely helpful."

Dr. Sai stood and shook her hand. "Take care. If you have any further questions, even after the case, don't hesitate to reach out." He handed her his card.

She slipped it into her bag, overwhelmed by a visceral need to reach Josh. Where had he gone? Was he okay?

She found him next to the station wagon, slamming his hands onto the hood. He kicked the tire so hard she worried he'd hurt himself. His face fell when he saw her.

"I'm sorry."

"You're allowed to be angry, Josh."

He swallowed hard, squeezing his eyes shut for a moment. "It's never going to go away."

Amy reached out and touched his arm, the skin as familiar as her own. "I know," she said. "But neither am I."

His shoulders slumped. He leaned against the car for support, his green eyes swimming with fear and grief. He sobbed once, a guttural sound of despair. His eyes filmed. He swiped at them desperately.

Amy'd never seen him cry before; not even close. She reached up and touched his face, feeling the rough stubble he'd neglected. "You don't have to do that with me."

As if unleashed by her permission, the tears came in torrents. His body sagged forward as he broke down, sobbing profusely. She gathered him to her, attempting to absorb his pain along with her own. He clung to her, burying his face in her shoulder as the scalding flood of tears soaked through her shirt; wet her hair.

Tightening her arms around her big, strong husband while he sobbed like a baby, Amy did the only thing she could do; the same thing he'd done for her not so long ago.

She held him together while he fell apart.

Chapter 35

Josh lay in bed, paralyzed. The words *paranoid schizophrenia* bounced around in his head. The other voices were ironically quiet. He'd been in bed all day, like he was sick. He *was* sick. He'd be sick every single day for the rest of his life. *Paranoid schizophrenia.*

The toilet flushed. The faucet turned on and off. Amy slid into bed beside him, resting her hand between his shoulder blades.

"I know you're not asleep."

He sighed, rolling over to face her. "How can you tell?"

"By your breathing. I spend a lot of time listening to it. It's the best sound in the world." She gave him a smile that he didn't return. Her hand brushed his cheek. "What is it?"

The damn tears. His eyes ached from the unfamiliar weight of them. Once they'd been released, they came without his permission. His voice was thick with them.

"Amy, there's something I need to ask you."

Her eyes widened. "Okay."

He took a deep breath and spoke over the pounding of his heart. He needed to know. "Would you have married me if you'd known what I'd become?"

"Yes," she said without hesitation.

"Why?" he asked. "I mean, how?"

"Because I know who you are."

He sighed, his body heavy with weariness despite his inactivity. "I don't even know who I am anymore."

Her hand rested on his cheek, warm and reassuring. "You're the same person you've always been. You just . . . get a little lost sometimes."

They fell silent for a moment.

"Josh?"

"Hmm?"

"Are you going to try to kill yourself again?"

He swam in the deep pools of fear in her eyes. "No. I didn't know what I was doing, Amy."

"I know. But I want you to come to me. When things get confusing? Trust me to tell you what's real when you can't trust your own mind, okay?" She bit her lip.

He smiled. "Deal." Josh let the quiet stretch again, not wanting to say what had to be said next. "Amy? I need you to promise me something, okay?"

"Anything."

He put his arm around her under the comforter. Comforter. Such a grandiose name for an object with no power to quell life's miseries. "If your parents win the case—"

"They won't."

"But if they do . . ." He forced the next words out in a rush before he could stop himself. "If the judge sides with them you have to divorce me."

Her eyes filled. "Josh, no."

His own throat thickened again. "Obviously, it's not what I want. But you're his mother. They won't take him from you."

"You're his father," she cried.

"I know, Amy. That's why I need to think of him first. He needs you even more than I do. He needs you more than he needs me. Your parents—they can't have him. I won't allow it.

He can't lose us both. Maybe I can still see him, and maybe when he's older he'll understand, but I need you to promise me. If they win, you'll leave me."

His words conjured memories not of his wedding—a lavish, plastic event orchestrated by Walt—but the night he proposed at 5-Mile Point Lighthouse.

He'd dropped to one knee on the beach, his senses heightened. The grains of sand shifting under him, the tide coming in, the seagulls screeching to each other, the sun partially obscured by the lighthouse—he wanted to record every detail. He pulled the box from his pocket. Amy gasped; her eyes wide.

"Amy, the first time we came here together we were strangers. You didn't know me, didn't trust me, but you gave me a chance. I'll be forever grateful for that chance and I hope I've done okay with it."

She nodded, her eyes misty, filled with shock and—what else? He filled his lungs with salty air and continued.

"Getting to know you was like getting to know myself. I felt—I feel like I've known you forever. Before, I was going through the motions, living a to-do list, and trying my best to ignore the monotony of my life. But with you, every day has a spark that wasn't there before. You make me want to be a better person." His voice cracked and he cleared his throat.

"I wish I could give you everything, but I'm a high school drop-out who works for his dad. I can only offer you a simple life, far different from the one you've known. I'll understand if it's not what you want. But I can tell you I love you and I'll always love you no matter what. Together, we can do anything. You and me against the world. I want a future with you because I can't picture one without you. Amy Richards, will you marry me?"

He focused on her face, ignoring the cramp developing in his back. She looked at the ring and then at his face. She wasn't smiling. His stomach flipped.

"Josh, there's something I need to tell you."

"You're breaking up with me." The words were like gravel in his mouth. Break-up. Shatter. Dissolve. He wracked his brain for what he'd done wrong.

"It's not that. I was never myself until I was with you. I want to be with you. I want to marry you."

"Then what? Whatever it is, you can tell me."

She'd pressed his hand to the flat plain of her stomach. "I'm pregnant."

Amy's tears made rivers down her pale cheeks, jerking Josh back into the present and flooding his heart with preemptive grief. She wiped her nose with the sleeve of her nightgown. "I'll never forgive them for doing this."

He gathered her to him. "I know."

"Will you be okay?" she asked, her voice muffled in his chest.

"I'll be okay," Josh lied.

"This case is frivolous. It's pure sensational hysteria."

Josh watched Julian Stein pace the family room, his gold Rolex casting a white light on the walls. He was tall and lean, and clean shaven with his dark hair neatly trimmed. He really liked adjectives. Josh's eyes felt heavy and tired from crying. His head ached. Caleb napped upstairs, blissfully unaware of the circumstances deciding his fate.

"Do you think we can win?" Amy asked.

Julian waved his hand as though shooing the question away. "I don't lose. First thing's first. We need to do damage control on the assault and battery charge. By itself we could pass it off as teenage misjudgment, but under the circumstances, it doesn't look great. "He snapped his fingers, continuing his one-sided conversation. "Then again, their whole platform is based on you going crazy. The assault happened before that. No correlation, see?" He smiled.

"My diagnosis," Josh said. "That's a strike against us, right?"

Julian shrugged. "Depends how we spin it. Don't take this the wrong way, but this case couldn't have come at a better time, what with the formation of the National Alliance for the Mentally Ill. They're crazy about advocacy, if you'll excuse the pun. I've been in touch with them. We'll get an advocate up there." He rubbed his palms together. "The diagnosis could as easily work in our favor."

Josh cocked his head to one side. "How's that?"

"Think about it. Without a diagnosis, you're a guy who snapped one day. Better to be a guy who got sick."

Josh stared at Julian. "So, you don't think I'm capable of hurting Caleb?" He hated how much he needed to hear the answer.

Julian shrugged. "Doesn't matter what I think."

Chapter 36

Her parents' lawyer, something Davis, grinned up at her as he continued his ludicrous line of questioning. "Amy, has Josh ever hit you? Ever forced himself on you?"

Amy looked at Josh. The hurt was heavy in his eyes. "Josh would never touch me like that."

"Maybe not in his right mind."

They'd said the same thing when Josh awoke in the hospital. He'd been so scared; couldn't they see that? He was scared all the time now.

"Not in his heart. Everything he does is for me and Caleb."

"Was attempting suicide for you? For your son?"

"He didn't mean to hurt himself." She'd say it as many times as she had to.

"Amy, are you familiar with the term 'predictive neglect?'"

She nodded. Julian had explained everything. Despite his cavalier demeanor, he was every bit as good as Bob had promised. "It means you feel Josh might neglect or harm Caleb even though he never has."

"It's not what I feel. Predictive neglect refers to the question of whether it's reasonable to assume neglect or abuse may occur based on what we know. We know Josh tried to asphyxiate himself. We all agree he wouldn't have done that in his right mind, correct?"

Amy nodded.

"You'll need to speak up."

"Yes, that's correct."

Davis spread his hands out, savoring his performance. "Okay, so if Josh did something that he wouldn't have done in his right mind, something that almost had tragic consequences, isn't it reasonable to predict that he'll do other things that he wouldn't do in his right mind? Things that might have tragic consequences for Caleb? Are you really willing to play Russian roulette with your son's safety?"

The white-hot rage nearly blinded her. "No."

"No, you're not willing to play Russian roulette with Caleb's safety?"

His magnanimous tone fueled her anger. It was good; anger left no room for guilt or fear. "No, it's not reasonable to assume Josh will hurt Caleb because he hurt himself."

"Why not?"

"Objection," Julian said coolly. "Asked and answered."

"Sustained. Move on, Mr. Davis."

"Amy, did you know Josh would hurt himself? Did you expect him to try to take his life?"

Her gut twisted. "No."

"If you'd known, you would've tried to prevent it right?"

"Of course."

"Looking back, were their signs?"

"Objection. Where is he going with this, your honor?"

"Your honor, we are talking about predicting Josh's behavior."

"I'll allow it. But get to the point. I don't have all day."

"I should've seen it. He seemed more stressed; upset. I didn't know he was sick."

"You missed the signs. You didn't think Josh would hurt himself. You don't think he'll hurt Caleb. Predictive neglect is about seeing the signs before tragedy unfolds." Amy waited for a question, but it didn't come. Davis turned his back on her. "You're up, Stein."

Julian sauntered up to the stand, adjusting his tie. The pinstripes on his suit made Amy dizzy. She rubbed her eyes.

"Amy, do you know why Josh assaulted a seventeen-year-old boy when he was eighteen?"

Amy wanted to duck under the bench and hide. "Yes."

"Josh didn't want to tell the court why he beat up the kid. Do you know why that is?"

"Because," Amy said, "I asked him not to."

"Recently?"

"No, back then. I mean, before he went after Michael."

"I see. Explain to us what it was you asked Josh to keep secret."

Amy folded her hands in her lap to still the shaking. She looked at Josh. His eyes were wide. He gave her a slight shake of his head, trying to protect her as always. But it was time. She'd held the secret long enough. She was ready.

The strength in her voice surprised her. "It started in the spring of 1975, the night I met Josh. My parents had arranged a date for me."

Julian raised his eyebrows. They hadn't rehearsed this part. Up until today, Amy didn't know if she'd be able to get the story out. "Was this common, for your parents to set you up on dates?"

Amy looked at Walt and Eileen, sitting like statues, staring at her, both eerily expressionless. "Yes. They wanted me to end up with a boy from a wealthy family."

"I see. Please go on."

Amy took a deep breath and looked back to Josh. He was as still as her parents, but his jaw was set tight, his eyes blazing with equal parts concern and fury.

"Well, the date was awkward. They always were. I'd never

met him before. My friend Gwen and her boyfriend met us at this swanky steakhouse. Michael was annoyed at me for trying to tip the valet. When we left the restaurant, he still seemed irritated. I was anxious to get home."

"And did he take you home?" Julian's voice was soft. The rest of the courtroom was silent besides the click and hiss of the heater.

"No. He stopped on some desolate road." She clasped her hands in her lap to still the shaking. Then she forced the memory of the night that changed her life out of the dark corners of her mind and into the revealing light of the courtroom.

Chapter 37

Civilization had disappeared. The fire-engine red Mustang convertible pulled to the side of the deserted road.

Michael turned toward her. "I haven't shown you a good time on this date, and I want to."

Amy's heart pounded in her throat and her stomach twisted with revulsion as he leaned toward her, eyes closed. She pulled back. She'd be damned if Michael Newman would be her first kiss.

"Michael, thank you." Amy made her voice as sweet as she could. "For the dinner, and, uh, everything. I should probably get home. My parents will be waiting up for me." She wanted to remind him of this.

When his eyes snapped open, they were filled with darkness.

"They know you're with me, doll. They trust my parents, and so by extension, trust me. See?" He laughed as though he'd told a hilarious joke.

"Well, if you don't mind, I'd like to go home now."

"Actually, I do mind."

Before she knew what was happening he'd hopped out of the car and come around to her side.

"What are you—"

He picked her up like a ragdoll and tossed her into the back seat. She gasped as her back hit the leather and she struggled to right herself. The stench of Marlboros and expensive cologne suffocated her. Michael was already crawling over her. Before she could react, his cold hand traveled up her blouse and under her bra.

"Michael, no!" She pulled at his arm and shoved him with all her strength. She couldn't get much leverage in her awkward position, but at least she succeeded in removing his hand. "Take me home, Michael!" She struggled to get out from underneath him, gasping for breath.

Michael struck her in the chest, nearly knocking the wind out of her. He shoved her into the leather and pinned her wrists above her head with one hand. This couldn't be happening.

"We go home when I say we go home." His breath was hot and heavy in her ear. She tried to kick but his weight pinned her.

She was helpless to writhe away as she felt his hand push up her skirt and between her legs.

"Michael, no!" She let out a yelp of shock and pain when he touched her, the intrusion sharp and unforgiving. He didn't stop.

"Oh, you haven't done this before." His voice was heavy in her ear. "Relax. You'll like it. It will only hurt at first." He kissed her neck lightly, in direct contrast to the ruthlessness of his hand.

Tears sprang from her eyes, running into her now tangled hair. "Michael, please stop!"

"Shh," he whispered. "You know you want it."

Amy squeezed her eyes shut, unable to bear looking at his triumphant face any longer. Memories erupted behind her lids. Running through a pumpkin patch with Gwen. Crawling between her parents in the darkness after a nightmare. Her dad's hand steadying her first two-wheeler. Everything before this. Amy understood her life would now have a "before" and "after". Whether or not Michael killed her, he'd already destroyed the girl she'd been.

"I don't want to do this. Please, take me home," she sobbed, "I won't tell anyone, I swear. Please don't do this."

"Tell whoever you want. No one will believe you didn't want it. Not in this little number." He tugged at the mini skirt Gwen had convinced her to change into in the ladies' room of the steakhouse.

The rough movement of his hand finally stopped. Maybe it was over. Amy let out her breath, but she didn't dare open her eyes. Then she heard the unmistakable zip. If his hand hurt this would hurt much, much worse. This was it, then. When Amy had imagined sex, it was never like this.

"No," she tried one last time. Then she'd stopped begging and braced herself for the inevitable.

Chapter 38

December 5, 1979

Amy raised her eyes and scanned the court room. Her mother's hands covered her mouth. Walt was whispering furiously in his wife's ear. Davis was suddenly very absorbed in shuffling and reshuffling his papers. Julian tugged on his tie. Amy had to look away from the pity in his eyes. And Josh. Josh held her gaze, his spine ramrod straight, her strength.

Amy expected the tears. She would've even welcomed them. But they didn't come. Now that the story was out there in the sterile air, its power over her loosened.

"Amy, I think I speak for the entire court in offering apologies for your experience," Julian said. "Do you need a break, or shall we continue?"

"No," said Amy, "I'm ready."

Amy held Davis's gaze as he approached the bench, adjusting his pin stripe tie.

"Amy, I'd like to echo Mr. Stein's sympathy for your ordeal."

"Thank you," Amy said despite his obvious lack of sincerity.

"I have to ask you—what were you wearing?"

Amy had left the house in the ankle-length flowery lavender

skirt her mother chose. *"Amy, don't be such a Pollyanna,"* Gwen said when she pulled Amy into the ladies' room. *"Put this on."* She whipped out a sparkly, black mini skirt. Amy stared at it.

"Come on. You'll look so foxy."

In the end she conceded. Gwen had a way of making people do what she wanted. Her friend shoved her flowery skirt in the bottom of the trash before Amy could object.

Julian's shout jerked Amy back into the present.

"Objection! Relevance?"

Davis rounded on him. "You're the one turning a custody battle into a rape trial."

Amy flinched. She glanced at Josh and feared he might launch himself over the railing.

"Mr. Davis!" The judge's voice boomed.

"Only after you turned it into a double-jeopardy assault trial." Julian said.

"Gentlemen, approach." The judge's eyes were hard.

Amy watched, detached as the lawyers shuffled up to the bench like scolded toddlers.

"You two will not turn my courtroom into a circus. Be seated. I'll take over the questioning."

Amy caught the glare the two men exchanged before stalking back to their respective places. She turned her attention to the judge. *I wonder how he keeps his black robe so smooth, no wrinkles? Why am I thinking about wrinkles?*

"Amy, I'm sure this is difficult, but it's important I understand Josh's role in this event. Do you think you can continue?"

"Yes," Amy said.

Chapter 39

Amy had tried to go somewhere else in her head. Anywhere else. Suddenly, Michael's weight was off her. She didn't dare move or open her eyes.

"Are you deaf, asshole? She said no." a deep, unfamiliar voice yelled.

"Who the fuck are you?" Michael's voice sounded strangled.

"I'm the last person you'll ever see if you try to touch her again."

"What's it to you? Mind your own fucking business."

"She said no." The strange voice bit off each word.

Amy forced her eyes open. Michael's bugged-out eyes stared back at her. A man had his arms pinned behind him.

Quickly, she averted her eyes from Michael, and they landed on the man behind him, towering over him. With his height and broad shoulders, he was much bigger than Michael. His hair was jet black and hung in unruly strands around his face. He looked at Amy. Something in his eyes, colorless in the dark, made the tremors in her limbs calm.

"Are you all right, miss?" His voice was free from the venom it'd held moments before.

Amy couldn't answer. She should get out of the car and away from Michael, but her body refused to move. She was terrified if she so much as breathed she'd feel Michael's hands all over her again. Would she ever stop feeling his hands on her?

"Are you hurt? Can you get out of the car? Don't worry about him. He won't touch you again, will you, buddy?" He jerked Michael backwards.

Michael groaned. "It's none of your business."

Amy noticed for the first time that the stranger held a large wrench in his other hand. It was like she was floating above herself or watching a movie. *What's going to happen next?*

"Here's what's going to happen," The stranger said as though answering her thoughts. He moved the wrench to Michael's throat, resting it against his Adam's apple. "She's going to get out of the car and come stand behind me. And you—" he wiggled the wrench. "You're going to drive away in your flashy car never to be seen or heard from again. Because if you so much as think about her again, I'll know, and I'll find you. Do we understand each other?"

An angry, guttural sound escaped Michael's throat as he stared at Amy wild-eyed.

"I said do we understand each other. You really ought to have your hearing checked."

"Fuck! You know what, she's not worth it. Amy, get the fuck out of my car. I'm leaving you with this psycho. Good luck."

Amy found her equilibrium. She pulled herself up and crawled over the side of the car, backing away from it like it was about to explode.

The stranger pulled the wrench back and shoved Michael. He pitched forward and caught himself on the side of the car.

"Get lost."

The Mustang sped away leaving a cloud of dust.

Amy lurched for the side of the road, barely clearing the bed of the large white pickup truck parked there. She fell to her knees and lost her dinner right there in the gravel. The weight of a hand on her back made her jerk away, spinning around.

"Don't touch me!" she screamed. She wiped her mouth on her shawl.

The stranger straightened, his hands out in front of him. He was no longer holding the wrench. "Sorry. I'm sorry. Can I help you?"

Amy stared up at him towering over her, his face etched in concern. Her fear made room for embarrassment. She must look pathetic. She straightened her clothes and tried to tug her skirt lower.

"I'm not going to hurt you." He stretched his hand out to her.

To her horror, Amy felt the tears again. Tears of embarrassment and fear, anger and relief. "I'm sorry," she said, turning her head away and wiping her eyes hastily. Her hand came away smudged with black mascara. Perfect.

The sound of footsteps retreating sent rapid waves of relief and then panic through her. He was leaving, and she had no idea where she was.

When she looked up again he was walking back toward her, a bottle of water in one hand and a box of tissues in the other. He crouched down in front of her.

"Hey. Hey, it's going to be okay. He's not coming back. You're going to be okay." He held the water and the tissues out to her.

Gratefully, she took them, splashing a little water onto the tissues and wiping her mouth and her scraped knees. After swallowing some water her stomach stilled and her throat cooled.

"I'm sorry," he said.

She cocked her head to one side and looked up at him. "For what?"

"I'd like to apologize on behalf of my entire gender."

She shrugged, the motion sending a sharp pain between her

shoulder blades. "It was my fault. I was stupid."

"It's not your fault. He hurt you."

Something flashed in his eyes. As she studied him, she realized he wasn't much older than her, and he was very good looking in a rugged way. His cheek bones were high, his shoulders were broad, and his hair was wavy without being curly. What really got her were his eyes. They were deep green with flecks of gold. They held a gentleness she almost wanted to trust.

"Thank you. It would've been even worse if you hadn't come along." Her voice trailed off and she shivered.

"Here." He took off his black jacket and handed it to her.

She put it over her shoulders, still warm from his body heat. It enveloped her like a blanket. A warm, safe blanket. She read the logo stitched in white letters on the breast. "Everett and Sons Construction. That explains the wrench."

"Yep." He held out his hand again. "Josh Everett."

This time she took his outstretched hand. "Amy Richards." She let him help her to her feet.

He straightened the jacket on her shoulders. "Sorry, it probably smells like sawdust. I did a lot of sawing today."

"It's better than cigarette smoke."

Her legs felt like jelly. He must've noticed because he reached out to steady her with a light touch on her arm.

"I don't smoke."

Amy inhaled deeply through her nose. That smell, an intoxicating blend of wood with a hint on cologne, was one she'd always associate with Josh.

He looked her over, but his gaze felt neither intrusive nor indifferent, the only way she could ever remember men looking at her. "Are you hurt? I should take you to a hospital."

Amy shuddered. The poking and the prodding. The questions. The frowns of disapproval. The phone call to her parents. Riding home in the back of her father's Bentley, listening to the disappointed whispers trickling conspicuously from the front. Her body hurt in places she'd never been touched before. Still, she figured she was mostly okay.

She shook her head. "I'll be fine. I just need to get home."

His dark eyebrows knit together. "I'll take you home, but we should stop at the police station and report him."

Amy shook her head again. The thought of anyone knowing where Michael touched her brought fresh fire to her cheeks.

"Your call. I hate to see him get away with it."

"He would anyway. His parents have a lot of money."

It was Josh's turn to shake his head. "I guess I don't understand rich people. I'll take you home." He started to lead her toward the truck.

Amy pulled back with a sharp warning in her stomach. Was she really going to get into another car with another boy she didn't know?

"What's wrong?"

"How do I know you're not a serial killer?" she blurted, although being murdered was no longer her top worry. She felt a steady parade of fire ants under her skin where Michael had touched her. She couldn't let it happen again. All she wanted was to go home, take a long hot shower and scrub Michael off her body, put on her longest, softest nightgown and crawl into bed. But how else would she get home?

Josh's baritone voice interrupted her internal debate. "I'm not a serial killer. I'm a construction worker."

"But how am I supposed to know?"

"You're right. You don't know me from anyone." He lowered the hitch of the truck and spread a blanket on the edge. "Come sit." He patted the blanket. He helped her into the truck bed and hoisted himself up beside her.

She inched away from him. "What were you doing out here anyway?"

"Getting rid of bodies."

She didn't return his impish grin.

He hitched a thumb toward the old boarded up general store. "I came to look at this building. It's been an eye sore for decades. My dad's doing a bid for a tear down. It's infested with mice. I was closing up the trailer at a job site a few miles east, so I promised him I'd stop by and get a lay of the land. I'll have to get rid of the mice first."

"You have to kill them first? Why don't you just knock it down?" It was a pointless question, but she was stalling.

"Oh, no, I won't kill them. I mean, I'll tell my dad and brother I did. Really, I'll trap them and release them in the corn field. He must've caught her quizzical look. "It's not their fault," he continued. "They don't want to hurt anyone; they're trying to survive."

Who was this stranger who wouldn't even kill a mouse? "How old are you?" she asked.

"Eighteen."

"Do you go to public school or did you graduate?" She was sure she'd never seen him around her school.

He looked down at his hands and she followed his gaze. They were rough and calloused, like he was used to working with them. "I uh, I didn't graduate. I missed so many days my senior year, helping my dad. I didn't want my brother to miss. I wanted to graduate but my dad needed me to work, and well, I needed to help support the family, the business. We were going to lose our house. I dropped out and started working full time. I *will* finish, though. Eventually."

Surprising herself, she reached out and touched his arm. "I think it's admirable that you work so hard and had to grow up so fast."

He smiled. "Yeah?"

"Yeah."

"Serial killing doesn't pay the bills."

This time she laughed.

"Listen, I can't in good conscience leave you here. You may

not know this, but Townshed isn't the best area. It used to be the bee's knees, but now not so much." He reached toward her and she froze. He put his hand inside the pocket of the jacket and pulled out a set of keys and held them out to her. "Take my truck. I can walk to the next town and find a place to call my brother to come pick me up. I can always get it back from you tomorrow."

Amy felt her mouth drop open. Was he crazy? "Why would you give me your truck?"

"Not give. Loan. I want you to feel safe."

"I want you to feel safe." It was the kindest thing anyone had ever said to her. She looked into her lap.

"I can't take your truck."

"It's fine. Really."

"No, I mean I—I don't know how to drive. I'm almost seventeen but, well, I haven't learned yet." Her cheeks had to be flaming. No way could she admit that her father wouldn't teach her. Her mother had never learned to drive.

Josh gestured behind him. "Then take the wrench or one of my other tools. If I do anything serial killer-ish you can clobber me with it."

"Why are you being nice to me?"

"Why wouldn't I?"

She sighed. It was getting late. Her parents were probably wondering where she was. *She* was wondering where she was. If he wanted to try something with her he could've done it already. He looked like he could overpower her with one hand. "Okay." She hopped down from the tailgate and got into the passenger seat.

Amy gave Josh her address. He reached across her and she jerked back, plastering herself against the seat, but he reached into the glove compartment and pulled out a map. *Calm down, Amy. Just get home.* She focused on steadying her heart rate.

"We're not that far." He showed her the map, tracing a line with his finger.

Amy could remember the most random facts, but she never could read a map.

"What do you want to listen to?"

"You're asking me?"

"You're the passenger."

She flipped to a Christian rock station, wondering if he'd think she was a Pollyanna, if he didn't already. In a moment he was humming along with the song. "You like this?"

"Truth be told, I'm more of a hard rock guy, but the band at our church plays this almost every Sunday. My dad says you're never too sick or too busy to miss church."

"My dad says those who fail to keep the Sabbath will face eternal damnation."

Josh snorted. "Similar message, different delivery, I guess. My dad tries to be tough but he's harmless."

"You're mom's lucky." Amy's mother tiptoed around and stopped to straighten the towels after she washed her hands.

"Actually, he raised us himself. My mom died when I was little."

"Oh," Amy gasped. "I'm so sorry. I didn't—"

He waved his hand. "It's okay. I don't remember her. She died during childbirth with my brother. I wasn't even two."

"That must be hard."

"It's the way it is. It's always been us guys. We get along okay. It's probably been hardest on my dad."

They drove in amicable silence. Amy's anxiety evaporated until they pulled up in front of the rolling mansion. She couldn't believe how quickly the drive had gone.

"This it?" He put the truck in park.

She turned to him, suddenly ashamed. "Josh? I'm not like that."

"Not like what?" He gazed at her and she drank in his features.

"When you said you don't understand rich people. I'm not

snobby or anything. I hate the whole pretentious charade."

"Oh, I didn't mean—"

"And I usually don't—I mean I *never* dress like this. My friend talked me into wearing this skirt she had in her purse. Who carries a skirt in her purse? What kind of girl wears a skirt that fits in a purse? I knew better."

"Amy, you don't have to explain anything to me. It doesn't matter what you're wearing or how big your house is. Why would I judge you? And I don't care if you were birthday naked. He had no right to touch you."

Despite the edge that had crept into his voice, Amy giggled. "Birthday naked?"

A smile softened his features. "Yeah, you know, as naked as the day you were born?"

"I get it, I've never heard anyone use that phrase."

"What can I say, I'm a square peg."

"I thought I was the only one." Amy felt lighter, as though she'd been living on a deserted island and discovered another inhabitant.

"You're not."

"You know, if you were a smart serial killer you would drive me home, memorize my address, then come back and slay me when I least expect it. Like on a dark, rainy night." She made her voice low and dramatic.

He furrowed his eyebrows and gave her an endearing half smile. "Miss Richards, I think you've seen too many movies."

"I do watch a lot of movies. I don't have many friends." She wanted to clap a hand over her mouth as soon as the words were out. *Smooth, Amy.* But Josh nodded.

"Yeah, me neither. The whole square peg thing."

They smiled at each other. Amy couldn't avoid going inside forever. "Thank you, for everything. I guess I better go in."

The floodlights flicked on, bathing the front lawn and the truck in harsh, accusing light. "Shit," Amy muttered under her breath. Immediately, she looked at Josh. "Sorry."

"*Ladies don't swear, especially in front of men,*" her mom's voice said in her head.

Josh shrugged. "Hell if I care. Do you want me to go in with you? They saw my truck. It seems kind of rude not to introduce myself. Maybe I could help explain. But I won't tell them," he added quickly.

"I can't ask you to do that," she said, even though the relief of having someone, even a stranger, in her corner was enticing.

"You're not. I'm asking you. May I walk you to the door and meet your parents?"

"It's not that I don't want you to, but they may not be very nice to you. I've never introduced them to a boy before. It's always been the other way around."

"I can handle it. I'm tougher than I look."

Amy doubted that was possible, but if she stalled any longer her father would come storming out to the truck. She nodded.

They walked side by side up the stone path. The curtains moved and her heart fluttered with them. She stopped in her tracks.

He put a gentle hand between her shoulder blades and guided her forward. "Don't worry," he whispered in her ear. "We serial killers are good at explaining suspicious circumstances."

She opened the door and led Josh into the vast foyer. He looked up at the chandelier. Amy saw her childhood home the way he must have. The cold marble. The gaudy chandelier. The excessive space.

"Mom, Dad, I'm home," she called as they walked into the sitting room where her parents were predictably sitting in matching leather chairs pretending they hadn't been waiting for her. Her father rose first, and her mother took her place behind him.

"Dad, Mom, this is—"

"You're not Michael," her father said.

Josh shifted from one foot to the other. "No, Sir. I'm Josh. Josh Everett." He stuck out his hand, but Walt and Eileen stared at him. Gaped, really.

He let his hand drop to his side. Amy felt bad for him. She was a coward. She should tell her parents then and there how Josh had rescued her from her "perfect" date. She should show them the bruises instead of letting them treat him this way to avoid her own shame.

"You don't understand," she told her parents. "Michael was driving me home. He stopped the car on some deserted road and he ... he ..."

Her face grew hot and she feared she might faint. She felt Josh's hand on her arm, stopping her. "Amy, it's okay."

She saw her father's steel gray eyes cut to Josh's hand on her arm. He must've noticed it too, because he pulled away.

"Amy's date had a little car trouble. I was heading through on my way home from a job and I offered to drive her home. It seemed like it was going to take him some time to fix his problem."

Amy looked at her parents to see if they were buying this. They were both frowning. Her mom was staring at Josh slightly wide-eyed as though Amy had brought home an extra-terrestrial being.

"What sort of car trouble?" her father asked. "It's almost a brand-new car."

Josh cleared his throat. "I don't know. I think his gear shift got stuck."

"I see," Walt said. "Thank you for getting her home safely, young man. I'll walk you out."

"I'll walk him out, Dad." Amy was shocked at her own boldness. Her father must've been too, because he didn't object.

"Thank you," she told Josh once they were on the front stoop. "I know that was painful."

His smile brought out the gold flecks in his green eyes. "It was worth it." They stood still for a moment, looking at each other. Josh pushed a loose strand of hair out of Amy's face. It had gone completely straight.

"It was curly at the beginning of the night. It doesn't cooperate."

"I like it this way. More natural."

"Amy." Walt's voice broke the moment. "Let the young man go now. I'm sure he needs to get home, and your mother and I need to talk to you."

Josh winced. "Good luck. Take care of yourself. It was nice to meet you." He held out his hand as though they were first meeting.

Amy had the sudden urge to hug him. Instead, she put her hand in his, memorizing the warmth and strength of it. He squeezed her hand once and then he was gone. She watched the truck pull away until she could no longer avoid going back into the parlor where her parents waited in their respective chairs, stationed like guards.

"Have a seat." Walt nodded toward the red suede love seat facing the chairs. Amy perched herself on the edge looking at her parents' hard faces. Had she ever gone to these people for comfort? Maybe as a small child with a scraped knee or an earache? Naturally, her father spoke first.

"First off, do you care to explain why you left this house looking like a lady and returned looking like a cheap whore?"

He may as well have slapped her. The sting would've faded faster.

"Walt." Her mother put a hand on his arm. He shook it off and gave her a look that silenced her.

"Gwen wanted me to try it on." Amy wished like hell she had on the long-flowered skirt and white slip Gwen had stuffed in the bathroom garbage can at the steakhouse.

"That girl is too fast for you," Walt said. His voice echoed through the uninviting parlor. "Why do you always invite her along on your dates?"

"I'm not comfortable going on these dates with boys I don't know." Amy couldn't help wishing Josh was there to back her up while she faced the firing squad.

"Yet you were comfortable getting into some rattle trap truck with a boy you don't know. He just so happened to be driving by?"

"Yes, he just so happened to be driving by. I didn't find him at Mulligan's."

"Obviously not, dressed like he was. And watch your tone, young lady. Why would you get into a car with a complete stranger?"

Amy wanted to say that was exactly what he'd required her to do a few hours earlier. "I thought it would be better than being stranded," she said instead.

Walt's eyes bored into her while Eileen sat mutely beside him. "I'm not sure I believe any part of this car trouble story but I'm not going to get to the bottom of it tonight. It's late. Get ready for bed. And throw that skirt in the trash, which is what it says about anyone wearing it." He rose as though dismissing a meeting.

Amy had barely closed her bedroom door when she heard a soft knock. Would this night never end? "Come in."

Her mother padded across the shag carpet and perched on the edge of her four-poster bed, knitting her fingers together the way she did when she had something she wanted to say. She cleared her throat. "Amy, what really happened tonight?"

Amy saw an opening. She wanted to crawl into her mother's lap like a little girl. "Michael wanted to do things that I didn't," she said, testing the waters. I told him no and he . . . he . . ." She stopped, seeing her mother frown.

"Well, Amy, can you blame him with what you're wearing?"

Expecting this response didn't make it hurt any less. "I made a mistake."

Eileen nodded, plastering an empty smile on her face. She stood and kissed Amy's hair lightly. "Well, I trust you've learned your lesson. Men are opportunists."

"Eileen!" Walt's voice carried through the walls.

"Speaking of. Good night, Amy." Eileen closed the door behind her.

Although Amy expected them, would've even welcomed them, the tears didn't come. Thoughts swirled in her exhausted head. It wasn't until she locked herself in her en suite and began to undress for the shower that she noticed she was still wearing Josh's jacket. She hung it on the hook inside the door before turning the shower water on as hot as she could stand. Crimson splotches stained her once pure white panties. She shoved them to the bottom of the trash can along with the skirt.

Once in the shower, Amy lathered her pink loofa with lavender scented soap and scrubbed until it hurt. When she closed her eyes to rinse her hair, Michael's leering face and reaching hand popped into her brain, and she snapped them open with a stifled scream. Even the sting of soap in her eyes couldn't entice her to close them again.

The pain between her legs was still sharp and hot. Would it bleed more? Who could she ask?

Even after her skin was red and raw, she could still feel Michael's hands crawling all over her. She clamped a hand over her mouth to keep from screaming, wishing she could tear her own skin off. She was so, so alone.

Finally, she toweled off and pulled on her softest cotton night gown. Her lids were heavy, but she was terrified to close them. She never wanted to see Michael again, even in her mind. If only she could erase him. Despite the steam-filled room, she couldn't stop shivering.

Josh's jacket brushed her arm when she reached for the doorknob. Without thinking about it, she pulled it on, her hands disappearing halfway up the sleeves. The fleece lining cushioned her skin. She zipped it up and crawled under the duvet. The sweet smell of pine and aftershave tickled her nose as she tucked one arm under her head.

Although she was afraid to close her eyes, afraid to invite dreams, when her exhausted lids finally forced themselves closed her only thoughts were of Josh.

Chapter 40

Josh put his tattered visor down and squinted into the sun, navigating the truck along the sparsely trafficked roads to Bob's house. Apparently Bob had something to tell him and Jason and it needed to be in person, on a Sunday morning no less.

To say Josh had a lot on his mind would be an understatement. For one thing, it was his son's last day as a one-year old. Amy was at the market buying ingredients to make a vanilla bean cake. The celebration would be small and bittersweet. Would this be Caleb's last birthday with his father? Josh shook his head to dislodge the thought.

On its heels were thoughts of Amy in front of that courtroom, telling her parents, the lawyers, everyone what Michael had done. Pride filled him. She'd done it for him, but also for herself. In the days since, she seemed lighter. Josh's tired brain was ready to explode. He tried not to wonder what Bob wanted to tell them.

"He called you here to tell you what a disappointment you are as a son. As a man. As a fucking human being. They all know. Run the truck off the road. Don't fuck it up this time."

"Shut the fuck up!" Josh turned up the radio as loud as he could.

The voice was coming from the radio. No, it wasn't; of

course, it wasn't. It was coming from his head. He hit himself in the side of the head. Relief and dread soured his stomach as he pulled up to his childhood home. Josh's mind had conjured up a million scenarios since his dad had called that morning asking him to come over to talk. If there was one thing Bob Everett didn't do it was heart-to-hearts. Josh had a headache from the task of untangling his own thoughts from the tormenting voices. The old house needed a new coat of paint. The front porch sagged. Josh let himself in.

"Hello?" he called.

"Hello." Jason was sitting ramrod straight on the couch, tearing a label off a bottle of Budweiser. He frowned at Josh.

"He hates you now."

"He doesn't hate me," Josh flopped down beside Jason.

"Who doesn't hate you?"

"You."

Jason slapped his arm. "Of course, I don't hate you. Why are they telling you shit like that? Tell them to stop talking shit about me."

Josh laughed, his shoulders relaxing. Jason referred to the voices like they were real, which to Josh, they were. It made Josh feel almost normal. Less alone, like when Jason and Josh presented a united front against the bullies who teased them about their thrift store clothes, sparse lunches, and absent mother.

"It can be genetic." Josh swallowed. Would he be able to give Caleb a sibling? Should he? He and Jason had such an uncanny connection. As children they'd have the same dreams, waking simultaneously from nightmares. Bob would find them in the morning both huddled in the same twin bed, blanket over their heads. At least the link between their brains hadn't extended to schizophrenia.

"You okay?" Jason nudged him with an elbow.

"Yeah, it's just . . . do you know what this is about?"

"Nope." He picked at a stubborn piece of the label.

Bob walked in from the kitchen, a sweating beer in his hand. "You want a beer?" he asked Josh by way of greeting.

Josh could almost taste the cool relief of a Budweiser, feel the subtle loosening of his muscles. "I probably shouldn't with the meds."

Bob nodded. Josh studied him. Was he sick? His face was ruddy and full, but he'd been coughing a lot; getting winded.

"Dad, are you okay?"

"I'm fine. There's something I need to tell you both." He looked down at them and Josh was reminded of sitting on this very couch with Jason, Bob towering over them demanding to know who'd broken the neighbor's window. It had been Jason; a wayward baseball. Josh had taken the blame, getting up and turning around before Bob even pulled his belt from its loops.

"For Godsakes, tell us," Jason said.

"Your mother didn't die during childbirth."

Josh looked around. He was hearing things. "Did you say Mom didn't die during childbirth?"

You killed her. It's your fault. You're evil.

Josh shook his head, trying to dislodge the disembodied voice. He looked around but didn't see Shane. This voice was more of a harsh whisper.

He'd been younger than Caleb when she died. Or had he? If Bob had been lying about how she died could he have lied about when?

"How'd she die, then?" Jason asked.

Your little brother's about to find out you killed Mommy.

For a second, Josh thought he was going to throw up. He snatched Jason's beer and drained it, setting the bottle on the floor. Jason didn't seem to notice.

"I lied to everyone," Bob said, almost to himself. I thought I was protecting her. Protecting you guys. Honoring her memory." He sighed heavily. "You need to know the truth."

"What is the truth?" Jason said each word slowly.

Josh expended all his energy focusing on his dad so he could hear over the background noise of the voices.

"She cut her wrists in the bathtub. By the time I found her..." A violent coughing fit interrupted him.

The thick silence that followed the admission disturbed him more than the voices. Josh broke it. "I'm sorry, did you say Mom killed herself? She slit her wrists and you found her?"

The scene made his stomach turn. His dad walking in the bathroom. His mom, faceless as she always was in his imagination, bleeding out. Bob Everett had lived with that secret for two decades. But why?

"Yes, he said she fucking killed herself," Jason said. "Do you want him to say it again? God!"

"Jason don't take this out on your brother. If you're going to be mad at someone, be mad at me."

"You're damn right, I'm mad at you. My whole life you let me think it was my fault."

Josh looked at his brother. His eyes were fiery with hurt and rage. Josh laid a hand on his arm, but he jerked it away.

Bob's eyes widened. "Your fault? Why on earth would it be your fault? I never said anything like that."

"You never said anything at all! We never talked about it! You never wanted us to talk about her! You never wanted us to talk about anything we were feeling!"

"That's not true." Bob rubbed the back of his neck. He stifled a cough. "Jason, how could it have been your fault? You were an infant."

"You said she died giving birth to me!"

"That wouldn't make it your fault. If anything, the fault is my own."

"It's no one's fault," Josh said.

"I appreciate that, Josh," Bob said. "But I'm not blameless. She was sick for a long time and I didn't know how to help her.

"Sick how?" Josh asked. "*Schizophrenia is sometimes genetic.*"

Bob stared into his eyes, pleading. "She started hearing voices. Shortly after you were born. She was only nineteen years old. She was terrified people were plotting to have her locked up, to take you. She'd sit in front of your crib guarding you until she'd literally collapse from exhaustion. She begged me not to tell anyone, so I never did. I never told a soul until now."

"You did nothing," Jason said.

"I didn't know what to do, Jason. When she got pregnant with you, she got worse. She thought she was carrying the second coming and demons would try to take you. She insisted on having you at home because she was so afraid of hospitals. She was so devoted to you guys."

"So devoted that she left us," Jason said.

Josh winced.

Jason looked up at Bob. "You turned a blind eye like you did when Josh got sick."

"Jason—" Josh began, but Bob held up a hand.

"No, he's right." He looked from Josh to Jason. "Look, you have to understand. It was the fifties. Mental illness was a skeleton you hid in your closet. People who heard voices were thought to be possessed."

Josh shuddered.

"*Get out of here! Run! The demons will get you, too!*"

What was it like, having no way of knowing what was happening to you? Nowhere to turn. How could he blame her for taking her life?

"Did you think if you ignored it, it would go away?" Jason asked.

"I thought if I loved her enough she could get better, but she kept getting worse. I didn't know what 'it' was. I didn't have a name for it until . . . until now." He nodded toward Josh.

"It's genetic," Josh said. "It might happen to Caleb."

"If it does, you'll get him help," Jason said. "Dad, why didn't you get Mom help?"

Bob's eyes flashed. "Do you know what 'help' looked like back then, Jason? People were locked up in asylums. Asylums, not mental wards. Crazy people were dunked in ice water, tied up in straight jacket, confined in padded rooms."

Josh flinched.

"He's getting mad. He's going to hurt you."

"Is that what you wanted me to do to your mother, Jason? I loved her. Maybe I didn't do right by her, but God knows I loved her the best I knew how." He coughed so hard his face turned red. He pulled out a handkerchief and wiped his mouth.

The voices blended together, bouncing off each other. Josh hit the sides of his head. He clamped his hands over his ears and moaned. If they could leave him alone; just for now. He needed to think. He needed to not think.

"Take a breath, kid," Sam, the man from the road, said from somewhere close by. "You're turnin' blue."

Bob looked at him, alarmed. "Josh are you okay?"

"Of course, he's not okay! Don't say 'crazy people'. What is wrong with you? You lie to us for our entire lives and now you're yelling at me? This is unbelievable." Jason shot to his feet and headed for the door.

"Jay, wait." Josh reached for him, but he jerked away. The door slammed behind him.

"Let him go. He needs time. Besides, he has every right to be angry. There's more I need to say to you."

"This is the part where he tells you you're dead to him. Hahaha."

Bob was watching him. "What are they saying to you?"

"You don't want to know."

"No, I do. I want to know what it's like. Help me understand."

Josh cleared his throat. The words meant everything coming from his dad. He thought about what he was going through in court. It wasn't so hard to understand why Bob had kept this secret. He dug his fingers into the rough fabric underneath him, trying to find the right words. Once he found them they kept coming.

"It's waking up one morning and someone has stolen part of your brain. Now you have to share it. It will never be yours again. It's having a roommate you can't evict. Sometimes he sleeps; sometimes he's quiet; sometimes he does his own thing and leaves you alone, but other times he looks over your shoulder, whispers or shouts in your ear, telling you you're worthless. It's waiting a beat to respond to anyone or anything, so you know it's real. It's being feared even though you'd never hurt anyone. It's people thinking you have multiple personalities, that you're a danger to your child, that you can't hold a conversation. It's fear." Josh sucked in a deep breath.

"That sounds awful," Bob said.

Josh shrugged. "It's not all bad. There are good parts too."

Bob looked hopeful. "Yeah?"

"Sure. You notice things other people don't. You appreciate the lucid moments. And you find out who your allies are."

"Is it too late for me to be your ally?"

"It's never too late."

Bob sighed. "I want you to come back to work, son. The truth is I can't quite run this project without you. I've got this guy, Blake helping to manage the project, but he misses the details you never did, and your brother's more cantankerous than a wet cat without you around. I need you back."

"I appreciate that, Dad, but I can't hide my illness."

"I'm not asking you to."

"But, aren't you embarrassed? "

"No. I'm proud."

Josh scoffed. "You're proud to have a schizophrenic for a son?"

"No, I'm proud to have you for a son. Schizophrenia's just part of the package."

Josh stood and reached for his dad's hand. "I accept the job, Mr. Everett."

Bob pumped his hand. "You're hired." Another coughing fit overtook him, nearly doubling him over.

"Jesus, Dad, you've had that a while. You need to see a doctor."

Bob waved him off. "I've got no time to be sick. We've got to get this house done before the ground freezes. Just a bug." He grabbed Josh by the shoulders. "Josh, you have to know I loved your mother."

"I believe you."

He cleared his throat. "You have to know I love you, too."

Josh considered this. "You know, I don't think you've ever told me that before."

"I'm telling you now."

"I think there's someone else who needs to hear it too, since you're becoming such a bleeding heart."

Bob slapped him on the arm. "You're right. If he ever wants to hear anything I have to say again."

"He'll cool off. I'll talk to him." Josh headed for the door, turning back when his dad called his name.

"When I saw you in that hospital bed, it all came back to me. I haven't slept a night through since I found her. Burying my wife nearly killed me. The thought of burying my child . . . I couldn't handle it. I'm too much of a coward. I drove up to those hospital doors so many times. So many times, Josh. I was too scared to go in. I was too scared of what I'd find. I regret letting that fear keep me away."

A weight fell from Josh's shoulders. "I get it, Dad. And I love you too."

Josh found his brother on the little wooden bench Bob had built in the back yard facing the little pond where they used to skip rocks and race matchbox boats. His shoulders were slumped, his eyes on the thin veil of ice encasing the water. Josh sat next to him, picking at a fleck of chipped white paint.

"This thing needs a new coat of paint." Jason didn't answer. "You okay?"

Jason shrugged. "I don't know. I don't know what I am." He scuffed his shoe in the dirt. Finally, he looked at Josh. "Aren't you pissed that he lied to us?"

"It sucks, but I get it. People don't talk about suicide. They talked about it less then."

"They should."

Josh nodded. "You're right."

"Either way, it's my fault."

"How can you say that?"

"She killed herself right after I was born. Maybe having another baby put her over the edge."

"She was sick, Jay. She was probably schizophrenic. It's in no way your fault. She wouldn't want you to think that."

Jason seemed to consider that. He searched Josh's eyes. "But if she loved us why would she do it?"

Josh chose his words carefully. "I think she loved us the best way she knew how. Maybe she thought we'd be better off. Maybe she thought it was the only way to make the voices shut up. The only way to make the pain stop."

"Is that what you thought?" Jason's voice shook.

Josh swallowed hard. "I don't know what I thought. I wasn't thinking straight."

They watched a pair of squirrels chase each other down one tree and up another, undeterred by the plummeting temperature.

"Josh?"

"Hmm?"

"Are you going to try it again?" He squeezed his eyes shut as if bracing for Josh's answer.

"No."

"I need your word on that, because I couldn't take it. I'm not strong enough. I'm not." He raked a hand through his hair.

The familiar flutter of regret took up residence in Josh's gut. How many lives would've been altered if he'd succeeded? He'd be forever grateful to Amy for pulling him out of that truck in time; forever grateful to God or intuition or whatever force had awakened her that night and compelled her to check the garage. He would've missed so much!

He put a firm hand on his brother's shoulder. "Jay, look at me."

His eyes met Josh's pained and pleading.

"I'm not going to hurt myself again. I swear. You have my word, okay?"

Jason nodded. "Okay." The tension visibly drained from his body.

"You know," Josh said, "Dad loves us too, in his own way, even if he can't express it."

"I was a little harsh. I'll clear the air with him. Life's too short, right?"

Shane came up behind him. He fired a rock into the pond, creating a nonexistent splash. "You're a pansy," he muttered.

Josh just laughed.

"What exactly is funny?"

"Nothing, it's just ... While we're on the subject—you know I love you, right?"

Jason rubbed a hand across his eyes. He broke into a grin, his eyes as shiny as a kid on Christmas morning. "We're all turning into a bunch of saps, aren't we?"

Josh laughed. "Yep. The whole family's gone crazy."

Jason bumped Josh's knee with his own. "You know, maybe that's not such a bad thing."

Josh smiled, leaning back against the cold wood. He knew it was the closest his brother could come to saying I love you too.

Chapter 41

"**W**alt will take the stand tomorrow. You can bet he and Davis are preparing to not only prove Josh's instability, but also highlight the discrepancies in your lifestyles."

Caleb toddled over and handed Julian a plastic dinosaur. Julian smiled, ruffling Caleb's thick blond hair. "T-Rex, huh? My favorite. That was my nick name in law school because no one stood a chance against me." He laughed, making the toy's mouth open and shut.

Amy relaxed back against the couch, grateful that Caleb was blissfully unaware of the preparations happening in his own family room.

"Discrepancies in our lifestyles?" Josh squirmed next to Amy, his eyes never leaving Caleb.

"I hate to say it, but money talks, and the Richards have plenty."

"I thought this was about me being a lunatic, not me being poor."

"Josh." Amy touched his arm, hating his self-deprecating tone.

Julian shrugged. "Well, sure. But every custody case comes down to the best interests of the child. Part of that is who can best provide for the child."

Josh got to his feet and began pacing. "Provide what, exactly? Money? Marble floors and oriental rugs he can't play on? Servants?"

Amy's face burned. His defensiveness was understandable, but his disdain felt personal.

"Look, Josh, it's not me who needs convincing. I'm here to prepare you guys, mostly Amy, for what's going to transpire. The best defense is a good offense, right? Are you guys receiving government aid?"

Amy cringed. Josh whirled around, his eyes blazing. "That is none of your business."

"It's all my business. It's all the judge's business."

"Josh, sit down," Amy said more harshly than she'd meant to. "You're making me nervous."

"I make everyone nervous. That's the point, right? Who knows what I'll do next?" He spun his finger at the side of his head.

"You're not helping. Walking around with a chip on your shoulder won't do any good."

"Easy for you to say."

Amy rubbed the back of her neck. Caleb pulled on Josh's pant leg and held up his arms. Amy watched him deflate, the agitation draining out of him like Caleb had pulled a plug. He lifted him above his head, spinning around.

Caleb shrieked. Josh pulled him close, wrapping his arms around him. His eyes filmed.

"I love you," he whispered into Caleb's hair.

See, Amy wanted to scream. *See how he is with him?*

Caleb squirmed in Josh's arms. "Down, Dada, down."

"Okay, okay." Josh set him down and returned to the couch. He wiped his eyes and looked at Julian. "How many times will I get to hold him? If the judge takes him from me, will they let me see him at all? Will I ever see him again?" His voice broke along with Amy's heart.

"If that happens, we can appeal. Worst case scenario, you'll get supervised visitation."

"So I could see him how often?"

"You could still see him regularly, but under supervision, like in a social service office."

Josh looked at Caleb, stricken. "That would be so scary and confusing for him. I can't do that to him. He's a baby; he won't even know who I am. Maybe it would be better for him if I let him forget me."

Amy laced her fingers through his and tried to still the shaking. "Josh, that's not going to happen."

"That's worst-case scenario, and T-Rexes don't settle for worse-case scenarios, right, Caleb? Roar!" He waved the toy.

The baby took the toy back from Julian. "Fine," Caleb said. Fine was his new word. Everything was always fine. If only.

"You said you had to prepare us, especially me. Why especially me?" Amy asked.

Julian looked at her. "Your parents and their lawyer are going to postulate that they can offer Caleb a better, more stable upbringing; that they're the right people to raise him. Our job is to show the judge that they're not."

"Okay." Amy pulled Julian's explanation through the thick fog in her head. "How?"

Julian grinned. He clasped his in front of him. "Slander. Give me the dirt. We show that they weren't good parents."

"That shouldn't be very hard," Josh muttered.

The heaviness in Amy's stomach snowballed. Her chest tightened like a sieve.

"Right." Julian leaned over and rummaged in his briefcase, pulling out a yellow legal pad. "Amy, tell me about any abuse you were subjected to as a child. Did your father or mother hit you? Use excessive punishment? Touch you inappropriately?"

Amy's face flushed. "No," she said to her hands. She picked at a cuticle until a drop of blood bloomed like a warning against her pale skin. Josh took her hands in both of his.

Julian shrugged. "That's okay. We don't need that."

That's okay? Was he disappointed her parents hadn't beat her? To him, this was a job, Amy reminded herself. But Caleb and Josh were her whole life. She wanted to rip the legal pad out of Julian's hands and tear it to shreds. She wanted to scream at him to get out of their house, their lives; to leave them the hell alone already. The only problem was her anger was misdirected.

"Why don't you tell me what it was like growing up with your parents?"

Amy looked at Josh. He tucked a strand of hair behind her ear. His tenderness, intended for comfort, poured gasoline on the embers of her regret.

What was it like growing up with her parents? Lonely was the first word that came to mind. But it hadn't always been that way. The slide show of her childhood ran through Amy's head. Swinging on the end of her parents' arms, their laughter when she dropped her weight without warning. Riding on her dad's shoulder through Disney World, held safely above the crowds. Walt's steady hand on the back of her two-wheeler. Her mother tenderly dabbing the blood on her skinned knee. The time her dad slept on her floor for an entire month because she couldn't be convinced monsters didn't live under her bed waiting to grab her ankles when she put her feet on the floor.

When had it changed? Middle school, maybe a little before. Walt "made it big". They'd packed up their cozy two-bedroom house and left it behind, an after-thought.

"You'll have all the things I never did, Amy-girl," her dad had said, smiling as he showed her the plans for the mansion.

Amy had felt the same emptiness at her core that she did now. How could she tell him that wasn't what she wanted at all? What she wanted was their tight-knit threesome and their cozy home. She couldn't. She didn't. They moved into the mansion and Walt moved up the ladder. He was gone more, and he smiled less, then not at all. Eileen traded her old friendships for superficial country club connections. Backyard barbeques gave way to stuffy dinner parties. The mansion had more living space but less space to live.

"Amy?" Julian broke into her trance. "I know it's a loaded question."

"I was lonely," Amy managed. My parents were gone a lot, and when they were there they weren't really *there*. I was closer to Maria, our cook, than I was to my own mother. It was her I went to for advice, and her I went to when I got my first—" she flushed. "Well, I went to her for girl stuff."

Julian scrawled furiously on his legal pad. "Good." He nodded to himself. "Good."

"But it wasn't always like that," Amy said. "It wasn't all bad." We used to go on family vacations all the time. Road trips where we'd tell stories, taking turns with the lines. We'd have family game nights and Mom would always cheat. For my ninth birthday, she decorated the house like a movie studio. She even got an actual red carpet. Then there was this one time—"

Julian held up his hand. "I get your parents weren't all bad, but they're the villains. I need to hear more about how you felt abandoned."

"Lonely, not abandoned."

"Dammit, Amy," Josh said, and she jumped. "Are you really going to defend them right now? I saw what it was like for you, living with them. They made you feel invisible. All they care about is their image."

Defensive tears sprang into her eyes. "You don't know everything. You met me when I was sixteen. There's a whole backstory that you don't know."

"I don't give a—" He glanced at Caleb. "I don't care that they once hugged you or they played games with you or took you on trips. It's their fault you always feel guilty for everything; you're always second guessing yourself. I won't have my son raised like that."

"Gee, Josh, it's nice to know you think I turned out so great."

"This isn't about me. Or you. Your parents waged this war, not me, not Julian, not you. Them."

"That doesn't mean it's easy for me to stand up and say they were horrible parents and people."

Josh threw up his hands. "They are horrible parents and people!"

"It's not that black and white!"

"In court, it is," Julian said. Amy barely heard him. She was watching Josh. A vein pulsed in his neck.

"They're still my parents. It's hard!"

"Yes, it's hard!" Josh shouted. "It's hard to be dragged through court, accused of being an unfit parent. It's hard to have someone try to rip your child out of your arms claiming they could do better when they messed it up the first time."

"Now you think I'm messed up?"

"Stop making this about you!"

Julian's eyes darted between them. Caleb was watching, but Amy couldn't reign this in. Don't make it about her? Well, it seemed *she* was the one being interrogated! She shot to her feet. "You don't know everything," she yelled at Josh. "You think you know every last thing about me, but you don't!"

Caleb's lower lip trembled. Fat, silent tears rolled down his cheeks. Josh went to him, lifting him. Celeb buried his face in Josh's neck. Josh was a more capable parent than she'd ever been. That's what made this whole thing so ludicrous. If anyone's parenting ability should be questioned it was her own.

He turned to her, bouncing Caleb. "What exactly is it that I don't know?" His voice was measured; the anger boiling below the surface.

Amy opened her mouth and closed it several times. "You don't know the kind of person I really am. You think I'm some perfect little flower who was a victim of her parents' shortcomings. I'm not. What my parents are doing sucks. But I'm not such a great person either."

She was reminded of a Bible verse she'd learned at Sunday school. "*Remove the plank from your own eye. Then you can see clearly to remove the spec from your brother's eye*" Brother. Her heart pounded. The confession torpedoed inside of her with all the velocity of an oncoming train.

"I know everything I need to know," said Josh.

"No, you don't."

Caleb whimpered, clinging to Josh.

"What is it, then? What don't I know?"

"I can't do this right now." Amy's head spun. An ache throbbed at her temples.

Julian got to his feet. "Maybe I should come back later."

"Maybe you should," Amy said.

"No, stay," Josh said at the same time.

Julian's head bobbed between them. "Amy, why don't you write down anything you think is relevant for me to know. Anything. We can reconvene at my office first thing tomorrow morning."

"But court's tomorrow," Josh said, an edge of panic in his voice. "We have to be ready. The Richards are very adept at manipulation."

"We get it, Josh," Amy said.

He looked at her sharply, his hand cradling the back of Caleb's head as though he was trying to shield him from her. "Amy they're using our son as a pawn. They've never wanted us to be together. You know that."

"We are, aren't we?" *For now.*

"Guys, we need to present a united front, at least in the court room. This is heavy stuff; I get that. Take the rest of the day. Spend time with that cute kid. Think about it. Get a good night's sleep. Court's not until four. We'll be fresh in the morning."

"Okay," said Amy, even though thinking a good night's sleep was the answer was like coming at a forest fire with a squirt gun. She needed Julian to leave, because she was coming unhinged. Listing her parents' shortcomings felt like hypocrisy when she hadn't admitted to her own. What if Josh knew that she'd kissed Jason? He wouldn't think she was so innocent.

Amy and Josh danced around each other for the rest of the day, talking in clipped tones over Caleb's head. Josh put Caleb to bed while Amy cleaned up the dinner dishes, her hands shaking so badly that she dropped two glasses. She couldn't slow her galloping heart. Josh came back into the kitchen as she was sweeping up the last of the broken shards. His expression was unreadable.

"He's asleep." He watched her dump the broken pieces into the trash.

"I know you're mad at me. I hate what my parents are doing. I'll do whatever I need to do to fight this." She paused, taking a deep breath. "But I still can't seem to make myself stop loving them."

He nodded, raking a hand through his hair. "Yeah, I get that."

Amy stared at him. "You—you do?"

He smiled. "Well, yeah. I mean, there's nothing you could ever do to make me stop loving you."

It was like he'd pulled the precarious block from the tower. Amy sank to the kitchen floor, put her face in her hands, and began to sob.

"Hey," Josh said, alarmed. "Hey, what is it?"

She sensed him crouch down next to her. He rubbed her

back and tried to pull her into his arms. She plastered herself against the cabinets.

"Don't," she sobbed.

"Amy, talk to me. I didn't mean to upset you."

She lifted her face to meet his eyes, preparing herself to erase the love from them. "It's not you. It's me. I did something. Something unforgiveable. And I don't see how you can still love me."

He rocked back on his heels, a shadow passing over his face. "I'll always love you. I have no choice. What could be that bad?"

Amy made herself hold his gaze. "Jason and I . . . we . . . I kissed him. I kissed your brother."

Chapter 42

"You kissed my brother." Josh almost laughed. The words were too ludicrous to be true.

Amy nodded, tears streaming down her face. Laughter boomed in his ears, mocking him for believing his marriage could withstand the erosion of his sanity.

"I didn't want to tell you until after the trial." She sniffled loudly. "But I couldn't keep it from you."

Shane wandered into the kitchen, tossing an apple up and catching it. That's not really Amy. She's been taken over by aliens. Or maybe it is her and she needed an upgrade. Hahaha." He bit into the red skin. Juice dribbled onto his uniform.

Josh reached for the counter and pulled himself up. "You kissed him, or he kissed you?"

She stared up at him, misery written all over her face. "I don't know. Both. Does it matter?"

He shook his head. He was hallucinating; he had to be. It was the only explanation that made sense. "I don't believe you. This isn't real."

Amy struggled to her feet. She started to reach out to touch him but let her arm drop. "I'm so sorry. I'd give anything to take it back."

"Did you sleep with him?" The words were bitter and rotten in Josh's mouth.

Shane nodded. "Yup."

"Shut up!"

Amy's eyes widened. "No! It was one kiss. It was a mistake."

"This isn't real. I know this isn't real. I'm hallucinating."

Her eyes were wide and glassy. "I wish it wasn't real. I could stand here and tell you that I was struggling to keep my head above water, that I let my loneliness take over, but that's an excuse."

He backed away from her. "I don't believe you."

"I did it, okay? I kissed—"

He held up his hands. "For Godsakes, don't say it again. Fuck." He raked his hand through his hair.

She looked like Amy, but she wasn't. It was so damn confusing. He was sick of being confused. The familiar sensation of the walls closing in on him made him dizzy with panic.

"I have to get out of here." He bolted for the door, scanning the key hooks. "Where are my keys?"

"Josh, don't." Fear flickered in her eyes.

"Where the fuck are my keys, Amy?"

She backed away from him, mutely pointing toward the junk drawer. He ripped it open, rummaging through the paper clips and lose change until his fingers closed around the reassuring lighthouse key chain.

"Please don't leave. Can we talk about this?"

The desperation in her voice only fueled his fury. What, was he behaving irrationally? What was a normal-person reaction to your wife telling you she frenched your brother?

"I can't talk to you. I need to find the real Amy." He fled, slamming the door behind him.

The air bit his bare arms. He wasn't going back in for a jacket. He stared at the waiting truck. Had he survived to lose everything anyway?

There was only one way to find out if this was real. He couldn't trust the fake Amy and he obviously couldn't trust himself. He didn't know where he was going until he was halfway there. Despite the chill, he rolled the windows all the way down.

Sam materialized in the passenger seat like a ghost.

"Shit!" Josh swerved.

"Careful." Sam nodded out the front window. "Eyes on the road."

"What the fuck do you want?"

Between Sam and the fake Amy, maybe he needed to up his dose. Or a different medication?

"There's not a pill for everything," Sam said. "For example, no pill in the world can temper the pain of a broken heart. No salve can soothe the sting of betrayal."

Josh glanced at him. "What do you want, Sam? Haven't you fucked up my life enough?"

"Hey, I'm one of the good ones."

Was it possible for a hallucination to sound offended? Josh laughed. "There are good hallucinations?"

"Sure, if you learn how to interpret them."

"Oh, yeah? How do I interpret an old man from 1900 sitting in my truck?"

"You're reading too far into things. Your hallucinations are just tactile manifestations of your own suppressed thoughts."

"I think about farmers from the turn of the century?"

Sam waved a wrinkled hand. "Forget me. Deep down, you've always feared you'd never be good enough for Amy. The voices tell you you're not. They tell you she doesn't love you. Now people are saying you're not fit to raise that baby. You wonder if they're right. The voices tell you you're robbing your son of a normal childhood."

Josh turned onto the familiar road leading to his childhood home. "Your point?"

"Amy went from relying on her parents to relying on you. Then you were institutionalized, and her parents wrote her off when she wouldn't write you off. That's a lot to handle, no?"

"I wasn't exactly having a party myself."

"If she didn't love you, if she weren't devoted to you, she wouldn't be standing beside you in court. Defending you. Risking everything to keep you."

"I know." Josh sighed. "That's why it makes no sense that she'd kiss Jason."

"Makes perfect sense. It happens all the time. They were grieving, stumbling around together trying to figure out what was happening to you. Boom! Forced intimacy."

Josh parked the truck in front of the dilapidated bungalow and turned to face Sam. "So you're saying—" The seat was empty. "Right. You're not saying anything. You're not real. You're not real!" he screamed into the still night as he slammed the door of the truck.

Bob opened the door before he knocked. He looked Josh up and down. "Josh, are you—"

Josh charged past him. "Where the hell is Jason?"

A door creaked open and slammed shut. Jason walked into the family room and stopped dead. As soon as Josh looked him in the eyes he knew the truth.

"She told you."

"It's true. You kissed her. You kissed my wife." Josh spat each word.

"Josh, it just happened, okay?"

"Really, Jason? A cliché? That's the best you can do?"

Bob came up behind Josh and put his hands on his shoulders. "Josh, why don't you sit down? Let's talk about this."

Josh shook him off. "Why does everyone always want to talk? I'm sick of talking! I'm sick of listening. Talk, talk, talk, all the damn time!" He clamped his hands over his ears.

Jason circumvented the couch to face him. You're right. Let's not talk. Go ahead. Hit me."

"Jason," Bob said.

"Why? Because I'm a violent, crazy person?"

"No, because you're a human being who found out your brother kissed your wife. I'd hit me."

"I'm not going to hit you." The flicker of relief was gone from Jason's eyes so fast Josh couldn't be sure he hadn't imagined it. "Do you have feelings for her?"

Jason hesitated long enough for Josh to have the answer. "So what if I do? She loves *you*. She's crazy in love with you. Any fool can see that."

"She kissed you."

Jason shrugged. "It was a weird time, okay? We were spending a lot of time together. We talked, mostly about you. I was trying to help, and—"

"You were trying to *help*? What the actual fuck is wrong with you?"

"Josh, slow down." Bob was in over his head. This was far deeper than any spat between them he'd previously mediated.

"What's wrong with *you*?" Jason fired back.

"We've already established what's wrong with me."

"Oh, don't play that card with me. You tried to off yourself, remember? Were you thinking of her then? Were you thinking of anyone when you started that truck? Anyone but yourself?"

The words hit Josh square in the gut so hard he almost doubled over.

"Stop it, Jason," Bob said. They both ignored him.

"You're trying to turn this around on me? You're mad at me?"

"You're damn right, I'm mad at you."

"I think he's actually scared. Easier to be mad." Sam perched on the arm of the couch, crowding the room.

The creak and slam of a door permeated the charged air.

Josh watched his brother for a reaction, but he didn't flinch. His stomach dropped even lower. Melissa strode into the room, her icy smile as real as the day in the trailer. Except it wasn't real at all. Josh understood the accuracy of the phrase "seeing red". He hadn't cheated. All that self-flagellation, and he hadn't cheated. And Amy had been filled with righteous indignation when he'd confessed his phantom affair.

Melissa waved her fingers at Josh, the nails painted neon yellow. How was a hallucination so detailed? "Hi, Joshie. I've missed you. Sorry about your brother screwing your wife. Now you can be with me guilt free and leave that floozy."

"Get out of here. I never want to see you again."

Jason advanced toward him. "Fine, I'll leave if that's how you wanna play it."

Josh put a hand to his chest and pushed him backward. "I wasn't talking to you."

Melissa's pout poured gasoline on the embers of Josh's rage. It felt like this whole thing was her fault.

"How much easier would it be to blame a hallucination," Sam supplied.

"Josh, I'm here for you. We can be together."

"Tell her," Sam said. "Tell her what you know. Look into your heart. Is she real?"

"Everyone shut up!" Josh screamed.

"No one's talking," Bob said, his voice almost a whisper.

Josh rounded on him. "I know that. You don't think I know that?" He gestured wildly. "Them—they look real. They sound real. I know they're not real." Lowering his voice, he looked at Melissa. "I know you're not real and you will leave me alone."

Melissa pouted for the last time. "If that's really what you want." She brushed past Bob and retreated.

Josh let out his breath and turned back to Jason, who was watching him like Josh was an angry cat about to pounce. "You, though? You're real. Your betrayal, Amy's betrayal is real."

"Josh, I know this is a lot," Bob said.

A sick realization dawned on Josh. He turned to his father. "Oh my God. You knew."

Bob raised his hands. "I didn't think you should hear it from me. It wasn't my place."

"This is unbelievable. You're all keeping secrets from me. You're all colluding against me."

"She was killing herself trying to keep everything together," Jason said, almost to himself. "Her parents totally dumped her, and finding you like that, and then not being able to bring you home from the hospital . . ."

"You waited until I was institutionalized and then swooped in to heroically save the day."

Jason's eyes darkened. His fists clenched. "Jesus, Josh. You never used to be such an asshole."

"He's got a point," Sam muttered.

Josh ignored him. "Dammit, Jason. Take some fucking responsibility for once in your fucking life."

Jason took a step closer, staring him down. "You mean like you did when you checked out of yours?"

Josh relinquished the last scraps of his composure. "Fuck you. You're dead to me." Silence hung between them.

"Josh," Bob almost whispered, "You don't mean that."

"No, you know what, it's fine." Jason shoved a finger in Josh's chest. "I don't need you. I don't fucking need either of you." He waved his hands wildly around the room. He shoved past Josh, knocking into his shoulder so hard he almost lost his balance. The front door slammed.

Bob winced. "That went well."

Josh turned on him. "Is there anything else you're keeping from me?"

Something filled Bob's eyes. Guilt and something else. Josh's stomach twisted.

"Oh God, what is it? Are you going to tell me you're not my real father or something?" Was anything real anymore?

Bob coughed. "Why don't you sit down, son?"

Chapter 43

"**I** will not sit down." An edge of hysteria crept into Josh's voice. "Tell me." As soon as Bob opened his mouth to speak Josh had the urge to clamp his hand over it.

"I'm sick." As if choreographed, a coughing fit overtook him. Josh's blood ran cold.

"Sick how?" he asked in the small voice of a terrified child.

"Sick like I went to the doctor this morning. I just found out."

"Found out what?" What would it take to make Bob go to a doctor?

"Congestive heart failure."

Josh stared at him. Only then did he recognize the look in his eyes as grief. He ran back over the days since he'd returned to work. Bob had been coughing more and more. Getting winded. Disappearing from the job site for hours. Had Josh really been that wrapped up in his own problems? *Were you thinking of anyone but yourself?*

"They can give you something for that, right? Medication? You'll take some time off. I can take care of everything. And then you'll be fine, right?" His voice was shrill in his ears, mingling with the incoherent, irrelevant chatter of invisible voices.

Bob shook his head. "Apparently I've had it a lot longer than I realized. It happens to people as young and robust as me." He smiled sadly. "There's nothing they can do."

Josh swallowed a lump in his throat. "How long?"

"Not long."

Everything hit Josh at once, shoving its way down his throat, suffocating him. He was losing everyone he loved. The tears were swift and instant. He made no effort to quell them, never mind that he was probably in preschool the last time his dad had seen him cry. "No," he sobbed. "No."

Bob's face crumpled. "Come on, kid. Don't do that. It'll be okay."

Blinded by tears, Josh was flung into an ocean of grief without a life jacket. He wouldn't survive. He wasn't sure he wanted to. "No," he sobbed again. It was the only word that came to him.

Bob put his hand on the back of Josh's head and pulled him against him. He smelled like cedar and after shave. Like security and childhood.

"What am I going to do?" Josh cried into his dad's strong shoulder.

"You're gonna be fine, Josh. You're more of a man than I've ever been. You've learned everything you need."

"I'm not ready." He tried to catch his breath.

"Neither am I, but we don't get to decide these things."

"You shouldn't be working."

"Don't worry about that. I'll keep working until I can't anymore. I want to."

Josh pulled away and wiped his eyes. "Does Jason know?"

Bob nodded. "I told him this morning. He, uh . . . he didn't take it well."

"*I don't fucking need either of you.*" Josh's heart wrenched. "Did he cry?"

"He punched a hole through the drywall. You know that

temper's all bluster, don't you? He was the same way the night Amy called us about you. Terrified."

Easier to be mad than scared.

"I'm not defending what your brother did. It was a shitty thing to do, period."

"Then why do I sense a 'but'?"

Bob sighed heavily. "Your brother's impulsive. I spent the first five years of his life trying to keep him alive. Every time I turned around he was trying to jump off something or run into traffic."

"Your point?"

"He can be a real knuckle head. But he's got a big heart. And he's full of it. He needs you. You two tough guys need each other whether you'll admit it or not. Especially once I'm gone."

Josh staggered backward as though he'd been struck. "Can you not say that?"

"It's recently come to my attention that reality doesn't go away if you avoid acknowledging it."

"How can you even joke right now?"

"I'm not dead yet."

"Dad, please."

"Too far?"

"Yeah, a little."

Bob coughed, his face turning red.

"You should sit down." Josh guided him to the couch.

Bob stared at the blank television before looking at Josh. "Don't look at me like that. I'm all right."

Josh swallowed the bitter irony of this claim. Afraid he'd start crying again, he looked away. "Where do you think Jason went?"

"He needs to blow off some steam." Bob studied him. "He cares about you. A lot more than he lets on."

"He's got a hell of a way of showing it."

"He didn't have to grow up as fast as you did. He's still got a lot to learn and he's liable to get himself into a world of trouble before he gets there." Bob pulled at a thread on the couch.

Josh heard what he didn't say. "Dad, I'm not going to let anything happen to him. I can't believe either of them would do this."

Bob nodded slowly. "When we were first married, a few years before you were born, your mother had an affair."

Josh rubbed his temples. How many more surprises could he endure?

"She slept with some guy she'd had a whirlwind romance with back in high school. It was a deal breaker for me. She admitted it to me. She cried. She got on her knees and begged me for forgiveness. I wouldn't hear it. I was hell bent on leaving."

"Why didn't you?"

Bob linked his hands behind his head. "Your mother wasn't perfect, Josh. But she was damn close. As close as they come. I decided to stay for the thousands of things she did right by me instead of leave for the one thing she did wrong."

Josh considered this. Amy applying for food stamps instead of taking her parents' help with strings attached. Amy saving his life. Amy facing a courtroom to prove he was a good father. A good husband. *Amy kissing Jason.*

"I can't tell you to forgive Amy. I can't tell you to forgive your brother either. But I hope you can. What you have with Amy doesn't come around very often."

"Dad, it's not that simple."

Bob studied him. He cupped Josh's face with his hand. "No," he said, "It never is."

Chapter 44

Amy sat at the table in the kitchen sliding a can of Tab back and forth, wishing she had something stronger. A mountain of tissues surrounded her. What was going to happen now? They were supposed to meet Julian in the morning, but she didn't know where Josh was or if he was coming home. If there was any way to make this up to him, she'd do it. She'd sit up in front of the courtroom, look her parents dead in the eyes, and list their shortcomings. She'd get on her knees and beg him to forgive her. None of it was enough.

She looked up at the sound of the door creaking open, squinting through swollen eyes. Josh entered the kitchen. He looked at her, his own eyes blood-shot and red-rimmed.

"Hey."

"You came home."

"I'll always come home."

"I thought—after what I did . . ."

He sighed heavily, rubbing the back of his neck. "It's going to take time, Amy. It's going to take me some time."

She nodded. What did that mean? Time to forgive her? He wasn't yelling at her; his expression was more sad than angry. She wanted to ask him if he still loved her, but she'd been selfish enough. "I know it doesn't change anything, but I really am sorry. I hate myself for it." She blew her nose, an ache spreading through her sinuses all the way to the back of her skull. She deserved it.

Josh kicked off his shoes, hung his keys on the hook, and dropped into the chair across from her. His face was etched with hurt and exhaustion. He rubbed his eyes. "Dad's dying, Amy."

She jerked her head up. "What? How?"

Josh stared into space.

"What do you mean he's dying?"

He rubbed his eyes, dull with exhaustion and grief. "Congestive heart failure. It's already advanced. There's nothing they can do." His voice broke.

Her worries about Josh forgiving her seemed petty and self-serving. And here she was moaning about slandering her parents when he was losing his only living parent.

"Oh, Josh." She reached across the table for his hands, but he pulled them back.

"Don't."

She swallowed hard, shoving her hands in her lap to resist the urge to touch him. Who was she to offer comfort when she was a significant part of the pain?

"I don't want to start bawling again."

Her heart ached. Fresh tears began to fall. "I'm sorry. I know how much he means to you. To me, too." The words felt wildly insufficient.

He nodded slowly. "How did it happen?"

"I don't know. I guess younger people can get it."

"No, I mean . . . The kiss. How did it happen?"

"You don't want to hear that."

"I do. Jason made excuses. I need to understand what led up to it." He looked her dead in the eyes. "You owe me that much."

He was right. She rolled the can of Tab between her palms.

"Jason was teaching me to drive, preparing me for the test. He went to the garage to get tools to tighten the station wagon's breaks. He saw the hose in the truck's tail pipe and he kind of freaked out. You should've seen his face." She forced herself to look up at him. His expression was hard.

"Anyway, he asked me what it was like the night I found you, so I told him. I still have dreams about it, you know? I didn't think I'd be able to bring you back. I guess when he asked me, well, I needed to talk to someone about it."

He raised his eyebrows. "And?"

She sighed. "And he was upset. And I was upset. Then he hugged me and . . . we kissed. I don't know who did it or why. I know there's nothing I can say to make this better. But I didn't mean for it to happen. I don't have feelings for him."

"And this happened right before I got out?"

She nodded.

"Were you planning on telling me?"

"Yes, of course. I told myself I'd tell you when you got settled at home, then the subpoena happened, and I told myself after the stress of the case passed. But then I got to thinking if you wanted to leave me why would you want to go through the trial? Then you were saying how you'd always love me and I just—I couldn't keep it from you."

"I will always love you."

Amy held her breath. He looked at her for a long time before pushing his chair back. "I'm exhausted. We'd better get some sleep. We have to meet Julian early in the morning."

He went upstairs. Amy remained frozen in place, listening to the sounds of him moving around; the toilet flushing and the water turning on and off. Finally, she dragged herself out of the chair, almost colliding with Josh on her way to the stairs. He had his pillow and a blanket under his arm. Her heart sank.

"You can sleep upstairs. I'll stay down here," she managed.

"It's fine."

She trailed him to the family room and watched him curl up on the couch, adjusting his pillow. She wanted to crawl on top of him, cover him, cling to him like a barnacle. For a moment she stared at him lying there. He'd never once slept on the couch. As an unspoken rule, they worked out their arguments before going to bed. This was not something that could be worked out before bed.

"Well, goodnight, then," Amy said, forcing her body to turn away.

"Amy?"

She turned back. "What?"

He propped himself up on his elbow. "If you thought I was going to leave you anyway, why'd you decide to fight your parents in court? Why'd you put yourself through talking about Michael and everything if you thought we might not be together? You know if you weren't with me they'd drop this whole thing."

"Because you're Caleb's dad." She cleared her throat. "Even if you can't be my husband anymore, that won't change. They need to know—the world needs to know that you're a good father. He's safe with you. We've always been safe with you. I won't let you lose him even if I lose you. I won't let him lose you."

His eyes were glassy. "Let's get through this trial, then we'll figure the rest out." He dropped his head to the pillow and Amy forced her way upstairs.

It wasn't exactly an olive branch, but he was here. She was getting into bed when the phone rang. She grabbed it off the nightstand on the second ring.

"Did he make it home okay?" Jason whispered.

"Yes. I'm sorry, Jason. I had to tell him. He's sleeping on the couch. I don't know what will happen next."

"You don't have to be sorry. It was gonna come out at some point."

"I'm sorry about your dad. How's he doing?"

"Oh, you know, it's hard to tell with him. He acts like everything's fine."

"And you? Are you okay?"

Jason gave a bitter laugh. "My brother hates me, my dad's dying, and I'm losing my only real friend. What do you think?"

Chapter 45

Amy perched on the witness stand, jittery from too much coffee. She'd barley slept the night before, thinking about Josh, Bob, Jason, and court. Davis approached the stand. Stale coffee churned in Amy's otherwise empty stomach.

"Amy, is Josh able to work consistently?"

"He is back at work, yes. He and his dad and brother own a construction company."

"I see. When he was hospitalized and after he was released he was unable to work for quite some time, is that correct?"

"Yes. But he's better now. He notices the details even more than before."

"Well, that's nice, but as we've heard from our experts, schizophrenia recovery isn't linear. He may need further hospitalizations, medications changes, things of that nature."

"Your honor, is a question hidden in Mr. Davis's speculations?" Julian said.

"Get to the point, Mr. Davis."

"Of course. Amy, when Josh was institutionalized—and in fact at other times, did you rely on your parents' financial assistance?"

"Yes, but they haven't helped since Josh was transferred to

the mental ward and they told me to divorce him."

"Fine. How did you pay the bills? Buy Caleb's clothes? Food?"

Amy looked down at her ragged nails. "I applied for social security. Food stamps. I also took on some in-home childcare."

Amy tensed, thinking of the conversation she'd had with Johnny's mom when this whole thing had started.

"We've made alternate childcare arrangements," the woman had told Amy, waving a manicured hand. "You neglected to reveal that your husband's a schizophrenic. Watch the news."

She realized Davis had said something.

"I'm sorry, could you repeat that?"

"Have your utilities been shut off?"

"Briefly, yes."

"You realize this case hinges on who is most capable of caring for the child. I'd say water and heat are pretty basic needs."

"Again, your honor, is that a question or is this the Davis show?"

"Careful, Mr. Stein." The judge pinched the bridge of his nose. "Mr. Davis, I'll ask you one more time to stick to questions. I graduated law school at the top of my class and I'm fully capable of drawing my own conclusions."

"My apologies, your honor."

It went on like that. Did Caleb grow out of clothes faster than she could buy new ones? Did they run out of food? Did she ever have to go without as a child? Did she have clothes, heat, space, toys, vacations? Did Josh's episodes ever scare Caleb? What about when he got older and noticed more?

"He always wants Josh," she told him. "He'll go to Josh before me. Josh will crawl around on the floor and play with him for hours."

Josh was getting so adept at filtering out his hallucinations that sometimes Amy could forget things had changed. If he answered a voice while playing with Caleb, Caleb thought it was part of the game.

Finally, it was Julian's turn. Amy was dizzy with exhaustion. She had to do this. Julian smiled reassuringly. He was the only person on their side of the courtroom who didn't look like he was about to fall apart.

"Amy, Mr. Davis painted a pretty picture of your childhood. You never wanted for any creature comforts, is that correct?"

"Yes."

"You lived in a modest two-bedroom home until about middle school, correct?"

"Yes."

"Where did you move after that?"

"My father had the mansion built. The home they live in now."

"Did you like living in the mansion?"

Despite Julian's advice to the contrary, she looked at Walt and Eileen. Walt's eyes were steely; defiant as he stared her down. Eileen clutched a rosary and looked from Walt to Amy and back again as if this were just another family meeting.

"No," Amy said.

Eileen's eyes widened. Walt's face remained etched in stone.

"No?" Julian feigned surprise. "Why not?"

"Well, first off, I was sad to leave our old life. I had friends and I had to change to a private school. We used to do things as a family. Road trips. Hikes. Neighborhood barbeques. That all stopped. My mom became more withdrawn and my dad was never home, he was so busy with work. He wasn't happy anymore either."

"If you had a problem as a girl, as a teenager, to whom did you turn for advice?"

"Sometimes my friend, Gwen. But she was the same age as me, so she wasn't always the best source. Otherwise, I went to Maria."

"Is Maria a family member?"

"Basically." Amy smiled. "She's been our cook for probably ten years. I mean my parents' cook. But she was so much more than that to me. She shared recipes. She took care of me when my parents travelled. She helped me with my homework and my problems."

"Aren't these things a mother would do? Why didn't you go to your own mother?"

Eileen's eyes were pained, but Amy shifted her gaze to Josh, eyes wide and bloodshot, and her loyalty was unquestionable. "I tried. I wanted to. But she wasn't supportive."

"Can you be more specific?"

"I'd ask her if we could bake together and she told me I didn't need to learn that stuff. If I had a problem, she'd tell me to get over it."

Julian adjusted his tie. "Amy, you were a teenaged mother. Will you tell the court how your parents reacted when you told them that you were pregnant with Josh's baby?"

Amy fought the urge to be sick as she recounted the day, sparing no detail.

Chapter 46

Nervous anticipation had tied a knot below Amy's rib cage. She didn't allow herself to imagine her parents' reaction. They'd be ashamed of her, obviously. The scandal of a Catholic school girl getting pregnant. But she was getting married. They could get married right after graduation, before she was even showing. Who needed a big, elaborate wedding? By the time the baby was born and those in her parents' circle bothered to do the math, well, it would be old news. This was their first grandchild. They'd be livid, but they'd come around.

Amy found Eileen in the exercise room stretching on a yoga mat, her hair secured in a severe bun. "Amy, I didn't expect you home on a Saturday. What's the occasion?" She sat up and mopped the sweat from her forehead with a purple sweat band.

Amy dodged the barb. "Is Dad home?"

Eileen's eyes narrowed. "He's in the office, working as usual. I don't expect to see him until dinnertime. Why?"

Amy forced air into her lungs. "Can we talk? All of us? In the sitting room? Josh is here."

Eileen looked momentarily stricken before she recovered. "I didn't want to believe it."

Amy took a step back, watching her mother in the mirror lining the far wall. "Believe what?"

"Oh, come on, Amy. I wasn't born yesterday. The weight gain. The vomiting. The feminine products not disappearing from your bathroom.

"You monitor my usage of feminine products?" Amy said, as if it was relevant at this point. "If you knew, why didn't you say anything? I've been wanting to ask you so many questions. Does the nausea ever end? When can you take me to the doctor?"

"Stop." Eileen held up her hand. "I'll make you an appointment first thing Monday morning."

Relief enveloped her. "Oh, thank you, Mom. Will you go in with me?"

"I'm not sure that's allowed."

"Why wouldn't it be?"

"We won't tell your father," Eileen said as though Amy hadn't spoken.

A sick feeling rose in Amy's stomach, but it wasn't morning sickness. Funny how they called it that when it lasted all day and all night. "What do you mean, not tell him? It's not like he won't find out. Like you said, I'm already gaining weight. I can probably hide it through graduation, but not much longer."

"You won't have to worry about that. I can get you in for the procedure within the week." Her eyes were fixed over Amy's head.

"Procedure?" Amy crossed her arms over her stomach. "Mom, no!"

"There's nothing to be afraid of Amy. You'll go to sleep, and when you wake up it'll all be over. You can go back to school the next day. It's painless. Honestly, you're lucky women have options now."

Horrified, Amy ran to her mom and grabbed her hands. "Mommy, please, I don't want an abortion."

When had she last called her "Mommy"? This was all going

horribly wrong. She had to make her mother understand. She needed her.

"It's legal now," Eileen said in a detached tone.

"That's not the point." She pulled on her mother's hands. "Can you please look at me?"

Eileen yanked her hands away. "Honestly, I can't, I'm disgusted with you and Josh for being such pigs."

She'd been a fool to believe her mother would be there for her. Amy refused to cry. She wouldn't give Eileen the satisfaction of her tears.

"We're getting married," she shrieked. "He asked me to marry him before he even knew about the baby."

"Amy, grow up. It's time to stop playing house with this boy."

"We love each other."

"That doesn't matter."

Amy fled from the room, ignoring her mother calling after her. She tore down the stairs and back to the sitting room. Josh bolted to his feet.

"Are you—"

"She wants me to get rid of it! She wants me to get rid of our baby!" She could hear herself hyperventilating.

He held out his arms to her. "Okay. It's okay. No one's getting rid of our baby. Calm down."

"Don't tell me to calm down!"

"What is going on here?" Walt entered the sitting room dressed for a business meeting. "What's all the yelling?"

Josh took in a sharp breath. He stepped between her and Walt, his arm jerking out in front of her protectively. "Mr. Richards, I want to marry your daughter," he blurted.

A torturous silence stretched between them. Walt's gaze moved from Josh to Amy. "Amy, what is he talking about?"

"Josh asked me to marry him."

"And?"

"And I said yes."

"Uh huh." His eyebrows knit together.

"Mr. Richards, I realize I'm not the man you'd pick for your daughter. I don't come from money and I'll never be able to give her this." He gestured around the room. "But I'll work as hard as I can. I'll honor and protect her, and I think—I know we can be happy together."

Amy nodded stupidly. Walt looked almost amused.

"Oh, really? Where will you live? You don't even have a diploma. Are you going to get one? Are you going to get a real job?"

"Dad!"

"It's okay, Amy. I'll always be with my dad's company. Eventually, it'll be my company. I'm sure as a developer you know there'll always be a need for someone to build the buildings."

Before Walt could respond, Eileen came in from the opposite entrance. She'd somehow managed to brush her long hair out, apply makeup, and change into a blouse and skirt. "Walt, honey, go back to work. I'll take care of this."

Amy stared at her. Terms of endearment? Between Walt and Eileen Richards? Eileen looked at Amy and gave an almost imperceptible shake of her head, her eyes as wide as if she were staring down an oncoming train.

Walt looked from one person to the other. "Someone better enlighten me."

Amy's head bobbed between her mother and her father. Eileen's expression wasn't one of anger or disappointment, but blind fear.

"Dad, Josh and I—" Amy began at the same time Josh said, "You see, Sir, it's like this—" They both stopped.

"Oh, hell," Eileen said. She jabbed a finger toward Josh. "He got your daughter pregnant!"

Time stopped. Amy looked back at Walt in time to see him

take a step toward Josh planted firmly in front of her. Before she knew what was happening, he swung, his fist landing with a sickening crack under Josh's right eye. Josh's head whipped around and he staggered backward. Amy caught him.

"Dad!" Amy cried, shocked. Walt was a hard man, but he'd never been violent. She turned Josh to face her, pulling his hand away from his face. "Let me see," she whispered, disregarding everyone else's presence. His eye was watering, the tender skin around it already bruising.

"It's okay, Amy," he said. "I'm fine."

Clearly, he wasn't. He straightened; shoulders squared. For a moment she thought he was going to hit her father back. She wouldn't have blamed him.

"This is real life, kid, not some romance novel. You think you can support a wife and a child? You think warm and fuzzies pays the bills? You think lust pays the bills?"

"No, sir." His muscles were rigid. Amy was close enough to hear his heart pounding. She touched his arm. His skin was like a furnace.

"But I've been helping support a family since I was big enough to swing a hammer."

"Walt, I'll take care of it," Eileen said from across the room.

Walt ignored her. "Have a seat." He pointed to the couch—a command, not an invitation.

Amy looked at Josh. A bolt of panic shot through her. Did he really love her enough to put up with this? Could she blame him if he ran out the front door?

"Are you going to hit me again?'

"No."

Josh shuffled to the couch and sat heavily. Amy was reminded of a phrase she heard often during lent. *Like a lamb led to the slaughter.* Unsure where her father was going with this, she sat next to Josh, their thighs touching. He scooted away from her.

Amy put her hand between his shoulder blades, making circles. It was more to soothe herself than him. What did it matter if her parents saw her touch him? They knew she'd had sex. She couldn't sink any lower in their eyes.

"Have a seat, Eileen." Walt didn't look at his wife. She perched on the edge of her chair, smoothing her skirt, her face tight with tension.

"She was a nice Catholic girl before she met you." Walt remained standing, pointing an accusing finger at Josh.

Amy felt a tremor go through him. For once, she didn't wait for her father to address her before she spoke. "Dad, that's not fair. It's not his fault. He didn't force me to do anything."

When he cut his gaze toward her she wished she'd stayed quiet. She tried to sink into the couch cushions.

"You know what's not fair? Your only daughter becoming a loose girl right under your own roof."

"Hey," Josh said, but Amy pushed her hand into his back in warning.

"All that money I spent on a Catholic education. What will people say?"

"Everyone will be whispering at the country club," Eileen added unnecessarily. "Honestly, Amy, did you even stop to consider how this would affect me?"

Amy hadn't done a single thing in her life, even something as miniscule as picking out an outfit, without considering her mother's feelings, but it would do no good to say so.

"I'm sorry, Mom, but it doesn't have to be that way. We can get married right after graduation. Months before the baby's born."

"Just listen to yourself. Do you honestly believe people are that stupid? It's basic math. Unless you have a time machine—" She held up her palms, eyebrows raised dramatically. "You wouldn't be the first wayward teen to pull a shotgun wedding."

Her words hit Amy like physical blows.

"It's the seventies," Josh said. "I really don't think anyone cares."

"Maybe not in your circles," Walt said.

A dull throb began at Amy's temples.

Walt nodded at Josh as though trying to work something out. "You want to make an honest woman out of her. I'll give you credit for that."

"It's not like that. I mean, I asked her to marry me before I knew about the baby."

"You know, respectable young men usually ask for a father's blessing."

"I figured I wouldn't get that."

"You figured right. You think you'll have a summer wedding and live happily ever after? What about college?"

"Dad, I already told you I don't want to go to college."

"Oh, so you'll rely on him?" He nodded at Josh. His voice dripped with disdain.

"I want to focus on raising the baby. What's so wrong with that? Mom didn't go to college." She regretted the words the moment they escaped her mouth.

"I didn't have the option, Amy. Women have options now. You have options. We'll take care of this. You can go to college. If the two of you want to get together and start a family, then at least you'll have something to fall back on."

"I don't want options. I want this baby." She looked at her mother. Her mouth was set in a hard line. No soft place to land.

"Let's be vigilant of what we rest on our own consciences, Eileen."

"But Walt—"

He held up his hand like a stop sign. "Enough. This isn't our sin. Let's not make it so." He turned to Amy, an impenetrable stone wall. "She made her bed. Let's let her lie in it."

"Walt, you can't be serious. You're going to let her marry him?"

Amy got the strange sensation she and Josh were spectators watching a movie play out rather than participants in the discussion of their fate.

"She's carrying his child. Let's let them learn the hard way. When it all falls apart she'll come home with a lot less fluff in her head."

"And with a baby. What will our friends say?"

"They'll say we threw the most extravagant wedding they've ever attended. Book the country club for the last week in June."

Amy's brain did several jumps and flips to catch up. Her dad was going to agree with this. Why did it feel more like a trap than a victory? She pictured a stuffy ballroom, hundreds of her parents' friends telling her they remembered her when she was a little girl. The questions. The advice. Sweat trickled down her back.

Finally, Josh spoke. "That's very generous of you, but we don't want—"

"I'm not interested in what you want. I'm not doing this out of generosity. I won't be embarrassed in front of my friends and employees. Make no mistake—this is nothing more than a very expensive sham."

Silent tears began rolling down her mother's cheeks.

"Mom, I'm sorry." Amy's shoulders ached under the weight of her mom's despair.

"I can't look at you anymore." She got up and left the room.

"Mom," Amy called after her.

"Walt shook his head. "Do you see what you're doing to your mother?"

"Dad, we don't need a big wedding. We can make it simple."

"Simple is the last thing you've made this. This conversation is over. And Josh, for Godsakes, get a haircut." He stormed out of the room. A moment later they heard the echo of the office door slamming.

"Okay," Josh had said after a beat, "That went well."

Julian rubbed his chin in mock contemplation. "So if your mother, who claims she can parent Caleb more effectively that Josh and yourself, had her way, Caleb wouldn't even exist."

"Objection! Mrs. Richards isn't the only mother who'd suggest her teenage daughter have an abortion. At that time the child was hypothetical."

"Over-ruled."

"That's right," Amy said.

"And your father punched Josh in the face. Did Josh hit him back?"

"No. Josh was calm. He sat there and took whatever my father threw at him."

"Interesting. Amy, did your parents travel often?"

"Yes. More often as I got older."

"Did they ever leave you alone?"

"Sometimes. Maria or the housekeeper would check in on me."

"And how old were you the first time your parents left you home alone for a few days?"

"Maybe thirteen."

"Interesting," Julian said again. "No further questions."

At the judge's nod, Amy somehow made it back through the gate and collapsed next to Josh.

"Your honor," Davis's voice boomed off the paneled walls. "I'd like to call Walt Richards to the stand."

Chapter 47

Amy's father was enjoying this. Of course he was. He loved the spotlight. He was certain he'd win. The dad on the stand bore no resemblance to the father who'd once sung Christmas carols and hunted for monsters.

"Mr. Richards, how are you today?" Davis began as though they were meeting for drinks.

"Fine. Yourself?"

"Very well. Let's get to it," he said as Julian was opening his mouth. "Why did you and your wife petition for custody of your grandson, Caleb?"

"He's in danger. It's our duty to step in as his grandparents and protect him if his mother won't. The child can't protect himself. He has no voice."

Amy stifled a scoff. Suddenly Walt Richards was concerned with giving people a voice?

"Josh, on the other hand, he has plenty of voices."

Davis smiled. Amy rolled her eyes. "When did you first become concerned with your grandson's safety?"

"When Josh was locked up we implored Amy to come home so that we could help her, protect her and Caleb. Josh was—is—in no condition."

"Prior to Josh's psychotic break, had you ever feared for Caleb's well-being?"

Walt straightened his tie. "Yes. It was apparent to us that Josh couldn't provide for the child or my daughter. She has a choice. Caleb doesn't. Amy brought Caleb over weekly. Often, he was in clothing that was tattered, torn, and too small."

"Is it true that you never wanted Amy to be with Josh?"

"Yes, that's no secret. You see, Amy's always been blinded by her infatuation with Josh. He's got some type of hold on her. She's willing to risk everything to be with him."

"Did you punch Josh Everett in the face?"

Walt barely suppressed a smile. "Yes. It was not my finest moment. I don't condone violence. I was a father informed his teenage daughter had been impregnated by a high school drop-out with a criminal record. I knew a baby would tie her to him forever."

"Did you think that Amy should have an abortion?"

Walt frowned, the lines between his eyebrows deepening. "We're Catholic. We don't believe in abortion. My wife reacted out of panic. We don't believe in fornication either, which is the only reason I went along with the charade of a wedding."

"Who planned and paid for the wedding?"

"I did."

"Who paid the bills and got the utilities turned back on when Josh was in the hospital?"

"I did."

Amy's body was like cement. His help had always come with strings attached. Now he was using those strings to hang her.

"Mr. Richards, were you absent often during your daughter's teen years?"

"Yes. Obviously, I regret that now. Maybe if I'd been more vigilant I'd have seen sooner what path she was headed down." He sighed. "We had such high hopes for her, my wife and myself. She's our only child." He pulled a handkerchief from his breast pocket and dabbed his dry eyes.

"Oh, for fuck's sake," Josh muttered.

"I had to work, though. It's a father's job to provide for his family. Josh can't fulfill that, the most basic role of fatherhood. I can."

Josh sat perfectly still, his back ramrod straight and his hands clasped together.

"He's wrong," she whispered. "You know that." He didn't seem to hear her.

"If you're awarded custody, who will care for Caleb during the day?"

"My wife. He'll be exposed to nutritious food, culture, enrichment."

"Will he have his own room?"

"Yes, of course. We have seven." He flashed a too-white smile.

"Where will he attend school?"

"St. Patrick's. Nothing like a Catholic education."

"Indeed. Your witness, Mr. Stein."

"It's almost too easy," Julian whispered before approaching the stand. "Mr. Richards, you seem like a smart man. Are you aware that punching someone in the face is considered assault?"

"Yes, of course."

"Huh, interesting, because you seem to be very concerned about your grandson being in a home with a father guilty of assault. Seems to me the only difference is Josh was prosecuted and you were not."

"Objection," Davis said. "Argumentative."

"Stick to the questions, Mr. Stein."

"I was attempting to protect my daughter," Walt said anyway.

Amy could practically hear Davis cringe. Overconfidence was Walt's Achilles' heel.

"Is that also what Josh was trying to do?"

"He was a jealous, hot-headed punk who beat up a minor."

Julian shrugged. "If you say so. Did you know that your daughter was sexually assaulted, Mr. Richards?"

He had the humanity to flinch. "No."

"When you arranged for Michael Newman to take your daughter out, did you predict he was the kind of guy who would commit sexual assault? Did you think he might be violent?"

"Well, obviously not. He was young. He behaved badly."

"And yet you didn't punch him in the face. Josh did it for you."

Davis was on his feet. "Objection."

"You're trying my already fragile patients, Mr. Stein."

"I apologize, your honor." He cleared his throat.

"You thought Michael would be a good man for your daughter. I'm sure you wouldn't have arranged the date otherwise."

"That's correct," Walt said warily.

Amy held her breath.

"Mr. Richards, did you misjudge Michael Newman?"

"I guess I did."

"Is it possible, then, that you misjudged Josh? That you aren't as accurate a judge of character as you thought?"

Shock and hope hit Amy simultaneously. Julian had accomplished what she hadn't seen anyone accomplish before. He'd flustered her father. *Her father the enemy.* She looked at Josh. His eyes flashed with vindication. Walt's mouth opened and snapped shut. His eyes darted back and forth, reminding Amy of a rodent that walked into a trap.

"He didn't see that coming," Amy whispered to Josh.

He nodded, never taking his eyes off Walt, who looked like he wanted to fly off the stand and wrap his hands around Julian's throat. The judge tilted his head and sized up Walt.

Looks like you don't have all the power after all, Amy thought, surprised by how avenged she felt.

"Mr. Richards, you'll need to answer the question."

Walt looked at him and back at Julian. His eyes were glazed. "Um, can you repeat the question?"

Finally, Josh looked at Amy. He raised his eyebrows, the hint of a smile on his face. Amy smiled back, then quickly looked away.

They're the enemy now. They waged this war, not you.

"Of course." Julian strategically waited a beat before clearing his throat. "We all seem to agree that you misjudged Michael Newman. Might it be possible that your judge of character isn't as iron-clad as you previously believed?"

"My judge of character?" Walt straightened, recovering his composure. "Look, Mr. Stein, I'm a developer. I employ many people. I make character judgements every day. Am I omniscient? No. But most of the time I'm right."

"Is it possible you misjudged Josh?" Julian persisted.

"I suppose it's possible, but I don't think—"

"All right then. We want Mr. Davis to stay awake, so I'll move on. Did you leave your daughter home alone for days at a time when she was as young as thirteen?"

"Yes." Walt's shoulder's relaxed. "Sometimes my wife would accompany me on business trips. Amy always had everything she needed."

"Are you aware that leaving a minor unattended for that length of time is considered neglect under the law, Mr. Richards?"

Walt's jaw worked back and forth. "She wasn't alone. Maria checked in on her. Our housekeeper checked in on her. To say she was neglected is preposterous."

"Was she alone overnight?"

"Sometimes, yes."

"Then to say she was neglected is simply citing the law, sir.

If you obtain custody of Caleb, will he be alone often? Overnight? For days at a time? How actively involved will you be in his daily life?"

Walt's eyes bulged. He tugged at his tie. "I—he—he'll be provided for!"

"What does that mean, exactly?"

"He'll have a cook. A tutor. People looking in on him. Everything he could ever want."

"How about love, Mr. Richards? How about support and acceptance?"

Walt's eyes darkened. "Love doesn't keep you warm at night. It doesn't put food in your mouth or clothes on your back."

"Do you love your grandson, Mr. Richards? Can you love him like a son?"

His face wrinkled in confusion. "Sure."

"It sounds like he'd be spending more time with house-keepers and the like."

"My wife would be with him all day."

"Would she be more present for her grandson then she was with your daughter?"

Walt sighed. "Amy was a needy child. She needed to learn some independence."

"But you didn't like when she asserted that independence by dating Josh."

"I didn't approve of him, no."

"Have the demands of your work changed?"

"It's very demanding. Money doesn't make itself. Look, plenty of kids grow up with one or both parents working a lot. It's not a bad thing."

"I'm not suggesting that it is, in general. I'm wondering how the dynamics will be different raising Caleb than they were with your daughter."

"There's nothing wrong with the way Amy was raised. She had an enviable childhood."

Amy recognized the defensive edge. He didn't like the way the conversation was going. Only this time he couldn't unilaterally declare it over.

"Okay, let me put it this way. Would you raise Caleb differently than you raised Amy?"

Walt stared at Julian as though he'd sprouted another head. "No. He'll have what she had."

Julian nodded. "Thank you, sir. That's all I needed to know. You may step down."

Walt worked his jaw. "Wait. We can provide the child with the stability that Josh—"

"Mr. Richards, please take your seat."

Her father stared at the judge for what seemed like a full minute before abandoning the witness stand, his body vibrating with rage. Amy watched him, but he set his jaw and stared straight ahead.

"Your Honor," Julian said once Walt was seated, "I'd like to call Maria Vasquez to the stand.

There was a commotion in the courtroom. Papers rustled. Amy turned in her seat. Maria strode down the aisle wearing a denim dress and beautiful turquoise earrings. Amy recognized them. They were her mother's; a family heirloom. Their monetary value was negligible, but as a young girl Amy felt special every time Maria had let her use them for dress up. What was Maria doing here now?

"Your Honor, what is she doing here?" Davis echoed Amy's thoughts. "I'm supposed to have a list of Mr. Stein's witnesses? Isn't that law school 101?"

Julian didn't miss a beat. "She came forward to testify. That's her right. I updated the witness list before lunch."

The judge placed his spectacles on the bridge of his nose and shuffled some papers in front of him. "I received the request late morning. We can call a recess and reconvene tomorrow to give Mr. Davis time to prepare."

Amy looked from Davis to Maria, who was frozen with her hand on the gate separating the gallery from the front of the courtroom. She caught Amy's eye and winked. Davis's eyes bugged out like a cartoon character.

Julian shrugged. "My apologies. I'm happy to reconvene if Mr. Davis needs time to prepare." He grinned.

"I . . . uh . . . no. I don't need to prepare. Go right ahead."

The judge nodded. "Ms. Vasquez, you may proceed."

The witness stand overtook Maria's small frame, but she sat tall, shoulders pulled back and almond eyes sharp with righteous determination. Julian strode up to the bench.

"Ms. Vasquez, how would you describe the home life, the atmosphere in the Richards' household?"

Maria stared out into the gallery. "Cold."

"Cold?"

"Yes. They show no love, no affection."

"Walt and Eileen, you mean?"

"Yes."

"Ms. Vasquez, who fed Amy?"

She frowned. "I made all the food."

"Who packed her lunch?"

"Me."

"I see. And you also helped her with her homework, got her off to school in the morning, and invested in her friendships, problems, and growing pains. Would that be accurate?"

"Yes." Maria rubbed her eyes.

Julian spun around to face the courtroom. "Food, supervision, emotional involvement, getting a child ready for school." He ticked off each item on his fingers. "They all sound like basic developmental needs and day-to-day parenting tasks." He turned back to Maria. "If you were providing these necessities, what exactly did Walt and Eileen Richards provide for their daughter?"

Maria's eyes flashed again. She looked directly at Amy.

Maria's strong voice rang through the courtroom. "Money."

"Very well. How much time did you spend in the Richards' home?"

"Mr. Walt and Mrs. Eileen liked me there first thing. I prepare breakfast, coffee and lunch for Miss Amy, and got Miss Amy off to school."

"At what time did you arrive, on average?"

"Five."

"And your day ended around what time?"

"I make dinner and clean. I finish about seven or eight. If they have a dinner party, later."

"Okay, so you spent an average of fourteen to fifteen hours a day at the Richards'. In your observation, are Walt and Eileen Richards fit parents?"

Amy held her breath. Her parents would be livid. Maria's courage touched her.

"Absolutely not good parents."

"Really, because Mr. Richards claims Amy had an enviable childhood. Can you explain what you mean?"

"Miss Amy had a pool, a closetful of clothing, big house, expensive education. Her parents require little of her but expect much. She had no chores, but no acceptance, no freedom." She looked at the judge.

"You mention neglect. You mention abuse. Well, abuse doesn't always leave bruises and scars. At least not the kind you can see. A child needs provision, yes. But a child provided for with things can be neglected. A child never hit may be abused. I grew up with little, no toys, few clothes my mama sewed—but I was loved. I was happy. Amy had everything money can buy, but Mr. Walt and Mrs. Eileen, they make her feel bad for who she is. Is that not abuse? Can we not predict, as you say, they will do the same to Caleb?"

After court, Amy caught up to Maria in the parking lot, folding the small woman into a hug. She hadn't had time to dwell on how much she missed her. "It's good to see you, but what are you doing here? You didn't have to do that."

Maria held Amy at arm's-length. "I talk to that man. Julian?" She cast a furtive glance around the parking lot. Flecks of snow stood out in her dark hair. "It's not right. You're good parents." She looked at Josh. "Both good parents."

"Thank you, Maria," Amy said.

She shook her head. "I say to Julian I can testify. I watch your parents raise you and I see you with that baby. Mr. Walt and Mrs. Eileen should not raise another baby. Caleb's yours."

Josh reached out a squeezed Maria's hand. "You don't know what this means."

Amy's heart thudded. "Maria, my parents. They'll fire you."

Maria's smile made her dark eyes sparkle. She leaned toward Amy and patted her arm. "Ah, without you I don't like job anyway."

Chapter 48

Amy fed the powder-blue beads of her rosary through her fingers and tried to settle in the stiff wooden chair of the courtroom. Someone coughed. Papers shuffled. The judge appeared. When she got to her feet her legs buckled. She had to grab Josh's arm to keep from falling. He wrapped his strong arm around her, and she almost wept with gratitude. This was it.

Her eyes scanned the galley. Her heart pounded in her ears and nausea churned in her stomach. She wiped her palms on her skirt. Seconds ticked by. *Say it,* she thought.

The judge cleared his throat. "You may be seated." He waited for the shuffling to fade.

"I've been a judge for thirty-five years. Thirty of those years I've spent in the family court system. Let me tell you, it's not for the faint of heart." He smiled sadly. "Judges don't have a crystal ball, which makes predictive neglect cases imperfect at best. Over the course of my career I've wished we had the chance to intervene sooner, before a child was subjected to abuse or neglect, the results of which leave life-long scars. Many of the children I've removed wind up in the juvenile court system. I've heard cases of abuse that would keep the hardest heart up at night. Sometimes this is a result of a parent or caregiver's negligence, drug or alcohol use, or mental illness."

"Shhh!" Josh hissed next to her. His fists were clenched at his sides. Tentatively, she took his hand. He didn't resist.

"Is there a cop over there?" he whispered.

Amy followed his gaze to the paneled wall at their left. "No one's there," she whispered back.

He nodded and gave her a grateful smile. A tiny seed of hope took root inside her. He still trusted her to tell him what was real. She told herself if she hadn't lost his trust she wouldn't lose him. But the future of her marriage, of her family, was a giant question mark. Oh, no, what was she going to *do?*

"Amy, breathe." Josh tightened his arm around her.

She realized she was hyperventilating. She had a clear vision of herself as a preteen sitting on the kitchen floor while Maria held a paper bag to her mouth. How was Josh holding them both together? He was the strong one.

"Sadly, some people are just bad people," The judge continued. "As difficult as those cases are, they're straight-forward. What to do when the parents are inherently good people, but illness may interfere with their ability to provide a child with stability? What do we do when we have an obligation to protect a child, but no harm has come to them? How do we predict which children will be harmed? The stakes are high. Predictive neglect allows us to step in before neglect has occurred. But, it's a slippery slope."

"Get to the point," Josh whispered.

"The mentally ill were once forcibly sterilized due to the belief that they couldn't participate in basic civil rights such as procreating. We now know that's barbaric, but we have a long way to go in our understanding and support. We've heard from doctors and advocates. We've heard statistics of hope and stories of horror. But Josh Everett isn't a story or statistic. This case is not about whether schizophrenics can be good parents.

This is about whether it's in Caleb Everett's best interest to remain in the custody of his biological parents, or if custody should be awarded to his maternal grandparents."

"I've agonized over this case, because while we recognize mental illness is not the fault of the sufferer, we also cannot ignore the discord an illness as serious as schizophrenia brings to families."

Amy squeezed the beads so hard her fingers ached. Was he purposely dragging this out?

"However, I don't see evidence that Josh Everett poses a danger to his child, or to anyone else, for that matter. Let's not forget the child has a mentally stable mother."

Amy wasn't so sure about that, but she loosened her grip.

"It would be an overreach to remove the child, to punish Amy Everett for supporting her husband in his illness, for fighting to keep her family together. Furthermore, we acknowledge the level of functioning Josh has recuperated. I'm hereby denying Walt and Eileen Richards' petition for custody. The minor child, Caleb Everett, will remain in the custody of his biological parents with the stipulation that Josh Everett remains under psychiatric care. Case dismissed. I wish you all the best." His gavel crashed.

For a moment, no one moved. Then Julian grasped Josh's hand, and her own. She looked at Josh. His eyes were brimming with tears. He pulled her to him. The world righted itself. "Let's go home," he said into her hair. He took her hand and led her from the courtroom.

Amy caught a glimpse of her mother as Josh led her down the center aisle toward the heavy wood doors. Eileen was alone. Amy sensed her following.

"Amy, wait," Eileen said when they reached the hallway.

Amy was struck by déjà vu. If this was some sort of peace offering, it was pathetic. She turned, barely recognizing the woman before her. Her face was pasty and free of makeup. Her hair hung limply around her face.

"We have nothing to say to you," Amy said. Josh's grip on her hand tightened. "You tried to break my family apart and you failed. If you think you can be in my life after this—"

"I don't. I know what we did is unforgiveable. I don't expect you to ever speak to me again. But there's something I need to say."

Josh stepped between Amy and her mother. "I think you've said enough."

"Please." Eileen looked through Josh. "Two minutes."

Amy put a hand on Josh's arm, feeling his muscle twitch under her touch. "It's okay. Why don't you get the car?"

He turned to her. "You're sure?"

She nodded. "I'll be right out."

Frowning, he turned and retreated down the hallway, his footsteps heavy. Amy turned back to her mother.

"Where's Dad?" she asked, not sure why she wanted to know.

"That's what I need to tell you." Eileen reached her hand out toward Amy, then thought better of it and let it drop. "I'm leaving your father."

This new information registered in her brain. Her parents had always been cool with each other. But they'd been a unit. It was impossible to determine where her father ended and her mother began. When Amy didn't respond, her mother continued.

"The truth is, I've always been jealous of your relationship with Josh. He's devoted to you. He loves you for who you are."

Amy scoffed. "That's what this is about? Jealousy?"

Eileen shook her head. She rummaged in her purse for a tissue and dabbed her eyes. "No. This is about me living in your father's shadow for twenty-three years. He said jump, I got out the trampoline. I got so good at being what he wanted me to be that I forgot who I was in the first place. I blocked out my own thoughts and feelings for so long, I adopted his until I was an extension of him."

"Your father never hit me," she continued. "But sometimes I think I would've preferred that." The corners of her mouth pulled up. "I had the picture-perfect life. What would people think if I left my rich, successful, handsome husband? Pretending was easier. Until pretending cost me everything. I never should have let him convince me to go along with this custody suit. I packed my bags."

Amy's head spun. "Why are you telling me this?"

"I had to."

"But why?"

Eileen straightened her shoulders and looked Amy in the eyes. "I hate what I've become. Seeing the strength you had to stay gave me the strength to finally leave."

Chapter 49

"Sh e's leaving your dad?" Josh pulled up to the house and his heart swelled. Their family was staying together.

"Yeah," Amy said. "Weird, right? She actually said she was jealous of our relationship."

"Huh." Josh cut the engine and looked at her.

Her face was pale and gaunt. Finding him dying in the truck, his descent into psychosis, her parents' ultimatum, and the stress of the trial must've nearly killed her. But she was so much stronger than she gave herself credit for. Strong, but still human. He tried to hold on to his anger at her betrayal, but it slipped through his clenched fingers like sand. *I decided to stay for the thousands of things she did right by me instead of leaving for the one thing she did wrong.*

"How do you feel? About the divorce?"

She sighed. "I don't know. I'm feeling so many things right now." She squared her shoulders and looked at him. "It doesn't matter. They're out of our lives. All that matters is you and Caleb." She searched his eyes.

He tucked a wayward strand of hair behind her ear. "I'm not going to leave you, Amy. I love you. That hasn't changed. If we could get through this trial we can get through anything. Together."

Her eyes filled with tears. "I'll earn your trust again."

He smiled. "I know. Listen, I need to run back to work and check on some things. I won't be late. I need to see him first, though."

Maria threw open the door before they reached it. Caleb peeked around her legs.

Amy ran to her and threw her arms around her. "We won."

"Oh, Miss Amy! I prayed so hard." She let go of Amy and hugged Josh.

"I'm so sorry you had to lose your job," Amy said.

"Now, don't worry about that."

"You don't have to go back to Guatemala. You can stay here, with us."

Josh grabbed Caleb and threw him into the air, catching him in a hug. "We won Caleb."

"Yay!" Caleb said, understanding only that "won" was an exciting word.

Josh set a squirming Caleb down and turned to Maria. "You'll always have a home here."

"I know. But it's time to go back. My mother, she's not well. But I come back. We're family."

Josh expected to be completely drained after the verdict. Instead, he drove back to work with renewed energy. A pile of bricks had been lifted off him. His meeting with the electrician would be a breeze. In light of keeping his son, any snafu that came up with the house project, he could handle.

Josh had left the project manager, Blake, in charge, with orders to keep workers out of the house until the electrician had had a chance to double-check the wiring. Even though Blake insisted it had been inspected thoroughly, Josh had noticed potentially faulty wiring in the grand fault circuit breaker.

"Look again," Sam had whispered over Josh's shoulder as he studied the grand fault circuit breaker, causing Josh to drop his heavy flashlight with a clatter. Josh almost hadn't listened, but Sam had been right.

Should be an easy fix, but the wires had the potential to oxidize the way they sat. Blake clearly didn't agree with Josh, but it was safest to keep the house clear until the problem was remedied.

Josh was a half mile away when he saw the curls of smoke in the sky. He rubbed his eyes. It was still there. Shit. He slammed his foot down on the gas. The old engine protested as the truck lurched ahead. His tires skidded on the dirt and gravel, fighting for traction as he careened up to the site and pumped his breaks.

His breath caught in his chest. Orange-blue flames licked the sky. The entire house was engulfed. Josh hit the ground running, not bothering to close the door of the truck. Smoke and ash burned his eyes and his nose. A strand of yellow caution tape blew across the dry ground. The roar of the fire was deafening.

"Get out of here!"

Instead, Josh ran toward the building, where Blake was standing at a safe distance, yelling something.

Josh grabbed his arm. "Where the hell's the fire department?"

Blake turned to him. The flames were eerily reflected in his eyes. "The phone line's down! I sent Jorge to get help."

"Okay, back up. That whole thing's gonna explode." He pulled Blake's arm, but something in his eyes made Josh go cold despite the inferno. "Blake, everyone cleared out, right?"

Blake responded with a blank stare.

Josh shook him, his head snapping back and forth. "Right?"

Blake's fingers dug into Josh's forearm. "It's Jason," he said. "Jason's in the house."

Chapter 50

Josh ran.

"Josh, you can't go in there!" Blake screamed. It's too late! It's coming down."

"Leave him. Save yourself!" Shane reached a burning hand toward Josh as a warning or threat, he wasn't sure which.

Josh ignored them both, running blindly toward the building. Flames illuminated the structure. Chunks of drywall cascaded to the dirt. He dodged a falling rafter, dropped to his knees, and crawled through the door frame. Thick smoke and brilliant flames clouded his vision and seared his lungs. He coughed violently.

"Welcome to hell."

Another voice, Josh's own, pulsed in his head. *"Fuck you. You're dead to me."*

He struggled to his feet, picking his way through the front room. A searing pain shot through his hand as he tossed aside a scorched beam.

"Jason!" His eyes watered. He coughed. "Jason!" His throat grew raw with his screams. Was his brother unconscious? Already dead? How long had he been in here? If Josh had told him about the faulty wiring, he'd have believed him. He wouldn't be in here. If only Josh hadn't dawdled at home.

He screamed his brother's name again and forced himself to pause, listening. Sweat soaked his hair. It felt like his skin was melting. Damn Blake. Why had he let Jason come in here?

He heard something through the crackling and roaring. A muffled scream. A weak voice calling his name.

The family room! The chopped layout of the house was burned into his memory. The doorway to the family room had collapsed. Josh climbed over the beams, nearly weeping with relief at the sight of Jason staring at him, his irises almost glowing like a cat's. Josh had only minutes if he was going to get them out of here alive.

Jason was flat on his back on the floor, one of the ridiculously ornate cement columns lying across his thigh, pinning him. Nearly slipping on the gritty floor, Josh rushed to him and tried to move the column with sheer force. His back screamed in protest.

"Josh." Jason's voice was ragged as though he'd been screaming for a long time. He grabbed for Josh's shirt. "Go. Get out. The house . . . is about to come down!" As if to illustrate, a popping sound erupted in the next room. "You . . . have a family. Leave . . . me here. Get out!"

Jagged coughs ripped from his lungs. Blood trickled from his mouth. A wheezing sound emanated from his chest as he tried to keep talking.

Panic assaulted Josh. Jason didn't have much time left. "Shut up, shut up! Don't try to talk."

Dizziness threatened his peripheral vision, and Jason had been in here a lot longer. He shook his head to dislodge the floaters, pulling the neck of his sweatshirt over his nose and mouth. He couldn't let his brother down.

He slid his hands under the heavy column. Jason struggled to sit up. He weakly pushed at Josh.

"Josh, what I did—" another coughing fit strangled his words. Josh's own panic was reflected in his inky pupils.

Shane crouched next to Jason, for once not wearing his macabre grin. "Deserves to die, don't you think?"

Josh barely registered him. "That doesn't matter right now. Your still my brother. I'm not leaving this building without you. Help me."

Jason must have realized Josh was serious. He pushed the column while Josh lifted.

"Slide your leg out," Josh choked, his arms shaking with the weight.

Jason slid his body backward with his hands, his face contorted in agony. As soon as he was clear of the beam Josh dropped it and turned his attention to his brother. He lay on his back staring at the ceiling, stunned. The pant leg of his jeans was soaked through with blood. Sweat ran into his eyes. His breath came in short, ragged breaths. His eyes were unfocused. *He's dying.*

Another pop. Cinder block cascaded inches from them. Josh's lungs burned. He couldn't decipher the hissing of the voices from the hissing of the flames. It didn't matter.

"I'm going to get you out of here." He slung Jason's left arm over his shoulder, wrapped his arm around his waist, and hoisted him to his feet.

Jason screamed, an animalistic sound of pain. His left leg dangled uselessly as he sagged against Josh. "Can't . . . walk."

"I've got you."

Josh's body protested as he half carried, half dragged Jason across the floor as it melted and warped under their feet. Jason used his uninjured leg to propel him forward, moaning in pain. The weight on Josh's shoulder increased.

"Tired," Jason gasped. "It hurts." His body went limp.

Josh didn't let go. "Stay with me. We're almost there."

"I can't Josh. I'm sorry. I . . . can't. Let me go."

He stumbled. Josh's arm tightened around him. "I won't. I won't let go." He didn't let go and he didn't slow down, not until he pulled his brother through what used to be the doorway and into the air.

A loud crack was instantly followed by a mighty explosion. They were both thrown forward, coughing and gasping. Josh threw his body over Jason. Something hard hit him in the shoulder. Without looking back, he scrambled up and dragged Jason away from the flames with his remaining strength.

"We need an ambulance!" he screamed.

People were running around and screaming. Who was real? Sirens moaned. He hoped to God *they* were real.

Dropping to his knees, he looked Jason over. Tears steamed from his eyes, making clean tracks in the soot caking his face. Blood was pooling in the dirt under his leg. Josh ripped his shirt off and wrapped it around his thigh as best he could. Jason moaned and thrashed; his eyes wild.

"I know," Josh said. "I'm sorry. I gotta slow the bleeding."

Jason's hand closed around Josh's wrist in a desperate grip. "It hurts," he cried. "Oh, God, it hurts so much." Sobs wracked his body, punctuated by coughs.

Josh had seen Jason pull a nail out of his hand and casually wipe the blood on his jeans. This had to be bad.

"Can't . . . breathe," Jason whimpered between coughing fits. "I don't wanna die." His body convulsed with agony and panic. "Am I gonna die, Josh?" He stared at Josh with the imploring, petrified eyes of a child.

Josh forgot the throbbing in his shoulder and the burning in his lungs. "Not on my watch, you're not. Here, squeeze my hand. There you go. That's it."

His wedding band dug into his finger as Jason's hand tightened like a sieve. "Where's Mom?" he asked. "I want Mom. Can you get her for me?" His voice faded to a whisper. His lids fluttered.

The pressure on Josh's hand went slack. *He's going into shock,* Josh realized. No matter how old or tough you were, there were moments in life when all that would do was a mother's comfort.

"You're gonna be fine, Jason. Do you hear me? You're gonna be fine. Stay with me."

Jason stared, unseeing, at Josh before his eyes rolled in the back of his head and he passed out cold.

Chapter 51

Josh got away with a third degree burn on his hand, a bruised shoulder, and smoke inhalation. He refused the pain medication they offered him. He wanted to ensure he was alert when Jason needed him.

Jason was still in surgery. Bob and Josh waited in a cramped room for what seemed like days. People rustled newspapers, did crosswords, or stared catatonically at the second-hand inching around the clock.

Blake entered the stuffy waiting room. He glanced around. His hair stood on end. Bob caught sight of him and struggled to his feet.

"You got a lot of nerve showing up here."

Blake looked everywhere but at Bob. He caught Josh's eye and looked at the floor. "Jason. Is he—"

"He's in surgery. Crushed his femur."

"Shit."

"Josh told you to shut the project down?"

"Bob, I can explain." Blake spread his hands in front of him, an ineffective shield. Josh almost felt sorry for him. "It was inspected by an independent company."

"I don't care if it was inspected by God himself. If Josh told you the building wasn't sound, why would you let Jason, or anyone for that matter, go in there?"

"Of course, in hindsight, Josh was right. But, you know, sometimes Josh . . . says things." He lowered his voice even though Josh was two feet away.

Josh raised his eyebrows. "I'm schizophrenic, not deaf."

Blake finally looked at him. "That's not what I'm saying."

"I think," Bob said, his voice dangerously low, "That's exactly what you're saying."

"Bob, I'm sorry."

"You're sorry? You're *sorry*? You almost got both my boys killed. You're done." Bob's breath came in angry gasps.

Josh vacated his chair. "I think you should leave."

Blake looked as though he wanted to say something but thought better of it. Without a word, he turned and walked away.

Bob dropped back into his chair. Josh paced the small room. A few people glared at him. A woman pulled her little girl close as though Josh was a caged animal that could attack at any moment.

"Josh," Bob hissed.

Josh knew he was acting weird, but he couldn't help it. He didn't want to help it. Was pacing stranger behavior than reading the freaking paper while waiting for a life or death verdict for someone you loved?

Josh's hands twitched at his sides. His thoughts tumbled around his head and spilled into his ears. Had the hospital gotten ahold of Amy? Would Jason survive the surgery? Anesthesia had to be risky with all the smoke he'd taken in. Could they fix his leg?

"You're being paranoid."

"Better knock it off, or they'll cart you off to the looney bin."

"Jason's dead."

Josh stopped pacing and looked at Bob. "What did you say?"

Bob glanced around. "Sit down and stop yelling."

"I'm not yelling."

A middle-aged man in scrubs opened the door. A surgical mask hung around his neck. Expectant faces turned.

"Everett?"

Josh and Bob followed the doctor out into the hallway. Josh poured all his energy into focusing on his words.

"The surgery went well. He's awake."

Awake. Alive.

"We were able to clean out the bone fragments and put a rod in. He's a tough kid."

Bob nodded. "Yes, he is."

"I'll be honest; he took in a lot of smoke. Tonight's essential. He'll be monitored closely. If he makes it through the night, I'll be optimistic, but the recovery won't be easy. It's unlikely that limb will ever bear weight again."

"I understand," Bob said.

Josh didn't. Jason was as stubborn as reinforced drywall. This wouldn't break him. "Can we see him?"

The doctor nodded. "He's still pretty out of it."

He led them down a maze of harshly lit hallways and left them in the doorway. Jason was in the first bed, the rest of the room curtained off. He was completely still, a white blanket pulled up to his chin. Tubes and wires snaked from various machines and disappeared under the blanket. His leg was suspended in some type of contraction.

Bob paused in the doorway, but Josh approached the bed, ignoring the antiseptic stinging his eyes and nose, unsettling the dust of hospital memories. Jason's eyes fluttered opened. He looked up at Josh and smiled.

Josh's legs went weak with relief. He gently tousled Jason's hair. "Hey, buddy. You hangin in there?"

"Yeah." Jason's voice was like sandpaper.

Bob made his way into the room. "How're you doing, son?"

"Never better. Josh saved my life."

"It was nothing. You'd do the same for me."

Jason shrugged one shoulder under the blanket, wearing a lopsided grin. "Eh, I might." He winced.

"What is it?" Bob asked. "Are you in pain? Should I get the doctor?"

"No, it's—" He looked at Josh. "I cried, didn't I? I'm so embarrassed. What a sissy."

"You were brave," Josh answered. "You did good, kid."

"Hmm." Jason's eyes closed again.

"When you get better, I'm taking you sky diving, and any other wild thing you can think of."

His eyes opened. "You're crazy. But I love you anyway."

Josh glanced at Bob to make sure he wasn't hearing things. "That's the morphine talking."

"It's good, but it ain't that good," Jason slurred.

"Josh, why don't we let your brother get some rest? He's been through the ringer."

"I want to stay with him tonight." Josh wouldn't let his guard down again. He adjusted the blanket. "You rest. I'll shut up now."

Jason grabbed his hand. His eyes clouded with tears. "I really am sorry, Josh."

Josh squeezed his hand. "I know. Me too."

"Josh." He blinked, the tears making rivers down his cheeks as embarrassment gave way to fear. "They said I'll never walk again."

Josh held his brother's gaze. "Jason, take it from me. Don't believe everything you hear."

Chapter 52

The call came in the middle of the night.

"It's time," Jason said. "You gotta come."

The drive was a blur. Amy'd offered to drive, but Josh needed something to do. Caleb slept in the back seat. He'd barely stirred when they'd transferred him from his crib. Amy settled him on Jason's bed while Jason led Josh to Bob's bedroom, his giant cast dragging across the wood floor. Bob wanted to be at home. He was sick of hospitals, he said. He was ready. He was the only one.

Bob was propped up on pillows. His skin was almost the exact gray of the peeling wallpaper. His eyes were sunken in his head. Josh couldn't reconcile the shrinking man in the bed with the big strong unstoppable force he'd always known. Bob coughed, the jagged sound tearing through the room Josh and Jason had retreated to when they were afraid.

"Josh," he whispered when the coughing fit subsided. He lifted his hand weakly.

Josh went to one side of the bed and Jason stationed himself at the other. They each took one of Bob's leathery hands, blue from lack of blood flow. "I'm here, Dad."

"It's just gonna be you two now. You gotta promise me . . ." He began coughing again. Wheezing leaked from his lungs.

"You gotta promise me you'll take care of each other." He gasped. "Don't let anything come between you."

Josh and Jason locked eyes over the bed.

"Don't worry," Josh said. "We got it from here."

Bob looked at Jason. "You got a lot to offer the world, son. You survived that fire for a reason. Don't let that anger get in your way."

"I'll try."

"And you'll ditch those crutches one day."

"I will," Jason managed. "I'm sorry for all the grief I gave you."

"Ah. You kept me young. You guys are gonna be fine."

Josh sensed Amy at his side. "I know you'll take care of him," Bob told her. "Make sure that baby hears stories about me."

"Of course." Amy's voice was thick with tears. She reached past Josh and squeezed Bob's arm. "Thank you for teaching me what it meant to be a part of a real family." She touched Josh's arm. "I'll give you some time."

Time. It moved too quickly and too slowly. It ceased to exist. The sound of Bob's labored breathing slowed and then stopped.

Jason tugged on his hand. "Dad?" Jason's eyes widened. "Dad!" He shook Bob's shoulder, his body swaying.

Josh let go of his dad's limp hand. He watched the scene from somewhere outside of himself as his brother continued to yell for his dad.

"He's gone, Jay." His own voice sounded flat in his ears.

Jason's head jerked toward him, eyes blazing. He propelled himself around the bed toward Josh, crutches cracking against the worn wood. Josh stepped away from the bed and turned toward him.

"You're lying!" Jason screamed at him, spittle flying from his mouth.

"Jason—"

"No. Shut the fuck up. You're a fucking liar! You don't know what the fuck you're saying."

He let one of his crutches fall. He hit Josh hard in the chest with his fist. "You don't know what you're saying," he wailed, striking Josh over and over again until he lost his balance.

Josh caught him, pulling him to his chest. Jason's remaining crutch clattered to the floor. His body buckled. "Sorry," he wailed. He grabbed fistfuls of Josh's shirt, sobbing into his chest.

"It's okay. We'll be okay." Josh did what he always did. He stood rooted like a tree, a rock, playing the hero in a tragedy. Trying to fix the unfixable. Josh didn't let go.

Chapter 53

Josh called the coroner. They holed themselves up in Jason's room, trying not to hear the zip of the body bag and the slam of the trunk. Long after Amy took Caleb home, Josh and Jason sat side by side on the tattered couch, shell shocked. Jason busied himself rolling a joint. Silence gave way to stories about Bob, about growing up, about where to go from here.

"You think we can handle the company?" Jason asked.

"Between your mind and my body, we make a full working person," Josh answered. "We'll make it." He studied his brother. "What about you?"

Jason raked a hand through his hair. "The house is paid off. I'll stay here. I'll be fine alone."

"You're not alone."

He looked at Josh. "I know. But it's time I found my own way." He was quiet for a moment. "I met someone."

"Where? Physical therapy?"

"Yes, actually. Her name's Rebecca. She's recovering from a car accident. We bonded over our mutual disdain for resistance bands." He grinned. "We decided to do our own physical endurance exercises."

Josh groaned. "Oh, God, please shut up."

Jason inhaled deeply before continuing. "Ya know, I realized it's not your wife I wanted. It's your *life*."

Josh cocked his head. "How's that?"

His eyes, half mast, slid over to Josh. "I don't know, man. I guess it's the way she looks at you. Like you walk on fucking water. And, you know, having a family and shit. I want that. I want someone to look at me like that."

"What are you talking about? Women look at you like that all the time."

Jason shook his head. "That's lust. I'm kinda tired of that."

"Hence the extracurricular physical therapy?"

Jason punched his arm. "Hey, man, I think Rebecca's different. We talk. I'm getting to the point in my life where I want more."

"Jay, you're twenty years old. You hardly have one foot in the grave."

"I almost did, though, didn't I? The doctors, they thought I didn't hear them when they said I shouldn't have lived, but I heard."

Josh swallowed hard. The what-ifs were too hard to contemplate, especially after watching his dad die.

"Don't look at me like that," Jason said. "I'm just saying, almost kicking it kind of makes you think about your life, you know?"

Josh nodded. "Yeah, I do." They were quiet for a moment. The voices talked amongst themselves, contemplating whether Josh was to blame for Bob's death. The repetition was ludicrous. "Focus on getting back on your feet. We'll figure something out. Maybe you can—"

Jason's eyes darkened. "Stop. Don't do that."

"Do what?"

"What you always do. Play the savior."

Josh leaned away from him, stung. "I'm not—"

"You gotta stop trying to save me. I'm not your project."

"Where is this coming from?"

"My whole life you've been stepping in, making things easy for me. You took care of the company so I could focus on school. And remember all those times you snuck my drunk ass home and sold Dad a bill of goods so ridiculous he only believed it because it was coming from you? How about the time you talked the principal into not expelling me after I got into that fight? Remember, they couldn't get ahold of Dad cause he was running a jackhammer all day?"

"What's your point?"

He looked at Josh through eyes red from crying and blood-shot from pot. "You're always looking out for me. Rescuing me. Fixing my mistakes."

"I'm your brother. That's my job."

Jason pointed the joint at him. "But see, it's not. I can figure shit out on my own. I'm the screw up and you're the prodigal son."

Josh laughed. "First of all, I think you need to brush up on your Bible stories. And second, I'm not perfect, Jay."

"Really, when have you ever done something wrong? Ever gone off the straight and narrow?"

Josh raised his eyebrows. "The straight and narrow?"

"Dude, I'm serious. You were always Dad's favorite, and who could blame him? You never gave him any trouble. He was worried about what would happen to me after he was gone. He told you that, didn't he?"

"Jason—" Josh felt a tornado swirling inside his head.

"Everyone expects me to fall flat on my face."

"Get over yourself," Josh snapped. "We're all falling flat on our faces. Dad's dead."

Jason straightened up. "You... You're so... You have everything figured out."

"I spent almost two months in a mental hospital. You watched me have a psychotic break, so I don't know where you're going with this."

Jason threw his hands up. Josh was afraid he'd send the joint flying. "I don't know! You just... Stop trying to be my parent. You can't fix everything. You sure as hell can't fix this."

Josh sighed. "Gimme that." He snatched the joint from Jason's fingers, brought it to his mouth, and pulled the smoke deep into his lungs. Instantly, his head swam. The world lost its definitive edges.

Jason stared at him, then burst out laughing. "Well, shit. Now I've seen everything."

Chapter 54

The irony of spring taunted Josh. The new life breaking through the soft ground. The influx of new projects. The cadence of life moving on without his dad. Josh was left with a constant urge to scream at everyone. How were they all going about their business? How dare the sun rise another day? Who gave a shit about building proposals anyway?

But life went on despite his silent protests, and he was left to run a company and a family when he couldn't even run his own mind. The spring and the housing development allowed him to hire someone to pick up the slack—a middle aged guy named Bubba who kept his head down and did what Josh asked. Amy came to the trailer some days to file papers and answer phones while Caleb played on the floor. She had to hate it, but she didn't complain. Rebecca followed Jason around, handing him his crutches and bringing him lunch. For someone who didn't want to be rescued, he ate up the attention.

After work, Josh joined the guys behind the trailer as they passed a joint, a trend he'd been naïvely blind to previously. Maybe Jason was right; he had to stop trying to be everyone's dad and boss. For once in his life, he was one of the guys. The first time he'd reached for the joint, a half a dozen pair of eyes focused on him.

"It's cool," Jason said. "He's one of us now."

For some reason, everyone thought this was hilarious. They all slapped Josh on the back and seemed to forget they were afraid of him. It felt, well, normal.

"You're a narc," the voices said.

"Not anymore," Josh answered.

"What's that?" the guy he passed the joint to asked.

"Oh, nothing." Josh tapped his temple. "They say I'm a narc."

Laughter rippled through the circle. "Even his voices know it."

Josh laughed along with them. He had ulterior motives for shooting the shit, though. There was a spy, or several, lurking around the job site and planning to sabotage the company. Josh didn't know who, yet, but everyone was a suspect. Could be Bubba, or Rebecca, or even Jason.

And then there was Amy. He'd caught her a few times shoving papers in a drawer as he walked in. She could be gathering information, but why and for whom? He made excuses to be in the trailer, listening, while she was on the phone. He skimmed through papers she'd had her hands on, but he couldn't figure it out. They were all trying to pull one over on him.

Amy was always watching him.

"Are you high right now?" she demanded one night when she greeted him after work.

"I don't do drugs," he said. "You know that."

She sighed, wiping Caleb's face and getting him out of his highchair. "I'm not stupid, Josh. For one thing, I can smell it on you. I know you're grieving. But you have to keep up with your treatment. Dr. Sai says you've missed your last two appointments, and you—"

Josh turned from the kitchen sink. Water sloshed over the glass he'd filled. "Oh, so you're talking about me now? What happened to confidentiality?"

"Don't start that. He called to ask if you were coming this week and if everything was okay since you missed the last two. Why didn't you go?"

"Because he's gathering information on me. He's recording what I say so he can use it against me later."

Amy stared at him. He couldn't miss the tremor in her hands. She was afraid of him, too. His own wife. She came to him, took the glass out of his hand and set it in the sink. She took hold of his arms.

"Josh. Talk to me. Please. What's going on? Are you taking your medication?"

"Yes, I'm taking my medication, *doctor*." He wasn't. What was the point? He could handle things on his own. He always had.

"Really, because you're acting paranoid."

"Do you want to fucking count them?"

"Shhh!" She looked over her shoulder, but Caleb had wandered into the family room, engrossed in some toy that made too much noise.

"Don't shush me. If we're lobbing accusations, why don't you tell me what you're doing with the information your gathering on the company? Who put you up to it? Huh?" His voice rose. The edges of the kitchen swam.

"She's the enemy. They're all the enemy. Run!"

Amy took a step back. Her face hardened. "I can't do this with you right now. I have to give Caleb a bath." She turned away. "Dinner's on the stove if you're interested," she called over her shoulder. "I didn't poison it, if you were wondering."

Josh bristled. She hadn't denied her involvement in some scheme. But what? She was right, though. It had to wait until after Caleb was in bed. Josh wandered into the bathroom. Caleb was patting the bubbles, giggling. Amy looked up at him from the floor, her expression dispassionate.

Josh knelt in front of the tub, an ache spreading in his

chest. He took a handful of bubbles and patted them on his chin. "Like my beard?"

Caleb looked at Josh, his eyes widening in delight. He brought bubbles up to his own cheeks. "Ho ho ho," he said.

Josh laughed. "Love you little man." He plopped a handful of bubbles on Caleb's head then straightened up, wiping his hands on a bath towel.

"Josh," Amy called as he turned to leave. "Take your pills."

His fists clenched. They were trying to drug him so he wouldn't know he was being taken. Not this time. He stomped to his own bathroom and opened the little mirror, studying the row of orange bottles. Fuck it. One by one, he unscrewed the caps and dumped the contents into the toilet, flushing it ceremoniously. The colors swirled together before disappearing. He dropped the empty bottles into the sink.

"Bad idea, Josh," Sam said, appearing in the doorway. "Some part of you must know that was a really bad idea."

"Leave! Get out of here! Run! They're all trying to trick you! Make you think your crazy! They're pretending to be on your side. Get out! Get out! Get out!" Shane stared at him from the mirror, replacing his reflection.

"Move," he said to Sam.

"Don't do it Josh. Don't throw it all away."

"Fuck you."

Josh barreled past him. He stood at the top of the stairs, listening to Caleb's splashes and giggles. His heart seized. "I'll be back, Little Man," he whispered. "As soon as I find the truth."

With no idea where he was going, Josh grabbed the keys to his truck and left the house.

Chapter 55

It took Amy less than twenty-four hours to start worrying about Josh. The empty pill bottles obviously left for her to find only infuriated her. He wasn't even trying! After everything they'd been through, he was going to risk it all? Out of what? Pride?

Fine, she thought when she noticed his truck missing. *Throw a fit and run away from home.*

He'd come back. He'd blow off some steam and come to his senses. This was all grief, she reasoned. The pot he thought he was hiding so well; refusing to take his pills; missing appointments; conjuring wild accusations. It wasn't him.

That's not him. Wasn't that what they'd said the first time he was hospitalized last summer, when his sick mind had completely taken over? By the second night, a low-level panic hardened in her blood. They'd been warned, hadn't they, that recovery wasn't linear? What was it they'd said? Noncompliance was high? But Josh knew better. Naïvely, she'd believed they were beating the statistics. The hard part was over. How stupid could she be?

"Where Dada?" Caleb asked.

His innocent face filled her with equal parts rage and fear. How could Josh disappear like this? What was he trying to prove? Where was he? How long had he been off his meds?

"I'm going to find out, Caleb." The brightness in her voice surprised her. She'd become a superb actress.

She dialed Jason's number, counting five rings before he picked up, his voice thick. Amy sighed inwardly. He'd be no help.

"Jason, is Josh there?"

"Josh?" he slurred.

"Yes, Josh. Your brother?"

"Naw, he wasn't at work today either. I haven't seen him since yesterday."

Amy wanted to strangle him through the phone. "He stopped taking his medication. He was accusing me of gathering information on the company. He left the house last night and I don't know where he is."

"Oh shit." She heard some shuffling and then another voice. "Stop that."

"Jason! What is the matter with you? Do you not hear what I'm saying right now?"

"See Amy, here's the thing. I kinda sorta maybe might've shared a joint with Josh the night Dad died, and he maybe kinda liked it more than I thought."

"I can't believe you."

"What? It's not like I forced it on him. Lots of people smoke pot, Amy. It's no big deal."

"Lots of people don't have schizophrenia!" she yelled.

"Okay, okay. You're right. I'm sorry. I'll come help you look for him."

A hard wall of resolve built in her chest. "Don't," she said. "I'll do it on my own." She hung up and immediately dialed Dr. Sai's emergency line.

"Hello, Dr. Sai."

"Dr. Sai, it's Amy. Josh hasn't been taking his meds. I don't know for how long. He's been smoking pot. He's paranoid."

"Oh, dear," Dr. Sai said, using too tame a term for the situation. "Marijuana can exacerbate psychotic symptoms. Can you get him to talk to me?"

"That's the thing." Amy smiled at Caleb as he lobbed a ball at a block tower. "He's missing. He left the house last night and I don't know where he is. I don't know what to do." Her voice cracked. "What should I do?"

"Hang up," Dr. Sai said. "And call the police."

Chapter 56

The road in front of him blurred. Tree branches morphed into arms and reached for the truck. The voices screamed at him from the radio, the air vents. Shane stuck his arm out the passenger window.

"Glad we left that buzz-kill farmer behind, Josh. I'm the only one really on your side. The only with the balls to give it to ya straight. Oh, here. Stop here."

Josh pulled over. He looked around him. Where was he? How long had he been gone? His stomach ached with a satisfying emptiness.

Shane glared at him. "Get out of the fucking truck."

Josh did, without questioning. He began to walk. Everything was loud and cold. He was far from home, maybe in a city. People bustled around him. The sun seared his corneas. Had he slept? What day was it? Who were all these people and why were the shouting at him?

Horns blared. People and cars blurred. They were all after him. He ran, each street corner copying the one before it. He couldn't get back and he couldn't get away. Only the terror was familiar.

Spent, he stopped at a crowded corner, watching the sign flash from a red hand to a stick figure and back again. What did it mean? It started to rain. People bustled around him, pulling out umbrellas. They jostled him on either side. They told him to move. They were all in on it, though Josh couldn't remember what *it* was. No one could help him now.

"*Trust no one.*"

"Leave me alone!" Josh screamed into the rain. Faces turned toward him. Bodies moved away. "Get away from me!"

The red hand flashed. Josh bolted. Horns blared. Someone screamed. A van came barreling toward him and Josh dove for the pavement. Searing pain jolted through his palms and ricocheted up his arms. Shiny black shoes materialized two inches from his face. He felt his hands pulled behind his back and the cold bite of handcuffs close around his wrists. *Not again.*

"Let me go!" he said into the pavement. He tasted blood.

He was hauled to his feet. He tried to run but shapes and colors were flying at him so fast he couldn't tell which way to go. Panic tore at his chest. Something bright and silver flashed in front of his eyes.

"New Haven police," a disembodied voice said. "You're coming with us."

Chapter 57

March 19, 1980

A my almost missed the call. She was trying to cajole Caleb into his shoes so she could take him to the toddler drop off at the library. The kindly lady who ran the program had decades of experience in childcare, she assured Amy. She'd found a program like this when she was a young single mom, she said, and now she was giving back. Caleb could come one day a week for no cost and be with other kids his age.

His shoe still in her hand, Amy answered the phone.

"New Haven Police Department. We've found your husband."

Amy drove north, her knuckles white on the steering wheel. Josh's truck had been found parked on the side of the road outside downtown New Haven. He'd been causing a "public disturbance", the officer told her. Ranting and raving. Scaring people.

He wouldn't hurt anyone, she wanted to say, but she didn't bother. *She* knew that, but she couldn't really blame people for being afraid. They didn't know him. All they saw was this six-foot-two guy ranting and raving at the wind. All they saw was the illness holding his mind hostage. As she braved the traffic,

· 318 ·

images of Josh sitting in a jail cell—again—wormed their way into her head.

The drive was eternal. Amy had to remind herself to breathe as she navigated the congestion she wasn't used to. She made several wrong turns and had to pull over to consult her map twice before she finally made it to the police department.

"Dammit, Josh," she muttered as she parallel parked, badly.

She held the anger until a bored-looking officer led her through a set of steel doors to the holding cell. Amy had never been inside a prison before. It was cold, and not just in temperature. Josh sat on a metal bench in a cinderblock cell, a statue. His hands were clasped in his lap. His hair obscured his face.

Amy wrapped her hands around the cool bars. "Josh."

He didn't move.

"He was running around downtown. Ran into the street and narrowly missed being hit by a delivery van."

Amy sucked in her breath. She turned to the officer, looking for compassion but seeing only indifference. "Is he okay?"

The officer shrugged. "Don't know. He's been like this since we got him here. He won't say anything."

"Is he—are you charging him with something?"

The cop shrugged again. "Not much we can charge him with, but we can't exactly have him running around on the streets scaring the day lights out of people, see? He on drugs or something?"

"He's schizophrenic," Amy said. "He went off his meds. He needs to be in the hospital."

To her surprise, the cop unlocked the cell. "You feel safe with him?"

Amy nodded, used to the question. He was too far gone for her to bring him back herself. But she *would* bring him back.

She knelt in front of him, brushing his hair back. The

painfully familiar vacantness in his eyes jolted her. His lip was bloody. "Josh, can you hear me?"

"I didn't do it," he whispered.

"I know, baby," she soothed. There'd be plenty of time to be mad at him later. "I'm going to get you out of here."

She tugged at his hands and he followed her, almost in a trance. At the front desk, they handed her his wallet. She held tightly to him as she led him to the car, afraid he'd bolt. He didn't. He dropped into the passenger seat and stared straight ahead.

"I don't know how I got here," he mumbled. "The white man and the red hand tricked me. They all tricked me."

"I know," she said again, although she had no idea what he was talking about. "Josh, why'd you stop taking the pills? They were helping you." It was no use, asking now, but she couldn't help it.

"They told me to," he muttered.

He stared out the window, glassy eyed. Her stomach knotted when they reached Fairview Hospital. What if he wouldn't go in? She maneuvered the car through the parking garage and parked as close to the doors as possible. He continued to stare out the window. What would she do if he ran?

"I need you to come with me." She touched his arm. He looked at her. His eyes filled with tears.

"No," he whispered, more pleading than defiant.

"It's going to be okay," she said. "But I need you to trust me."

"Trust no one," he said in that robotic voice she'd hoped to never hear again.

One thing had worked before. "They're all trying to get you," she said. "You can hide here. You'll be safe."

He looked at her so intently that for a moment she thought the tempered glass would fall from his eyes and he'd come back to her. "You know about them?" he said.

Amy swallowed hard. "Yes. I know about them. And I'm going to make them leave you alone."

Chapter 58

March 20, 1980

The smell of bleach and latex tickled Josh's nose. It was quiet; so quiet, save a gentle drip. Something scratchy rubbed his wrists. A sharp ache pierced the crook of his arm. His body was heavy. He didn't want to open his eyes.

His lids felt gritty, but he forced himself to crack them open. Fluorescent light leaked through. He raised his hands to rub his eyes, but they were caught on something. His eyes flew fully open. Starched white sheets. An IV pole. A white board. A curtain. Dingy blinds closed against the outside world. Hushed voices. Real? *The hospital.*

Josh back peddled in his mind, trying to force the memories. The swirl of pills in the toilet. Starting the truck. And then, nothing. He tried to sit up. His mouth was dry. "Hello?" he called. What had he done?

The curtain pulled back. "Oh, good, you're up," said a woman in pink scrubs and a white paper hat who looked vaguely familiar. "Your wife is on her way. She'll be happy. Your brother was here earlier, feeling really bad about something." She offered a kind smile.

"What day is it?" he asked.

"Thursday." She rolled a cart beside the bed, poured water in a paper cup, and handed it to him, undoing the Velcro around his wrist. The cool liquid coated his throat. She busied herself. Something tightened around his bicep.

"Taking your blood pressure," she said. "Do you know what year it is?"

Josh pictured the calendar tacked up at the jobsite. "1980."

"Good. Who's the president?"

"Jimmy Carter."

"Okay then. Do you know where you are?"

"The hospital?"

"Yep. You had a psychotic episode. We've had you on some heavy-duty meds here." She tapped the IV. "Things should get better."

"How'd I get here?"

"You're wife." She frowned. "Any thoughts of hurting yourself?"

Josh shook his head.

"Thoughts of hurting anyone else?"

"No."

She looked toward the way she'd come. "He's awake. He's pretty lucid." She smiled at Josh, then backed out of the room.

Amy moved the curtain aside and pulled a chair up to the bed. Her face was set in hard lines. The half-moons under her eyes had returned. Because of him.

"What did I do?" he asked her, not sure he wanted to hear the answer. "Did I hurt someone?"

She shook her head. "You were wandering around downtown New Haven. You ran into the street. The police picked you up."

Josh winced, grateful he couldn't remember that part.

"What's the last thing you remember?" Amy asked, as if reading his thoughts.

"Flushing my pills and getting in the truck."

"That's it?"

He nodded.

She sighed, absently straightening the sheet he was apparently allowed to have this time. "Why did you stop taking your meds? Why'd you start smoking pot?"

"I wanted to be normal." He felt heat rise to his face at his lame excuse.

"One of the stipulations for keeping Caleb is you remaining in treatment. Do you really want to risk it?"

The heat spread to his chest. "I don't want the government feeding me pills."

"Dammit, Josh. I can't help you if you won't let me. You're sick. You can't run away from that. I won't stop fighting for you, but you can't stop either."

He looked at her. Her green-blue eyes were stormy. Last time this had happened, she'd turned to Jason. How many times before she turned away from him completely?

"You'll stop loving me," he said, like a child.

Her frown deepened. "You know what, Josh? That's the craziest thing you've ever said." She pushed her chair back and left Josh alone with the weight of his mistakes.

Epilogue

Josh looked in the full-length mirror in his bedroom and adjusted his pinstripe tie.

"That tie's funky. You look like a tool," Sam's reflection said behind him.

"I don't think so." Josh glanced at him.

"Don't think so, what?" Amy came into view, nearly stepping on Sam, but of course she wouldn't know that.

"Sam," Josh answered. "He thinks my tie's too funky."

"Well, tell him I think it's perfect." She spun him around to face her and placed a lingering kiss on his mouth.

Sam groaned. "Get a room."

"This is our room."

"Here." Amy reached for the water glass on the nightstand, then opened her hand and held out three oblong shaped pills.

"Thanks." Josh tossed the pills back and chased them with the water; one more thing he'd never be able to keep track of without her.

"You don't have to take those," Sam said. "I'm leaving."

"I do have to take them. And they won't get rid of you—just push your jabbering into the background."

Amy frowned. She put up with him talking back to his

hallucinations to a point, but she'd stop him when she got tired of sharing his attention with someone she couldn't see. He was grateful for that; grateful that the rhythm of their relationship allowed for it. It had taken a long time to get to this place. Somehow despite the arguments and frustrations over medications, paranoid delusions, and what was real and what wasn't, they always managed to come back and repair the fissures in the foundation in their marriage with cement that was stronger than before.

Josh had to redefine normality and grieve the promise of a simple, predictable life. He hadn't let go over night. He may never be free of the voices, but he could manage them with a strict routine, medications, and appointments. He relied on Amy when he couldn't differentiate symptoms from reality. He trusted her. That, too, had taken time to rebuild. It had been worth it. *She* was worth it.

Amy took the glass out of his hand and returned it to the nightstand. She firmly gripped his shoulders.

"Josh, are you with me?"

The question brought him out of his head. Some days, his symptoms were nonexistent; but others, like today when he was nervous, they were more pronounced. He gave Amy what he hoped was a reassuring smile. "I'm with you."

"Are you okay?"

"I'm fine. A little nervous." He took in her black dress and gently curled hair. "You look beautiful."

She smiled. "Nah. You're seeing things." It was a joke that never got old.

He brought his calloused hand to her smooth cheek. "Maybe you're right; you're too perfect to be real."

He stared into the deep green-blue of her eyes, seeing the love there despite what any voices said. She was the voice of reason in his life. In many ways, she always had been.

He closed his eyes as his mouth met hers. The room was

blessedly silent, punctuated only by their breathing. Too soon she pulled away.

"We'll be late," she whispered.

Josh loved her habit of whispering when she was turned on. Except when he didn't have time to pursue it. He checked his watch; the same watch his father had never taken off.

"Dammit. "I guess it would make us bad parents to be late for our own son's college graduation."

Amy shrugged. "He's only valedictorian. No big deal." She took his hand. "Let's go."

Josh winced at the onslaught of noise as they entered Yale University's wood-paneled auditorium. Excited conversations blurred together. In these situations, it was impossible to discern real voices from hallucinations. He gripped Amy's hand and she squeezed back, grounding him. *You can do this*, he told himself. *For Caleb.*

Jason hurried down the aisle toward them with all the exuberance of a Labrador puppy, his limp almost imperceptible. "Hurry up. Rebecca saved seats up front and she's getting the stink eye." He led them to a spot to the right of the student body.

Josh gazed at all those shiny maroon hats, living vicariously through the graduates. Jason's wife Rebecca struggled to her feet to hug Amy, then Josh.

"Any day now, right?" Amy asked.

Rebecca cradled her belly. "Hopefully not late, like these two." She nodded at their eleven-year old twins.

"Dad, Bobby keeps snapping pictures of me on that thing," Olivia wrinkled her freckled nose and glared at her brother.

"Hand it over, Bobby." Jason held out his hand. With an exaggerated roll of his green eyes, he dropped the phone into his father's hand.

"Hey, Uncle Josh." Bobby stared up at him, his eyes free of the phone.

Josh smiled and settled into his seat. He fixed his eyes on the stage in anxious anticipation. The lights dimmed and the chancellor appeared on the stage looking like royalty with his black robe and silver hair. Josh squirmed through the chancellor's opening. His voice boomed off the wood-paneled walls. Josh barely listened as he droned on about the history of the school. Finally, he finished.

"Without further ado, I'd like to introduce our valedictorian." He pushed his glasses up on the bridge of his nose. "It has been the utmost honor and delight to have this young man in our program. A scholar who has consistently presented with the highest marks in the field of psychiatry. He will pursue a doctorate in this subject, an endeavor at which I have no doubt he'll succeed. Please join me in welcoming Caleb Everett."

Josh felt the exhilarating blend of terror and excitement, like waiting in line for a roller coaster. Mercifully, the whispering in his head dissolved with the applause. He'd assured Caleb he could talk about his mental illness. He hoped he was ready to hear what his son had to say.

Caleb approached the podium. He exuded confidence; his broad shoulders pulled back, his stocky six-foot-two frame owned the space. Caleb pushed his thick brown hair off his forehead and adjusted the microphone while looking out at the crowd. Josh swelled with pride. He put his arm around Amy.

"Our baby," she whispered. Her eyes glistened.

"Thank you, Chancellor," Caleb began.

When Caleb spoke, it was impossible not to hang on every word, which was exactly what Josh did as the rich tenor of his son's voice flowed through the auditorium.

"My name is Caleb Everett. Some of you know me. Many of you don't. I've spent a lot of my time here with my head stuck in books."

A ripple of laughter.

"I guess I'm supposed to give you all some words of wisdom

to take with you after graduation. Well, I'm only twenty-two; I don't have the secret to a happy, successful life. I'm around the same age my dad was when his life changed forever. His life was never easy, but at twenty-one, it became exponentially harder."

Caleb paused. Someone coughed. Amy squeezed Josh's knee.

"I'll get to that in a minute. If I'm presumptuous enough to give you advice, fellow classmates, I'll share what I've learned. Your life can change in an instant. The life you've planned can shift irrevocably overnight. Some changes will be good; others not so good. How we handle these changes, how we face the moments we can't plan for—that is what defines us."

"I learned this from my mom, Amy. She's the glue that held our little family together. I was a baby when our lives changed. I don't remember much about that time. Over the years I remember seeing my mom cry. Hearing her worry. Sometimes she got frustrated balancing everyone's needs before her own. The one thing she never did was give up. I was much older by the time I realized how many battles she fought, often alone. She didn't hide her struggles behind fake smiles; she owned them. She's my hero."

Amy wiped her eyes. Josh tightened his arm around her. "Mine, too," he whispered.

"The other lesson I want to share with you is one of tolerance and acceptance. As human beings, we're afraid of what we don't understand. If you're afraid of something, learn about it. Find all the information you can. Expose yourself to it. Don't avoid people who are different from you; people who look different, act different, think different. They will teach you the most about the world and about yourself. Don't assume someone's story; if you're wondering, ask. Most people would love nothing more than someone to listen. Be that person. Even when it's uncomfortable. Especially when it's uncomfortable."

The room was mesmerized. Silent. Josh let out his breath.

"We all have our journeys after we leave the insulation of this fine institution. Whatever you do, do it with all your might. I'll be moving to Massachusetts in the fall to obtain a doctorate in psychiatry from Harvard. My dad continues to be my motivation to pursue this passion. He gave me my unquenchable thirst to learn everything about everything, and an open mind and heart."

Josh stared up at Caleb. It was no mystery why he'd chosen psychiatry. Caleb was unusually inquisitive and accepting. But Josh had wondered if his relentless pursuit of education was his way of escaping a difficult childhood. Like Josh, Caleb had been forced to grow up too fast and take on wisdom and responsibility beyond his years. He swallowed the familiar brick of guilt as Caleb continued.

"My dad started hearing voices. He didn't realize no one else could hear them. He started seeing people who weren't there. Sometimes they tormented him. Now we know he experienced a psychotic break. The typical age of onset is late teens and early twenties. If your mood or behavior changes, if you have thoughts of death or see or hear things, speak up. Getting help is never a sign of weakness."

"For my dad, it wasn't easy. It was 1979—the year the National Alliance for the Mentally Ill was founded. There were so few resources, so little understanding of mental illness, particularly psychosis. My parents were confused, scared, and alone."

Josh was transfixed. This man confidently addressing a lecture hall full of peers was his son. Caleb paused for a drink of water.

"We've come a long way in recognizing and treating mental illness, but we have a long way to go. That's where I come in, and hopefully you, too." Caleb grinned. "This is the part where I say, 'we are the future.'" He made his voice deep and dramatic, stretching his arms out over his classmates. His audience laughed.

"I want to become a psychiatrist, work with the chronically mentally ill population, and promote further research. My rather lofty goal is that no family suffer the confusion, misunderstanding, and isolation mine has."

His deep emerald eyes stared imploringly out into the crowd. Josh swallowed a lump in his throat. This meant so much to his son.

"But I'm one person." Caleb put his hand on his heart. "In order to accomplish this goal, I need you. Each one of you. You don't have to be a mental health professional. Let go of fear. Refuse to allow taboo. Talk. Listen. Can you guys do that with me?"

Thunderous applause echoed off the thick walls. Rebecca reached around Jason and flashed Josh the thumbs up sign.

"Thank you. I know I've been jabbering at you for a while now. That I may have gotten from my uncle."

Jason elbowed Josh. "See," he whispered, "it really was all me."

"Good," Josh whispered back. "You can pay the student loans."

"In closing, I'll answer a question I've been asked repeatedly throughout my life. What is it like to grow up with a dad with paranoid schizophrenia?"

Josh braced himself, the voices and memories threatening his fragile composure. He'd never forget the day his son had come home from school wide-eyed and innocent, and asked, "Daddy, what's a nutter? What's a schizo?"

The whispers and stares at school functions. Friends' parents who wouldn't let their children come around the house when Josh was home. The girlfriend who'd suddenly developed a stomachache and excused herself in the middle of dinner when Josh started answering questions only he could hear.

Thirteen-year-old Caleb screaming at him, "I want a *normal* dad!" Those were things he'd never forget. He forced himself to block it all out and listen to the one voice in the room that mattered.

"I think it's a lot like growing up with any other dad. You see, I was still a baby when my dad got sick, so for me there was no 'before' and no 'after'. My dad's my dad and I love him. He taught me how to play baseball and football, how and when to stand up for myself, and how to fix pretty much anything with my own two hands.

"He also talked to people who weren't there and listened to voices that weren't real." Caleb shrugged again. "That's the way it was."

Josh let out a breath he didn't know he was holding. That Caleb didn't remember him before his break was one of his greatest regrets. But maybe it didn't matter? Maybe the timing was merciful.

"Some people believed my dad was unfit, that he would hurt me, neglect me, become violent. If I could talk to these people today, I'd tell them that they were unequivocally incorrect. Whenever possible, my dad was there for the big moments in my life and all the little moments in between. I'd be lying if I said it was easy. I hated when he had to be gone for weeks at a time. I couldn't visit him in the hospital. Sometimes he was in his own world. Sometimes I was embarrassed, or even jealous of the hallucinations because of how much of his attention they got."

"But you know what? The hardest part wasn't schizophrenia. The hardest part was people's reactions. The friends who stopped coming around. The kids who whispered in the halls. The parents who were afraid. The family members who turned on us. Those people made it harder, not my dad."

"My dad's this big strong guy. Seeing him brought to his knees and tortured by an invisible adversary tore me up. But he always got back up. Even when he had nothing left to fight with, he kept going. Even when my parents fought, I could tell how much they loved each other. How much they loved me. I'm gonna get sappy on you for a minute and say there was never a lack of love in my family."

"To date, no cure exists for schizophrenia. My dad continues to fight the same battles every single day. But he gets treatment. Mostly, he's good. So that's what it was like. Now, class of 1999, I'm going to carry the perseverance I learned out into the world. In my little family, it was us against the world. Let's change that. Let's change the world. Thank you."

A thousand people jumped to their feet simultaneously. Applause, whistles, and shouts ricocheted off the paneled walls. "Go, Caleb!" someone shouted.

Amy linked her arm through Josh's. She smiled up at him. "We did it."

"Yeah, we did." Josh savored the nugget of peace in his chest. The tightness would return soon enough.

The rest of the ceremony was a blur. Once they escaped the stuffy auditorium, Josh extricated himself from the crowds and waited for Caleb to make his way through. Families snapped pictures and cradled flowers.

"They all know your secret now."

Josh looked over his shoulder. Shane wore his ever-present smirk.

"Well, guess that means it's not a secret anymore." He waited for a retort, but none came. "You know, Shane, I can't believe I ever thought you were real. For one thing, real people have versatile affect."

Shane flipped Josh the finger before turning away.

Josh returned his attention to the crowd. And stared straight at Eileen. Neither he nor Amy had seen or spoken to her in twenty years, but Josh would recognize her anywhere. Her hair had gone gray, but she was otherwise unaffected by age. She locked eyes with Josh.

"Hallucinating my estranged mother-in-law," Josh muttered to himself. "Now that takes the cake."

"Mr. Popular will get to us eventual—" Amy was at his side. He looked at her, but she was staring in the direction of the Eileen hallucination, her mouth hanging open. Josh followed her gaze. The Eileen hallucination was hurriedly retreating.

"My—my mom?" Amy said.

Josh gaped at her. "You saw her too?"

"Of course, I saw her."

Josh rubbed his eyes, trying to keep up with this shifting reality. Amy was still staring at the spot where her mother had been.

Josh touched her shoulder. "Are you okay?"

She nodded. "I never dreamt she'd come."

"Are you going to say something to her?"

Amy looked at him. "No," she said. "I think she heard everything she needed to hear."

Acknowledgments

I'd like to thank my family, Jim, Aiden, and Elliott for your unending support, encouragement, and willingness to listen to my stories. Thanks to all those who allowed me invaluable writing time through baby-sitting offers, especially Beverly Steele and Carole Clark. Thank you to my friends for your endless support of and excitement for my book. Thank you to my sister-in-law, blog partner, and writing mentor Jan Steele for convincing me from the beginning that I am in fact a writer and dragging myself and my social anxiety to writers' conferences. Thank you to Michael Steven Gregory, Wes Albers, and everyone involved in the Southern California Writer's conference, where I learned everything I know about being a writer. May I continue to write more and suck less.

Thank you to Josef Malik, LL.M. for guiding me through the process of writing an authentic custody trial. Many thanks to Wayne Klein and Wayne Klein II of Klein Construction for sharing your extensive knowledge of the planning, building, and inspection process.

A big thank you to Joshua Youmans for constructing my website. Thanks to Marla Miller, Oz Monroe, and Holly Kammier for your editing expertise. Without you this book would not have been possible. Finally, I'd like to express deep appreciation for Holly Kammier and Jessica Therrien of Acorn publishing for believing in me, answering my endless questions, and holding my hand throughout every step of the editing, publishing, and marketing process. Thank you for helping me turn my dream into a reality.

Author's Note

In 2020, we have more resources for and knowledge of mental illness than Josh and Amy had. More people are sharing their mental health journeys now than any time in history. That said, we have a long way to go. Recent cuts to Medicaid in the United States leave countless individuals and families with inadequate mental health care. Although progress has been made, we still have work to do to remove the stigma and fear surrounding mental illness. In the media, we see violent acts linked to mental illness, when in reality those living with psychotic disorders such as schizophrenia and other mental illnesses are far more likely to be the victims of violent crimes than perpetrators. According to mentalhealth.gov, "... only 3%–5% of violent acts can be attributed to individuals with serious mental illness. In fact, people with severe mental illness are over 10 times more likely to be victims of violent crime than the general population."* Yet fear, shame, and ignorance continue to persist. By writing about these topics, both in fiction and nonfiction, I hope to raise awareness and be a part of replacing judgement with compassion, fear with understanding, and stigma with acceptance. Like Caleb, I'm just one person. I invite everyone to be a part of the changing attitudes toward mental illness. It starts with an open mind and a willingness to learn. Mental illness has touched myself and my family in a variety of ways. From my observation, the most difficult aspect has been the lack of understanding and the snap judgments. We can change that. We can save lives.

A portion of the profits from this book will be donated to help fund programs for mental health care for the chronically mentally ill population.

*https://www.mentalhealth.gov/basics/mental-health-myths-facts

About the Author

Kat Clark is an award-winning writer with a degree in psychology and a passion for storytelling. She found writing on a frigid winter night while holed up with a crying baby, a travelling husband, and a precocious three-year old.

Kat has been a stay-at-home mom to her two sons for eleven years. She also homeschools and advocates tirelessly for awareness of and accommodations for special needs. Her free time is spent volunteering with various church ministries including working with children with a variety of needs. Her personal experience with mental illness and her previous work with the chronically mentally ill population sparked her determination to remove the stigma from mental illness.

Kat is a contributing author for The Mighty website. She also shares a You Tube channel (Sonny Mom INC.) with her son and a blog with her sister-in-law at www.killingjunecleaver.blogspot.com. She lives in the Chicago suburbs with her husband, two children, two large, obnoxious dogs, and two cats who hate each other.

You can visit her online at
WWW.AUTHORKATCLARK.COM

Available From Acorn Publishing
WWW.ACORNPUBLISHINGLLC.COM

Made in the USA
Monee, IL
07 July 2020